Let It Go

by Eliza Jonas

Eliza Jonas

Cover Design – Kellie's Cover design

Editor – Scarlett's Proofreading Services

Dedication

This book is dedicated to my Besties for the Resties. You know who you are, and you kept me going.

Table of Contents

Content Warning

This book contains explicit sexual scenes including dirty talk, squirting, and two men with one woman. This book is not intended for those under the age of 18.

While Let It Go is not a dark romance, there may be themes that are triggering to others. Please be aware that this book contains references and experiences with **anti-fat bias** and a main character with **anxiety**.

If either of those items are triggering to you, please be very cautious before you proceed. Your mental health matters.

From the Author

Let It Go is a story that bubbled in the back of my mind for quite a while. When I went on a journey to love my own body, I started learning about the concept of anti-fat bias and it gave my story life. I did not set out to create a book to educate on anti-fat bias. I set out to create a story of love (and smut, let's be honest), and showing how pervasive anti-fat bias is in the world. Adding in the anxiety component felt perfect for Charlotte as I considered her journey through life in a larger body. Not everyone with a larger body deals with anxiety, and not everyone with anxiety lives in a larger body.

No two experiences with anti-fat bias or anxiety are the same, so while Charlotte's experience cannot speak for everyone, I hope it sparks conversation and learning. Everyone is worthy of being heard and every body is worthy of love.

If you'd like to learn more about anti-fat bias, I recommend:
- Fearing the Black Body by Sabrina Strings
- "You just need to lose weight" and 19 Other Myths About Fat People by Audrey Gordon

There are a multitude of resources out there, but these are two that I felt I needed to share.

 # Chapter 1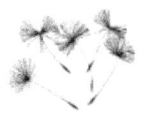

Charlotte

The radio's blasting as I drive down the road, and my voice is singing along as loud as I can get it. Singing in the car is perhaps one of my favorite things to do, which is why I don't mind that our weekly girls' night is happening at Amy's apartment this week. Well, Amy's house, I suppose, since she lives with her parents. Amy and I have known each other for about seven years now, and she has quickly become a close friend. Not a label I easily pass out. She earned it in spades, and I am more than happy to return the friendship. Olivia is joining us tonight, and I have known her as long as I can remember. She immediately welcomed Amy into our friendship; her heart seems to know no limits when it comes to love.

The next song starts as I turn onto Amy's street, my singing showing no signs of improving or quieting. It's easy to pretend I'm amazing when singing by myself. I'm on par with the greats on my own, just my empty seats to hear me, and I love feeling like I am the center of attention for an invisible crowd. No pressure, just fun. The fact that it drowns out the weird clunking noise happening is a bonus.

I park on the road next to Amy's driveway, trying not to be obnoxious and block anyone in. I grab my bags and start walking towards the door. The dogs' barking sounds through the door and a smile immediately spreads across my face. I love the chaos of Amy's house. It's full of love and there is *never* a dull moment. Without knocking, I push right in; there's no standing on ceremony with this family.

The dogs come at me, gleeful for a new person to lavish them with time and attention. The three of them are medium-sized, varied mutts they've adopted over the years and are just the sweetest. When they aren't having the occasional dominance battle. Bunch of bitches. I hold my bags up and smile at them.

"Hey Cerberus!" I greet them using my group nickname for them, making kissy faces and cooing over each of them.

I hear my name shouted. "Lotte!"

Looking up, I see Amy's mother in the kitchen, cleaning as though she hasn't already cleaned twice today. The woman is a bit obsessive. I set my bags down on the table and focus on her.

"Hey Sandy, how's it goin'?"

"Oh good, except I can never seem to get this dang counter clean! There's always one stain or another, and I'm starting to suspect that Corbin is doing it on purpose. I wouldn't put it past him. Need to get back at that little punk."

My head tips back in laughter. "I'm sure he's pulling a fast one on you. Don't let him get away with it! Maybe kiss him in the drop off lane at school and yell 'Mommy loves you, baby!'. I bet that would do it."

"Oh, you're devious, public humiliation for a teenager. Brutal!" Sandy replies, chuckling.

I hear a door open to the right and look over. Amy's opened the door to her upstairs apartment and is on her way down. She eyes her mom and my bag of goodies.

"Mom, are you trying to steal my friends again?" she asks.

"Not my fault they like me better, honey. Gotta try harder," Sandy retorts.

Amy squints her eyes at her mom, vengeance promised with the look. I try to keep a straight face but never can. They always manage to have these jokes going with straight faces, and I have no clue how they do it. It gets me every time.

"Don't worry Sandy, I love you too," I say as I pick up my bags and head Amy's way.

"Who doesn't? You girls have fun. Let me know if you think of anything good to get back at Corbin!"

"What did he do this time?" Amy asks her mom while I start up the stairs.

"He keeps leaving stains on my counters!"

Amy starts slowly backing up the stairs. "Okay, crazy lady, whatever you say."

I cackle as we get up the last few steps and close the door.

"There are never any stains. I have no idea what the hell she's looking at," Amy whispers.

Amy has the upstairs to herself. Her parents renovated it, so she has a small kitchen, bathroom, and a studio style living area. She has a couch and TV, but in the same space is her bed. She's not as tidy as her mom, and a large part of me suspects it's her way of rebelling, but she'll never admit to it. I set my haul of goodies on the coffee table she uses for eating and socializing. She doesn't have a formal living room since there wasn't room for it during the build, but her space does well enough without it. We set out the supplies for girls' night. Chips, candy, nuts, and cookies all appear from my bags, and I always feel like Mary Poppins when I bring this much food.

"Jesus. We always go so fuckin' overboard when we do these things," Amy says.

I pretend to scold her. "Hey, you never know what we're gonna be in the mood for. We have to be prepared! That's what the Boy Scouts say, right? Be prepared?"

"Pretty sure that's *Lion King*," she shoots back.

"Still applies."

She chuckles and rolls her eyes, setting out our snack fest with me. We just put the last bag of chips out when the door opens and closes quickly. Olivia leans against it, panting.

I raise my eyebrows at her. "Dramatic much?"

"Those dogs are out to get me, I swear!"

"Aw, Cerberus wouldn't hurt a fly," I tell her.

"Cerberus was a terrifying dog from hell! There are three of those things, not just one!" she protests.

Amy laughs. "I honestly don't think I've ever heard them even growl at anyone. I think dogs just make you uncomfortable."

"That or the chaos they create," Olivia grumbles.

She flops on the couch, sighing as loudly as she can. I shake my head and sit on the other end of the couch with her while Amy takes the bean bag. We could all three fit on the couch no problem, but it's always annoying trying to look at whoever is on the opposite end when we do that. It's easier to see everyone with some space.

"What do I owe you?" Olivia asks me as she pops a chip in her mouth.

"I dunno. I'll request it on Venmo later when I actually look at the receipt," I reply.

"Fair enough. What are we watching tonight?"

"Well, are we feeling like it's gonna be a chatterbox night, or do we want to actually pay attention?" Amy asks.

Olivia and I look at her like she's grown a third head.

"It's like you don't even know us," I tell her, pouring as much pout as I can into the words.

"Shut up, bitch." She laughs and throws a pillow at me.

I grin as she flips through the bad horror movies and puts on *Killer Sofa*. We've seen it enough times that it becomes background noise as we chat through the chair trying to kill everyone. We still can't decide why it's called *Killer Sofa* when the movie depicts a chair, but considering the chair is alive and killing people, it's probably a moot point anyway.

"So, what's the big sigh for tonight, Liv?" I ask before popping a chip into my mouth.

"Ugh! Bad date this afternoon. I agreed to meet him for an afternoon coffee since I had a light afternoon—"

Before she can finish, both Amy and I are all over her.

"A DATE?!" Amy yells.

"You didn't TELL US?!" I ask, astonished.

She rolls her eyes and holds out her hands, palms toward us as she tries to placate our excitement and disappointment over this unknown news.

"Okay, okay, look, I didn't say anything 'cuz we just matched on whatever dating app I have on my phone, and I figured why not do an in-person coffee date instead of all the texting?" she says with a shrug.

"How do you still not remember your dating app's name?" Amy asks her.

"Ugh, it would require brain power and I used all of mine for today." She brushes off the question.

"So, what the hell happened? Did he spill his coffee on you?" I ask her.

"I wish. That would have been easier to deal with, I think. No, the entire time he kept making comments about my weight"—we groan as she says this—"like he was amazed that I looked so good for my size. Or had I considered doing workouts? He said he'd love to workout with me."

"God, I hate men," Amy states.

"Your girlfriends would definitely clue us into that even if you didn't explicitly state that," Olivia deadpans.

Amy gathers both girls and guys and has a small polycule that is always open to meeting new people. Her relationships honestly are goals to me. They are all super open and honest with each other and make decisions as a group. Not everyone is with everyone else. For example, Amy isn't seeing any guys right now, but they still respect the rules and participate in the discussions. It's beautiful to see. She's fought hard to accept herself, and the group works hard to maintain what they really want.

I chuckle at Olivia's comment and gesture for her to continue. I know that while commenting on size was a trigger for her, she's willing to work past it if the person is willing to learn.

"Anyway, yeah, I told him that no, I haven't because I don't particularly enjoy workouts. I like going for walks and being active, but not straight workouts. I mentioned I'm very healthy according to my yearly physicals, so I haven't explored anything more. I like my body and unless I need to address a health issue, I don't see a need to change my lifestyle."

"Amen!" Amy yells.

Olivia raises her water glass in a cheers motion and they both drink. I smile and shake my head, unsure how to react to them. The topic of weight always makes me so uncomfortable, but Olivia and Amy never seem to shy away from it. My anxiety means I always overthink things and when it's a loaded topic, that means my brain goes into overdrive.

"So, his response? I needed to really keep my overall health in mind, not just what my doctor said. He also said that he has friends that love to shop and would be willing to shop with me for new clothes if I wanted. The worst part?"

"It gets worse than that?" I ask in disbelief.

She nods solemnly. "He ordered decaf," she says, in a tone reserved for when you talk about taboo subjects.

"Oh God!" I exclaim. "Are you ok?"

Amy laughs. "*Of course* that's what you two focus on."

"Look, there are standards to be held and if someone can't stomach caffeine in the afternoon, they seriously need to reevaluate their life choices," I tell her.

Amy chuckles. "While I don't disagree, I do think this might be why you don't date enough."

"What do you mean 'enough'?" I challenge her.

"I mean, you criticize everyone before you even get to a first date point. I'm surprised you let us in enough to be friends, let alone some guy who might want to love you. You never let anyone in."

I shrug. "I don't have time to be disappointed in people. It's easier to just not."

Olivia cocks her head and looks at me.

I never like it when she gets that look on her face. Like she knows more than I want her to, and she usually does.

I like my safe bubble of not opening up to people. That way, my anxiety doesn't pester me to keep thinking about how they'll probably just leave me anyway. I can't pinpoint when I started to think and worry about people leaving me, or what triggered it.

My parents are still together, my older and younger brothers both love me and are around if I need them. Nobody in my extended family has shunned me. I wasn't left at the altar at a young age. I just always worry that people will leave me. It's probably something I should talk to my counselor about, but I figure she'll just tell me it's my anxiety lying to me. So, I just try to breathe through the thoughts and focus on the good. It's worked so far. Mostly.

"She's not wrong," Olivia chimes in, still giving me that look. "You get all weirded out when people try to get you to open up and actually, I don't know, try to care about you?"

"You guys know me, and I let you in," I defend myself.

"Only because we gave you no choice," Olivia argues.

"Even if someone gets in, *you have* to find something that's wrong with them and end it, even if they're fine," adds Amy.

"How did we start talking about me? Can we talk about Ames' shortcomings now?" I grumble.

Amy looks disappointed. "Aw, I was having fun with the banter."

I laugh and chuck a handful of popcorn at her. She chuckles and tosses an Oreo back at me in retaliation. I love these girls with all my heart, and while we dropped the topic, I know I'll keep thinking about it. I'm confident that Olivia will bring it up again. She doesn't drop shit like this when she knows she hit a nerve.

 # Chapter 2

Charlotte

I leave my house, looking forward to having some time with just Olivia and me. I know she won't let the conversation from earlier this week go, but at least there will be alcohol around this time. My car starts fine and when I pull onto the street, I have hope that maybe the noise won't happen this time. I go over a bump in the road and that damn clunking noise starts up.

Motherfucker.

I know this is something I can't keep putting off. In the meantime, I can at least car karaoke and forget about the noise.

I pull up to Olivia's apartment building, music still blaring, and text her to come out. A good friend would go up and get her. That's not how we roll. Bitch can come downstairs on her own. I'm not slogging up three flights of stairs just to come right back down after she steps out. Forget that noise. Not a minute later, I see her come out the main door, holding it open and smiling widely at an older neighbor who was on their way in. I scoff. Olivia doesn't smile at people like that when she's being nice. That's her toothy smile of death.

I can't wait to hear this story.

She walks up to the car and hops in, rolling her eyes from the interaction with her neighbor.

"Hey bitch," I greet her as she slips into her seat.

"Sup, ho?" she says back, leaning over for the obligatory awkward car hug.

"What's the story with the old lady?" I ask, with a small smile on my face.

She rolls her eyes. "THAT was Mrs. Johnston, and *she* is the crabbiest old bitty I've ever met. Seriously, I was watching a movie the other night with Jordan, and she had the audacity to come to my door and ask me to keep it down. The TV was at like volume three and we had subtitles on!"

I snicker. "I mean, was she complaining about the movie or your noisy extracurriculars?"

"Shut it, that's not the point," she replies, laughing.

"I didn't realize you're still seeing him," I tell her.

"It's more of a 'hey I'm horny, are you? Cool, let's go' type of situation." She shrugs.

"Good for you!" I smile as we turned out of the complex and onto the main road.

We hit a bump as I turn, and that damn clunking noise starts up. It clunks for a moment, then slowly dies out.

"Soooo…" she says slowly. "What's up with the weird noise?"

I lean my head back on the headrest. "Ugh, I don't wanna talk about it."

"Dude, is the car going to get us there? It might fall apart with that noise."

I force a smile and don't reply. My stomach sinks a little at her words. Olivia and I have been through so much bullshit that there's an understanding there. Just about anything is fair game for teasing. Who has time to go through life without a little fun? Not us.

This one, though, is hitting closer than I'd like. She's not wrong about the noise, and we *do* always tease each other, but I'm feeling sensitive about not taking care of my shit.

Maybe I am procrastinating on my car, but I wouldn't drive it if it wasn't safe. I thought she knew that.

Thoughts keep swirling in my head, and I argue with myself about whether or not it was really just a joke when I see her fingers snap in front of my face.

"Hey. Was a joke. I'm sorry," she says.

We're at a red light, so I look over. "Yeah, I know, it just hit me weird and then the spiral started," I tell her, embarrassed about the stupid way my anxiety infiltrates my life at times.

"Girl, don't apologize. I should have gauged where you were at better." She waves me off.

"That's not your job—"

"No, but I know better, and I was all worked up remembering friggin' Mrs. Johnston and her prudish shit."

"Okay, well, I'm sorry, you're sorry. Let's go drown our sorrows in some tequila." I say with a smile.

"That sounds like a fabulous idea!" she agrees with a grin. "Maybe pick up a hottie or two? Yeah?"

"Ehhhh, we'll see," I hedge.

The idea of letting some drunk, smelly guy try to put his hands on me does not sound appealing. Assuming any of them even take the time to look past my extra rolls. Olivia still hasn't found someone to take up space in her life for more than an evening, but I don't doubt she'll pick up just the right guy. She's got something to her that people just can't seem to resist.

We pull up to the bar and park in a brightly lit area. We aren't dumb, no walking in the dark after drinks, even if it is just to the car. Since it's only 9 pm, we have a decent selection of where to go, and we choose a small high top, big enough for two, but we could squeeze a third if needed. We move the tall chairs nearer to each other so we can sit side by side and scan the room while we chat. People watching is a favorite pastime. Who doesn't like watching drunk people make fools of themselves? Impatient for some alcohol, I go to the bar for the first round, since last time she grabbed first round.

I walk up and try to get the bartender's attention and wait a few minutes. He glances at me once or twice but hasn't come down this way yet, still focused on the girls where he's standing, their boobs lifted to their eyes by push-up bras.

I feel sorry for the bras; that looks like a lot of work.

"Excuse me?" I call.

He finally walks over, looks me up and down, and asks me what I want. What I want is for him to lose the attitude, but maybe he isn't giving me any attitude and I'm assuming. I give him a friendly smile.

"Could I please have two gimlets with vodka?"

He nods at me and starts pulling out the necessary equipment to get started. I see his eyes dart back to the boob girls and they titter and whisper to each other as I wait. Probably should have just waited for the waitress to come get our first orders, but I need that damn drink. I assumed this would be faster. He sets the drinks down and I hand him some cash, telling him to keep the change.

"Might want to take it easy on the drinks, yeah?" he says as he takes the cash. "That simple syrup can add up quick."

My face flames and I grab the drinks quickly and gently and go back to the table.

One of these days I'll speak up, but today is clearly not that day.

I set the drinks down on the table and Olivia looks at the bartender with a little more malice than I'm comfortable with.

"Whatever you're thinking, don't," I warn her as I sit.

"I'm not thinking anything!" she protests.

"I know that look in your eye, and I don't like it."

"I wouldn't have this look if people would mind their own fucking business. We're not coming back here."

"He's one asshole. You can't get fired up every time someone makes a comment about the things we order."

"Well, if people didn't make dumbass comments, I wouldn't have to get fired up! He doesn't need to have any kind of say about what we put in our bodies!"

"You couldn't even hear him from here!" I protest.

"Didn't need to hear the words to know what he was saying," she mutters and picks up her drink.

"You know what?" I say, wrapping my hand around my own.

"What?" She looks at me, glass in the air.

"Fuck that guy," I say and clink my glass to hers.

She grins and loudly echoes me. "Fuck that guy!"

As we laugh, the server comes by with a basket of chips and salsa, gives us her name if we need anything, and hurries off to her next table. We spend some time people watching, making up stories about how their days may have gone, what their lives might be like. We also enjoy the awkward moments that are always funnier looking back, but those poor people in the moment are not amused. We don't laugh outright at them, and if there's a real need we'll help, but we smile, and chuckle and swap memories about when shit like that happened to us. Olivia points out that we never got tequila, so she orders a round of shots, and we each order another drink. After our refill, Olivia turns to me.

"So, really, what's going on with your car?"

"What do you mean?" I try to act like I don't know what she's talking about.

She sighs. "Bitch, don't play dumb with me. There's no way that weird clunking noise is normal. It sounds like someone's lifting weights in your car and letting them smack together."

"Do you even know what that sounds like?"

"Shut up!" she says, laughing. "I go to the gym more than *you* do."

"Doesn't take much to win that achievement." I chuckle. "But yeah, I know. I keep hoping it'll go away."

"How's that working?"

"I don't need your logic. I have my own that's been failing me for years," I protest.

"Do you even have a mechanic you go to right now?"

"No... I could probably ask my dad, but with the hour drive to each other's house and then the amount of chatting we *always* do; it doesn't leave much time for looking at the car. Plus, I know he's getting older, and I can't keep relying on him for stuff. He's enjoying retirement, and I'd hate to make him waste a day if it's something he can't even fix."

"So go to a shop," she says, like it's the obvious solution. I mean it is.

"I hate going to car shops. They're always run by skeevy old men who either leer at me the entire time or talk to me like I have an IQ of two."

"Pretty sure you'd be dead if that were the case."

"Pretty sure that's not the point and the old guys probably wouldn't understand what an IQ even is."

Olivia laughs at that. "Maybe you need better recommendations for shops."

"Okay fine. Where would I even start?"

"Lucky for you, I have one in mind! My parents found it a few months back and they've actually had really good experiences there overall. Decent prices, they explain everything to you, they give you the option to upgrade but don't try to sway you. It's actually just information they're sharing instead of trying to get more money."

"What's the catch?" I ask. "There's no way that's a real shop."

"No catch that I've heard yet. I suppose the only thing is that it's new. I think they've only been open for like six months. Not a lot of business or reputation yet."

"I guess, if that's the worst it is, I can always tell them no to the service and go somewhere else. I could have my dad come for a weekend, which sounds horrible."

"Yeah, he'd be a total pussy block for you with all those men you're courting," she deadpans.

"Hey, you don't know! I could have a harem at home!"

"But you don't."

"That's beside the point." I sniff. "FINE, I will take my damn car in. I'll have to call Thomas and see if he can give me a ride home from the shop this week. I should be able to just work from home for a couple of days."

"The perks of working in an office!" Olivia cheers. "Why not just call Graham? Doesn't he live a bit closer?"

"I am *not* dealing with a ten-hour lecture from Graham on why I didn't immediately have someone look at my car. Nobody has time for that."

Olivia cackles. "Too true!"

 # Chapter 3

Jax

I open the shop doors, appreciating the quiet of the garage before the day really gets started. Business has been steady lately, which is awesome, and there is something serene about walking through the space, opening the bay doors, and getting things in order.

After all the shop doors and bays are open, I boot up the computer at the desk and in my office. I check emails in my office and decide nothing is earth shaking. So, I move out to the front desk and start reviewing any appointments we have on the books. We have three appointments today, all basic oil changes, so nothing too crazy. That's good. We can focus on the car in Bay 3 that needs more intensive diagnostics. We had the new guy start on that one, but I think it's going to be more than he can handle. I'll need to have Roman jump in and assist with that. I probably should offer since it's my shop, but I like to be the face when customers call or come in.

I mean, I do my share of repairs; last week I had to replace someone's fuel pump. The previous shop quoted the person $3,000. The most it should cost is like $1,300. We low-balled them at $900 and didn't make as much profit as we could, but I'm hoping it gets more business through the door. I don't make it a habit to low ball like that, but when I heard that ridiculous quote, I had to have their business. I wanted them to have a positive experience with a mechanic. Since my name is on the shop, I took care of the replacement and took the hit from my income.

I hear the employee entrance door bang open and shut again. Probably Roman, he was scheduled to come in early today, but the new guy isn't until mid-morning.

"How's it going, man?" I hear Roman call out as he walks toward the employee lounge.

Lounge is probably overstating it. It's an 8x10 room with some chairs, a mini-fridge, and a couch. Someday we'll even put in a TV like a fancy place would. My employees would be so lucky. Well, they would if there were more than three of us. I can't wait to hire more; it'll be a mark of success.

"Sup bro?" I call back at him.

"Living the dream," he replies. Roman puts his lunch away and walks over to stand with me at the main computer. He looks over the schedule and grimaces. "Only three appointments?"

"Yeah, but we'll pick up more. Plus, we have that mystery repair in Bay 3 that we have the new kid on. I might have you help him; I can handle the oil changes." I tell him.

"New kid has a name," Roman insists.

"He's new kid 'til he's been here more than three weeks."

"Pretty sure he's an adult."

"Pretty sure none of us are adults." I say with a laugh.

Roman smirks and heads over to where he keeps his tools, ensuring everything is where he wants it to be and that they're clean and ready. The man is meticulous about his tools, but that's part of what makes him so good. He probably cleans them twice a day, which means they look pretty dang new. Of course I give him shit for it.

What kind of mechanic has clean, shiny tools? A showoff, that's who. Don't get me wrong, I take care of my tools, but Roman treats them like they're worth more than gold. Showoff.

I glance at the clock, seeing that we're supposed to open in ten minutes. I go ahead and turn on the open sign early. We don't exactly have a line out the door at 8 am, so may as well do it while it's on my mind.

The day passes without much fanfare. We get the oil changes done and pick up a new replacement for shocks and struts. Easy stuff, but do it with quality work and they last you longer than overpriced and mediocre efforts.

The last of our three scheduled oil changes leaves and I glance at the clock, noting it is almost 4 pm. I look over through the window separating the shop area from reception and see Roman pointing out something to the new guy. I smile to myself a little and open the window so I can shout out to them.

"Hey! Did you get that done yet?" I bark.

Roman glances over and raises his brows at me, silently communicating to fuck off. The new guy isn't as sure how to respond.

"Uh, not yet, but we're getting there," replies new guy.

"I'm not paying you to sit around and look at cars. I'm paying you to work!"

"I promise we're doing the best we can!" he protests.

"Do better!" I slam the window shut.

The new guy immediately puts his head back into the car and Roman flips me the bird, not even looking my way. I start chuckling and can't wait for the new guy to figure out I'm just pulling his leg.

The door is open when I look back and I about stop breathing. The girl, no, woman, standing there, hesitant in the doorway, looks like she is straight from my fantasies. Tall, the bluest eyes I've ever seen, and legs that go for days. Her cheekbones are high with a straight nose that screams Romanesque beauty. I see her lips moving, but all I hear is static as my world fades to her face, which is starting to frown, and her nose scrunches up.

"… have the wrong place?"

Oh crap, she's actually talking.

"Hey, I'm sorry. I, uh, was thinking about a car I need to fix."

Hopefully she buys that bullshit.

"I'm Jax. How can I help?"

"Oh, uh, this is Jax's repair shop?"

"Yup!"

She lets the door close behind her and the ringing sound of a new customer chimes as the door reconnects to its frame. She stands there for a moment before straightening her spine a little and walking over to the desk.

"My friend said you guys have reasonable prices? And you're good with cars?" she asks.

I can tell she is a mix of nervous and defensive. If I had to guess, she isn't used to dealing with mechanics, and if she is, then she's used to douche canoes. I suddenly need to fix whatever she's bringing to my shop. I want her to not be afraid to ask for help from a mechanic. Everyone should be able to have a car that works, and you shouldn't have to be nervous to ask for help or pay out the nose to get said help.

I'll show her a good time… I mean mechanic. Good mechanic. Christ, this is gonna be a rough conversation.

"Yeah, we do our best and keep our prices reasonable, at least in my opinion. I'll give you all the facts about what's wrong and your options for fixing it. I'll never try to upsell you or coerce you into fixing what you don't need. You can choose if you want the fancy repair or the standard or the cheap. I'm all in your hands," I tell her, hoping it doesn't come out too desperate or rushed.

She starts smiling a bit, and I can tell she's trying not to giggle. "Does that mean you'll do what I tell you?" she asks.

"Absolutely!" I say, enjoying her giggle.

She chuckles more and I smile along. Then I realize what I said. "Oh, I mean, yeah, like, I'll do you right. No, I mean, I'll fix you good. Dammit!" I lean my elbow on the counter and cover my face with it, bracing my other arm on the counter as well.

She outright laughs now, the tension seemingly forgotten. "I know what you mean," she says, a kind smile on her face.

"Thanks," I breathe out. "That was, uh, unprecedented. I swear I'm not a creep."

"No worries." She giggles some more.

I standup straight again and can't stop myself from blurting out the next comment. "I really like your hair. It looks awesome."

"Oh, thanks," she says, running her fingers through it. "I wasn't sure what to go with, but blue just seemed to call to me."

"Do you do that kind of color all the time?" I ask, desperate to keep her talking. The minute we start talking about her car will mean we're close to ending any conversation.

"Oh, uh, I like to switch it up. Keeps things fun," she says.

We stand in silence for a moment, looking at each other. I can feel the tension between us and if we were in a bar, I would be doing my best to get my hands on her.

We're not a club. We're at my place of business. Professional. Be professional, dammit.

"What seems to be the problem with your car?" I shake myself out of the stare.

"Well, uh, my car's been making this noise for a while and I'm not sure what it is, but it won't go away, and I figure I should probably get it looked at. I, uh, don't have the best history or luck with mechanics, but a friend said you guys are reasonable and know what you're doing."

"Yeah, for sure. What's it sound like?"

"Um." She screws up her face a little, trying to think about it. "It's kind of like a clunking noise? I think?"

I smile. It's a stereotypical girl response and I can't handle how much I love it. "Is it rhythmic?" I ask, lowering my voice a little.

I hope that she'll pick up on my flirting and when she blushes just a bit on her cheeks, I give myself an internal high five. I give her a small wink. Her blush spreads to more of her face, and that blush is now my favorite color.

"Or is it more sporadic?"

"Um, a little of both? It happens once in a while and it starts off pretty steadily, but eventually… runs out of steam." She looks up at me through her lashes as she says that last part, a small smirk on her face.

Holy shit, is she flirting back? I don't even care that it was a slam. I'm all about this.

I lean forward on the counter, resting my weight on my elbows. "Hmmm, sounds like a stamina issue. Definitely need to fix what's going on there. Is there a trigger? Something that really gets it goin'?"

"Well, usually if I go over a bump or something, that'll start it off," she says, more business and a little less flirtatious.

I'm not about to give up the flirting. There's some serious chemistry here. "Well, I've definitely got some skills with my hands.

I bet I could get her to make some noise for me," I tell her, raising my eyebrows and a small smile on my face.

She blushes a little harder, looking flustered, and bites her bottom lip just a bit.

Well, fuck me, that's hot.

"How long would it take you to determine what's wrong with it?" she asks, officially business mode now.

"Not long, maybe a few hours. She's in good hands here, I promise, Sunshine." The endearment rolls off my tongue with no effort. She is radiant, and it fits.

"Sounds good. Do I just give you my keys, or…?"

"You can give me your number." She pauses and I reach under the counter for a clipboard and our general client form. "Just fill out your info at the top and leave your keys with me," I tell her with a flirty smile.

She laughs a little and grabs the pen I offer. I can't help but watch her while she fills out the form. If she notices, she doesn't react. Her brows contract slightly as she concentrates on making her letters visible on the tiny form.

"Sorry it's so small. It's hard to find forms with more space for client information," I tell her.

Not that I've tried, but she doesn't know that.

"Oh, it's no problem." She glances up and gives me a smile.

I smile back at her. I can't help it; it's like an instinctual reaction to her. That and blurting out words to try to keep her talking. She hands me her keys and I add the label to them, writing Sunshine on it. I promise to call her tomorrow when we have a better idea of what is going on with the car.

Maybe I can convince her to go on a date? Plus, there's a guy out there waiting for her. I really hope she's not taken.

"Thanks so much," she tells me, her face more relaxed than when she arrived.

"No, thank you. I appreciate the business, Sunshine. Is, uh, is that your boyfriend out there? He giving you a ride home?"

She glances out where a tall, lanky guy leans on a truck, alternating between glancing at the shop door and staring at the sky.

She giggles a little. "No, definitely not my boyfriend, but he is my ride home."

"Oh, good, then," I say, hoping she catches the fact that I'm glad he's not her boyfriend. I don't want to come off as a total creep, so I leave it. "Have a great day, beautiful."

She blushes a little again, smiles at me, and turns and leaves the shop. I watch her ass sway as she walks and blow out a breath.

I need more time with that woman.

As I look down at the form she left, I thank God for this counter. I was sporting a semi that entire time.

 # Chapter 4

Charlotte

Thomas pulls into my driveway on Friday afternoon, looking like he's just rolled out of bed. The thing with Thomas is that you never know if he did. He likes that lazy style and isn't ashamed of it. Thankfully, it works for him, or he'd have a lot harder time finding a job that pays well. I step out of the front door and lock it, then walk to his car as he rolls down the driver's side window.

"You owe me," he grumbles.

"I promise, on my life as your big sister, I will buy you Star B's," I tell him, holding my hand in the air like I'm swearing into court.

"I'm ordering a venti," he threatens.

"I'm sure you'll earn it," I tell him and walk to my car.

We back out of my driveway in our cars and head for the shop. It's about a fifteen-minute drive, so not too bad. Far enough I can't walk it without extra time planned in, so I'm grateful for my little brother helping me out. I mean, he's been taller than me since we were in high school, but I always tell him he'll be littler than me. It always earns me a pinch in the side and attempted tickles. We may be adults, but we're not grown up. We pull into the parking lot of the shop and Thomas gets out of his car with me.

"Want me to come in with you?" he asks, not sounding particularly enthused.

"No, I think I got this," I tell him.

"You sure? I know you hate mechanics."

"Only if they're old and skeezy and treat me like an idiot."

"Fair enough," he relents and yawns. "I'll wait here unless you send up a smoke signal."

"What would I even use to make a smoke signal inside the shop?" I ask him, confused.

"I don't know, that's not even the point! Stop making me think, go inside," he fires back.

I laugh and walk toward the door, glancing back to see him leaning against the side of his car, waiting. Apparently, he meant he'd wait there literally. He's a better sibling than I am. I'd be sitting in the car enjoying the controlled temperature.

I open the door and immediately am assaulted by the sound of yelling.

"I'm not paying you to sit around and look at cars. I'm paying you to work!" The guy at the front desk is yelling out of the window overlooking the rest of the shop.

"I promise we're doing the best we can!" someone shouts back.

"Do better!" He slams the window shut.

Maybe this was a bad idea. I don't think I want to deal with a shop where yelling at your employees is normal behavior.

I hesitate in the doorway with the door still open, trying to decide if I'm going to walk in or just bail. The guy at the counter turns back around and freezes when he sees me.

Hot damn, is he gorgeous.

He's tall, and I can tell he's strong under that shirt. He doesn't appear to have chiseled muscles, at least not that I can see, but I'm so okay with that. Men with chiseled muscles usually are high maintenance. This guy has the brightest blue eyes I've ever seen, and a neatly kept beard on his face. I can see small laugh lines around his eyes, indicating that he does smile a lot despite what I've just heard.

Maybe he won't be so bad after all?

"Hi, um, I was looking for Jax's Repair Shop? My car needs to be looked at, but I'm not sure I'm in the right place?"

I am sure I'm in the right place, but I'm a little unsure if it's the place for me. I guess it'll depend on his response. He seems to shake himself out of it and smiles at me.

Pretty sure I just melted inside.

"Hey, I'm sorry, I, uh, was thinking about a car I need to fix. I'm Jax. How can I help?"

"Oh, uh, this is Jax's repair shop?" Stupid question, but I'm not even sure what to ask at this point. The man has me all flustered.

"Yup!"

His voice is nice, deep, but not in an intimidating way. I decide I need to bite the bullet and just go in. He seems decent and even if he *is* cute, there's no reason to drool.

It's not like I'm here to get a date. If he even wanted to date me. There's no guarantee of that; we don't even know each other. I wouldn't mind getting to know him, though.

I straighten my shoulders a bit to boost my confidence and walk fully into the shop, letting the door close behind me.

\#

I walk out of the shop, floating a little as I walk back towards Thomas. I may or may not put a little extra sway in my hips. I hope Jax is looking, but he's probably not. Even if he's not, the motion gives me a little confidence. I think he was flirting with me, but he could have just been really nice. I tried to reciprocate a little, but I felt awkward doing that, so I tried to go for nice.

The things I want him to do to me land way above nice. More in the ecstasy region of feelings.

Thomas pulls himself out of the lean he had going on his truck. "All good?"

"Yeah, I think this will be a decent shop. The guy at the counter seems nice," I tell him.

"Glad to hear it. The other two mechanics in there look like they're working hard, so hopefully that's a sign that this place knows what it's doing. Some places I swear they just stand around and talk."

I frown a little as I walk over to my side of the truck and climb in. "Yeah, I heard him yelling when I went in, so I was a little worried."

"Nah, you know dudes who work with their hands. They're always pullin' that kind of shit with each other. Those guys are probably just a little more gruff than you're used to," he says with all the confidence of someone who just *knows* they're right. The man works as a warehouse manager. I don't think he's done hard work with his hands… ever.

I roll my eyes at him. "Maybe so. Anyway, I owe you some coffee. Let's hit Star B's and get caffeinated."

"Now you're talkin'," he says, pulling out of the parking lot.

We get our caffeine fix and start heading back to my place. It's close to the end of the day, but Thomas usually works thirds so this is a bit early for him. Me? I just have a problem. I don't have to worry about work until Monday. Thankfully, my job is flexible and I can work from home for a few days next week while my car is repaired. The perks of working in an IT environment. I don't actually fix computers. I'm a project manager, so I just make sure people do their part to get the work done.

I glance over at Thomas. "Soooo… anything exciting happen lately?"

He shrugs.

"You know, some people say it's hard to get you to talk, but you never seem to shut up around me."

He chuckles but remains silent.

"Come ON, you're caffeinated now. Give me SOMETHING," I beg him.

I doubt he actually has much to update me on, but harassing him for information is most of the fun here. It's my duty as the big sister to be overly invested in his life. Or at least pretend to be. He lets out a long sigh, suffering from having to deal with me.

"Uh, I went out for drinks with some chick the other day," he says.

I scoff. "I meant something fun, not your hang outs with Courtney."

Courtney is his best friend. They met in high school over their mutual hate of exercise and have been inseparable since. I think it's been about ten years now. I see him roll his eyes at that.

"Any dates lately?" I jab at him.

I don't know if he's even seeing anyone, but his last boyfriend was a piece of shit, so I'm hoping he gets back out there soon.

"I mean, there was a cute guy at the bar. Courtney tried to get me to go after him, but I don't know if I'm ready," he says in a rare moment of vulnerability.

"Nobody can decide that for you, but if you ever need an extra wingman, I'm here for you. Courtney does pretty well, though."

He smiles gently. "Yeah, she does. She's pretty great."

"I'm glad you have her. We should hang out soon. It's been ages since I've seen her."

He scoffs. "You're so dramatic. It's only been like a month."

"Still too long," I sing-song at him.

"Maybe we can make it a whole sibling thing and go out with Graham, too. Well, at least invite him and understand he won't actually show," he offers.

I laugh a little as we pull into my driveway. Graham is our big brother, and he's awesome. Incredibly responsible, he's always there for us, and we know he loves us. He has faults though and two of them are a huge stick up his ass and chastising us any chance he gets for not being more mature or responsible.

"Sounds like a plan." I smile at him. "Thanks again for the ride, bro. I really didn't want to deal with a Graham lecture."

"No prob, get out so I can go home and game," he says with a smile.

"Not working tonight?"

"Nah, swapped with someone, so I'll work Sunday night instead of tonight."

"What the hell? You guilted me into coffee, and you're not even working tonight??"

He smiles. "Yeah, you fell for it too."

"Asshole."

"Love you too," he says.

"Well, enjoy World of WarCraft. Chat with a cute boy."

He looks at me in disgust. "It's Call of Duty. I can't believe you think you know me!"

I laugh and wave him off.

After I'm inside, I look at the time and decide it's time for dinner. I take another sip of my latte and realize I'm going to be up for hours at this rate. I call the girls, because if I have to be awake, I may as well be entertained. Olivia and Amy say they'll be over in an hour, and I look through my fridge for food. I consider ordering out, but with the car repair cost, I decide not to. That guy didn't say how much it would be, and I don't want to get crazy with spending until I know how much I'm going to have to shell out.

I decide on some pasta and chicken with veggies on the side. Simple, easy, and who doesn't love pasta? I'm pan frying the chicken when I hear someone come into the house.

"WHAT DID YOU COOK ME?" a familiar voice yells across the house.

Liv then.

"Nothing! It's all for me!" I shout back with a smile.

She comes in, cake in hand from the store and sets it on the counter. I look from her to the cake and back again.

"Did… did you go to the store for me?" I ask, pretending to tear up.

She rolls her eyes. "I *can* go to the store, you know. I just prefer not to. People are assholes."

I giggle and agree, turning back to the chicken. As I'm putting it all together, Amy comes strolling in, two bottles of wine in hand.

"Sup bitches?" she says as she sets the wine on the table.

She immediately heads for the wine glasses as I dish out pasta and veg on three separate plates. We sit at the table and dig in. Olivia groans as she eats, and I smile a little.

"How are you so good at this?" she asks through a full mouth.

"It's just chicken and pasta," I protest. "It's not that hard."

"Yeah, well, we're not all gifted with the ability to cook," she grumbles.

"Just 'cuz *you* burn everything." Amy cackles at her expense.

Olivia tosses a piece of broccoli at her, but Amy is ready for her and catches it in her mouth. We laugh and finish eating, then clean up the kitchen. Olivia grabs three forks and the cake, then we migrate to the living room. I look at her and back to the cake and forks.

"Don't we need plates?" I ask.

Amy laughs. "Who do you think you're talking to?"

Olivia's grin is full of the mischief that comes with eating cake straight from the packaging. She sets the cake down, takes off the top and digs in. It looks amazing, yellow cake with chocolate frosting and sprinkles on the sides. I sigh like they're putting me through hardship and grab my own fork. We all take up spots on the floor surrounding the coffee table.

"So you finally got your car in?" Olivia asks as we stuff our faces.

"Yeah, I took it to that Jax place you told me about."

"What's up with your car?" Amy asks.

"It kept making this weird clunking noise when I went over bumps and Liv finally convinced me I should get it looked at," I explain.

"Tell her how long it was making the noise," Olivia butts in.

I give her the side eye and mutter, "Three weeks. "

"Excuse me?" Amy holds her hand to her ear like I'm not a foot away.

"Three weeks."

"Seriously? That's bad even for you," Amy scolds me.

"I know, I know, but I figured if it wasn't doing it all the time, it's not that bad, right?" I look between them, hoping for support.

Spoiler alert: I get none from either of them.

"Girl, you need to get over this mechanic bullshit," says Olivia.

"I hate how they look at me and talk to me like I'm dumb," I complain. "It was just easier to let Dad deal with it and I haven't had any car issues since they moved last year."

"What do you mean?" Amy asks.

She wasn't around in college when I first tried to go to the mechanic on my own. My dad had insisted it was a life skill I needed to develop, so he pushed me to take it in myself, but he was there for moral support.

I sigh. "The first few times I tried to take my car into the mechanic in college, it was almost always some older dude. That's not so bad, right? Except they would always look me up and down, either with a judging face or a creeper face. THEN they always, *always* called me girlie. They also talked to me like I didn't understand how cars work."

"I mean, do you?" asks Amy.

"Well, no, but they don't have to be dicks about it."

Olivia and Amy both start laughing. I smile a little, admitting it is a bit ridiculous. I put my fork down, full for the moment.

"I got tired of being treated like a piece of meat or like a stupid girl, so I just twisted my dad's arm to get him to do it for me," I explain.

Olivia coughs something that sounds suspiciously like "Daddy's Girl", and I chuckle.

"So how was this guy then?" Amy asks, thankfully changing the subject away from my creepy old mechanics toward the new sexy mechanic.

"It was good. I was kind of nervous, but he was really nice and seemed to know what he was doing," I tell them.

"Why are you blushing?" Amy asks.

Where Olivia is practical, Amy is painfully blunt. That's part of why I love her though. You don't get that from a lot of people who are also good people. Most blunt people are just assholes, but Amy also actually cares.

"I'm not blushing," I insist.

Maybe I am a little. Maybe.

"You're blushing." Olivia backs her up, pouncing on the opportunity to harass me.

I groan in frustration and lean back against the couch. They wait patiently, not taking their eyes off me. I finally sit back up a little and adjust myself so I'm just sitting against the couch instead of a full-on avoidance lean.

"Well, he was really cute," I finally admit.

"I think the word you're looking for is drop dead gorgeous," Olivia says.

"That's three words," Amy points out.

Olivia flips her off.

"You've met him?" I ask.

"No, but if you're saying he's cute, then he's definitely high on the scale. Was his smile nice? You can always get a feeling for a person based on their customer service smile."

"Oh, I don't know that I got that smile," I say, thinking back. All his smiles had seemed genuine to me.

"Oh, he didn't smile?" Olivia asks, confused. "But he was still nice, right?"

"Yeah, super nice, but he did smile," I tell her.

"So, you got a *real* smile," Amy says, a suggestive tone in her voice.

Before I realize it, a smile is spreading across my face.

"OK, spill ALL the details," Olivia insists, pushing the cake away.

"I don't think there's a lot to tell. He was really nice, but when I walked in, he was yelling into the car repair area and then laughed when he closed the window. I was worried he was like, super mean and enjoying it, but Thomas said that's just kind of how those guys are?"

"Yeah, they like to razz each other. I've been to a few garages that operate that way. It's kind of fun to watch when you can see both sides," says Amy.

"Oh. Well, I'm glad to know that. He seemed pretty flirty, but I'm not sure if he was actually flirting or if he was just being nice. When he smiled, you could see his eyes crinkle at the edges."

I honestly can't understand why he would want to flirt with me. I like who I am and how I look, but I know it's not "beauty standard". I've had enough guys tell me I have a great personality to understand that I probably won't catch anyone long term. I'm okay with that; I'd rather be alone than with some jerk. Been there, done that.

The girls are looking at me expectantly, so I explain what I thought were innuendos and his slip up saying he was in my hands, and the fumbles after. I tell them he asked about my hair, how he was leaning forward, but that a lot of people ask about my hair, and he was probably just resting his body from being up and moving all day.

Olivia and Amy look at each other, then back at me.

"You're, like, super obtuse, you know?" Amy comments.

"Well, I don't know if she's obtuse as much as in denial," Olivia offers.

Amy snaps her fingers. "That's it! Totally in denial."

"What are you guys talking about?" I ask.

"Girl, he was totally into you," Olivia says.

"No, I'm sure he was just being nice. It's good for business, you know?"

"Guys don't ask about your hair unless it actually interests them," Olivia insists.

"They do if they want word to spread about their business. He was being nice and showing interest, so I can tell everyone about the shop and how it felt comfortable there."

"It felt comfortable?" Amy asks. "You never feel comfortable when you're doing basic human interaction outside of us."

Olivia smiles. "It's true babe. You always feel kind of awkward, even if it's just a little."

I think back to the shop and talking to Jax. I really was comfortable. I didn't feel like he was going to be inappropriate, and I actually let my walls down for a moment.

"Yeah, but that doesn't mean he's into me," I insist.

"Oh, he is, trust us," says Olivia with confidence.

"Guys, seriously, nobody's gonna be into me," I tell them. "And I'm okay with that. There's nothing wrong with being on my own."

"Of course not!" Amy says vehemently. "That's not why you're alone, though. You're alone because you have convinced yourself that you're not worth someone's time and attention just because of your size and your anxiety. It's a lie and you need someone to show you that."

I look down at my hands, emotions starting to swell, and I fight back some tears. Amy and Olivia come and sit on either side of me, our bodies touching. We sit there like that for a few minutes, enjoying some human contact while I get myself back under control.

"Yeah," I rasp, throat still a little tight. "I get it. I just don't know how to believe it."

Amy puts her head on my shoulder. "We'll get you there."

"We're always here for you," Olivia adds, her head on my other shoulder.

I grab their hands and wonder how I got so lucky to have these amazing women in my life.

 # Chapter 5

Jax

I've taken Charlotte's car for a few test drives so far this morning and I think I have the problem down. I need to do a little visual inspection just to be sure, so I make sure it's aligned in the bay lift properly and get her into the air. As the car lifts, my mind drifts to yesterday when she walked in, not realizing how much she rocked my world. After she left, the first thing I did with her form was find her first name. Perfect name for the perfect girl.

Roman and the new guy are still working on that other repair, but new guy actually identified the problem and today they're starting on repair. Roman made the new guy call the owner and give the quote and get permission. I have to admit, he did well. I think he's actually going to fit in well here. I'm glad that's the case because hiring people is a hassle and I hate it.

After I get Charlotte's car fully raised, I start looking around underneath and I think I'm right on the issue. I'll need to take it apart a little to validate, but I want to give the new guy one more test and this feels like a good opportunity. I look over and see Roman's taken over for the moment and decide now is the time. Roman won't mind me pulling him away for a moment.

"New guy," I bark.

He looks over at me, a little surprised and a little apprehensive. "Um, it's Dan," he says, with more force than I would have expected.

"Dan, come over here and look at this with me. You come to the same conclusion as I did and I'll stop calling you new guy," I offer.

I probably would either way, but he doesn't need to know that.

Dan walks over and looks up. "What do you know so far?" he asks.

"Makes a clunking noise when you go over bumps. Starts out frequent but slowly dies away."

"Kind of like a bouncy ball does," he comments offhandedly.

"Yeah, I'm pretty sure I know what's up with it, but curious what you would check."

He looks for a moment, thinking. "I would check the subframe bushings. I'm assuming the noise is from the front, since that's where you're standing, and that's the first thing I would check with those symptoms."

I shoot him a smile. "That was my thought too, man. Help me out a second."

I give him the pliers to use, and he clears my line of sight so I can see that the bushings are going bad. We won't be able to see how bad it is until we get in there, but at least I know what we need to repair, and I can give Charlotte a call. A quote too, but I'm looking forward to the call more. I want to hear her voice again. It's been a day and I'm already a sucker. I pat Dan on the shoulder, tell him thanks, and head towards the office to make the call.

As I walk away, I hear, "Were you actually nice to Dan?"

"I'm a nice guy!" I insist, turning to look at Roman while walking backwards.

"You've called him new guy since he started!" Roman argues, like I don't know that.

"So? That's what he was."

"You're a dick," Roman says.

I shrug and nod, grinning, then turn and walk all the way back to the office and the phone. Pulling out Charlotte's file, I dial her number and feel a flutter of excitement in my belly as it rings. I'm afraid it's going to go to voicemail when I finally hear her pick up.

"Hello?"

She sounds breathless. I *want to make her breathless.*

"Hi, is this Charlotte?" I ask, but I already know.

"This is," she says, all business.

"This is Jax from Jax's Repair Shop. I wanted to get in touch with you on what we need to repair and what the cost could be."

"Oh, great! That was quick."

"Well, we haven't fixed it yet, but I at least know what we need to do," I say with a smile.

"Oh, awesome. Well, what's the problem?"

Suddenly, I can't resist pulling her leg a bit. Especially with how she answered the phone.

"Well," I start. "We actually found a vibrator under the passenger side seat of your car."

Silence.

"Charlotte?" I ask, wondering if maybe I took it too far.

"Are you KIDDING ME?!" she shrieks.

I almost chuckle. But manage to hold it in.

"Yeah, I mean, it's a pretty powerful device. I can imagine how much noise it would have made."

"Oh my God, I am mortified," I hear her mumble to herself. She clears her throat. "Would you believe me if I said it wasn't mine?"

At that point I can't hold back the chuckle. She fell right into it, and I don't want to take the joke too far.

"I'm serious!" she insists.

"I believe you," I say, still laughing a bit. "I was just pulling your leg."

Silence again.

"I'm sorry if that was too far. I couldn't resist," I confess.

She huffs a laugh. "God, you really had me going for a minute!"

"Do you want to know what was actually wrong?"

"Yes please," she says, and I can hear her smile. "Hopefully no vibrators stuck somewhere else in the car."

I can't help but laugh out loud at that one. "No, but it looks like your subframe bushings are bad and need to be replaced. It's something that really isn't safe to drive around with, so I would highly recommend fixing it. It's not optional, in my opinion. Cost-wise, we're looking $250 minimum, but could be more depending on if there's additional damage."

She's quiet for a moment, but I can hear her moving around a little. Maybe pacing? I can't help but wonder what she's doing.

"Well, at least it's not a stuck vibrator. Okay, let's go ahead and fix it. But will you please let me know if it's more than $500 before you do anything?" she asks, her voice suddenly timid.

Huh, she sounded way more confident at first. Now she sounds like when she first arrived at the shop yesterday. Why is she so nervous? Maybe money? Hopefully, I can ease her concerns. I was hoping the joke would make her feel better over the whole situation.

"Yeah absolutely, I won't do any repairs if it's going to be more than $500 unless you give me the okay," I reassure her.

"Thanks," she says with a small sigh.

"I'm gonna guess it'll be Monday afternoon when we're done with it but could be Tuesday if things are more complicated than I anticipate. I'll be sure to call you if that's the case though. I don't want you to be caught off guard."

"Oh, well, thank you." She sounds surprised, and I wonder what kind of shops she's dealt with in the past.

"No problem, I'll talk to you soon," I tell her.

"Thanks again, bye," she says, and I can hear the smile in her voice.

I wanted so badly to keep her talking, but I know if I do then I'll never get to repair her car and I'll come off like a creeper. Not good for my business OR my end goal of getting to know her better. I sigh after I hang up the phone and decide I need to get to work. Then I realize I never asked if she needed a rental car and wonder if I should call her back.

No, no, I need to leave it and go get her car fixed. I'm sure she would have asked if she needed one.

I talk myself out of calling her again and turn to leave the office. I've got a car to fix.

 # Chapter 6

Roman

My alarm goes off for the second time and my knee jerk reaction is to throw the damn thing across the room. The problem is my phone is my alarm and I can't really afford to throw that. So, I restrain myself.

"Fuuuuuck," I say to nobody.

I turn off the alarm and swing the blankets off, hoping to motivate myself out of bed. It's a shop day, and I love the shop, but I hate mornings. People who like mornings are crazy, I'm convinced of it. I stretch my body and scratch up and down my torso before dragging my ass out of bed and running through my morning routine.

I think Jax is finally giving the Lexus back to the girl he calls Sunshine today. He even put that stupid nickname on the key tag. Sappy. One of us needs to be, I suppose. I didn't get a good look at her when she dropped the car off since I was busy working with Dan on some stuff, but Jax is totally smitten.

I heard him call her with the diagnosis and when he told her it was a vibrator in the car; I huffed a laugh. There's always a joke around for him to tell. I don't think he goes through a day without making a joke or trying to get someone to smile. We're pretty opposite and that's why I like him. Nobody needs two broody bastards all the time.

Locking up my apartment, I head out to my beat-up truck, grabbing yesterday's mail as I go. I toss it on the seat next to me and fire my baby up. She's falling apart, but I've had her since I was eighteen and learning to fix cars. Giving her a minute, I look over at the mail and groan. I can already see the red letters.

More overdue shit, just what I need.

My little sister begged to go to college when she graduated high school, but our parents weren't in a place to help with that, considering my dad was dead and my mom took off at the first opportunity with a new guy. My sister did a lot of the legwork on her own initially, but I agreed to co-sign a couple of her loans. Here's a life lesson, kiddies, don't co-sign on shit unless you read the fine print. Juliet skipped out on college after two years and then skipped out on her bills.

Now I get to deal with her student loan payments I can't afford and listen to my mom bitch about the credit card Juliet took out in her name. At least, when she deigns to call me. I'm sure she'll shove that off on me at some point. Our parents named their daughter after a tragedy and she's certainly fulfilling that role. Shaking my head, I get my truck in gear and pull out of the apartment complex, heading toward the shop.

At least I can fix shit there instead of just piling on the problems with no solutions. My late bills can wait, my financial problems can wait, and I can focus on fixing other people's cars.

I arrive with some coffee and see that Jax has begun opening the shop. He's early, which means he's probably nervous. I'm not sure what he's so nervous about, but I would guess it's the girl coming for her car today.

He needs to get laid. Hopefully she's game.

I walk into the bay he's in and hand him a coffee. He grabs it with a small bit of gratitude thrown my way and starts drinking it immediately. He's busy looking over the Lexus. Again.

"Want me to get the office open and computer on?" I ask.

"You hate doing that shit," he replies, glancing at me before looking at the car again.

"Someone around here needs to actually work," I quip as I walk to the office area.

I feel something smack the back of my head and then a metallic "ting" as it hits the ground. Turning, I see the quarter that Jax got me with. Leaning down, I pick it up, nod my thanks, and keep walking.

"Asshole!" Jax yells, but I can hear the smile in his voice.

Smirking, I hold up my middle finger as I keep walking.

The day passes pretty quickly. Dan is absolutely proving his worth to this shop. He's already caught a few things that I missed on the initial inspection of some cars we're doing oil changes on. I would have caught them, but he got it sooner. Clapping him on the back, I tell him he's doing great and turn to see what else is in the bay that needs doing. It's then that I see a girl with vibrant blue hair walking toward the office.

Not only is her hair vibrant blue, but she walks with a mix of confidence and trepidation and the combination fascinates me. She's got full lips, fantastic tits, and legs for miles. She has a friend with her, but my brain barely registers her existence before focusing back on the blue-haired beauty.

I start for the office. Whoever this girl is, I need to meet her. It feels like she's calling to me, which makes me feel like a sappy idiot. Jax hurries past me and holds his hand up, telling me he's got it. I force myself away from the office and back to the car I'm working on. That lasts all of a minute before my feet are taking me closer to the office. I stand next to the window, just out of sight, and pretend to look for a part while I listen in on what conversation I can catch. Unfortunately, it's not much.

Jax is explaining the repair costs to her, and she sounds surprised that it's easy to understand and actually affordable.

Fuck, I wanna know which mechanic made her uncomfortable in the past and punch him or her in the face. Double fuck, Jax is asking her out.

I smirk since he's borderline stumbling over his words, trying to be smooth.

"Of course, like I said, any time. Hey, uh, I wanted to ask you something but, I don't wanna come off wrong or like make you uncomfortable." He's babbling a little by the end.

"Okay…." she responds.

"Could, I, uh, call you sometime? I'd love to get to know you more over drinks or something?"

"Yeah, I'd like that."

Of course she would. Jax is an upbeat dude. He doesn't really have a hard time getting girls, he just has a hard time deciding to go for one.

Fuck. I don't want to cause problems and chase after the same girl, but she's going to live rent-free in my head.

"Here, I have a pen, so you can write your number down." He's babbling again.

"You already have it." I hear her sass him and then the door dings a moment later.

I step quickly away from the wall to watch her walk out to her car. I'm standing next to one of the cars, watching her sashay away from the shop like a total creeper.

Do I care? No. I want to watch that ass swing all day long.

She glances down at her phone, then back at the shop with a smile on her face. Her eyes drift to where I'm standing and she freezes, staring right at me. The smile on her face changes from a happy smile to something a little more sultry, and she bites her lip a little.

Oh she's interested.

I smirk at her and nod my head toward her.

I'm game if you are, baby. I have no problem sharing.

After she leaves, I make my way into the office. Jax is on his phone, smiling as he types away. I sidle up to him and look over his shoulder, waiting to see if he notices me. It takes him another two texts before he finally realizes I'm there and jumps.

"Fuck Roman! You scared the shit out of me," he says.

I shrug. "Been here for five minutes, not like I just got here."

"You could say something!"

"Nah, this is more entertaining," I tell him.

Jax huffs a laugh and shakes his head at me. "What's up?" he asks.

I jump right to it. "Who was that?"

"That was my newest obsession. Her name is Charlotte, and I am dying to get to know her," he confesses.

"She's hot," I tell him, not even trying to hide it.

He gives me side eye. "I saw her first, asshole."

I can tell suggesting sharing isn't going to go well yet, so I leave it alone and clap my hand on his shoulder.

"Alright, alright, I get it. No touching…. for now." I add the last part under my breath.

The shop is just about done for the day and Jax helps me get the last couple of oil changes completed and the owners notified. Once everything is packed up for the night, I clear my throat and look over at my best friend. He looks up and frowns at me.

"What's up?" he asks. "You don't usually linger unless you got something to say."

"Yeah, uh, I wanted to ask you something."

"I'm all ears, man."

"Remember the offer you made, like six months ago, about renting me a room?"

"When are you moving in?" he asks.

"Are you sure?"

Jax puts on his unusually serious face. "Dude, I know what you've been dealing with from your sister's shit. My house is always open to you. You've been by my side for the last twelve years. Let me be there for you."

I clear my throat.

I'm not about to cry, I swear. I don't have feelings like that. Better clear my throat again to be sure.

"Yeah, I really appreciate that, man. My lease is up next week. Is it ok if I just bring stuff over a little every day? I don't have much."

"Yeah, let me know if you want help. We can use the basement or garage for storage. I still haven't finished the damn basement so it should be used for something."

He pulls me into a hug and holds me a little longer than I'd normally let him. For someone as obtuse as he is, he really does know what someone needs at times.

 # Chapter 7

Charlotte

Since Saturday morning when Jax called, I've been anxious. I just want my car back. I like my freedom and independence, so it's hard to be without, even just in my head. Not that I have anywhere to go, but it's the lack of choice that really gets me wound up. Thankfully, my vibrator wasn't actually stuck in the car, so I was able to use that to unwind.

Come to think of it, I should have seen his teasing sooner than I did. The car definitely was not making a buzzing noise. Smiling to myself, I lock my computer, ready to take my lunch break, and my phone rings. I pick it up from my desk and stand up, looking at the caller ID.

Ugh, it's Graham. Do I pick up the phone and expose myself to a potential lecture, or do I just let it go? I'm not sure I'm really in the mood to deal with it since I've been a little on edge waiting for the call that my car's ready. I'll call him back later. He'll survive.

Phone in hand, I venture to find food. Not two seconds after I make it into the kitchen, the damn thing rings again. I roll my eyes and slide my finger across the screen to answer.

"What?" I answer in a flat voice, not looking forward to whatever Graham has to say.

"Hi, is this Charlotte?"

Oh god, I know that voice. It's Jax, I can't believe I didn't look at the Caller ID. Who doesn't look at the Caller ID? Classic bad romance novel move.

"Oh, hi, yes, I'm so sorry. I, um…. hi," I finish lamely.

"Hi." I hear a laugh in his voice. "This is Jax from Jax's Repair Shop. We've got your car fixed up, it's ready when you are."

"Oh, great! Um, how late are you open today?"

"We close at six."

"Okay, wonderful. I'll try to be by this afternoon, if that's okay?"

"Sounds perfect, I'll be waiting. I mean, I'll be here," he says, sounding a bit flustered.

I smile. "Okay, thanks again! Bye."

"Bye, Sunshine."

OMG, he called me sunshine again. Maybe the girls were right, and he was flirting. Then again, he's probably just being nice. Like, don't all shop guys treat girls like that with silly names? Yeah, probably. I'm reading too much into this.

My phone beeps, notifying me that Graham left a message. I finish making my lunch and pull up Graham's voicemail while I eat.

"Hey Charli, I see you're avoiding me…"

How the fuck does he always know?

"…but I wanted to call and ask about your car. Thomas mentioned you had to bring it in. I know the mechanic shit is hard for you, so I figured I'd be nice and ask. I mean, you should have brought it in way sooner than you did, but at least you brought it in. Thomas also said we should all go out soon, and I wanted to let you know I'm in. Been thinking I don't see either of you enough. Call me later."

Well, color me stunned. Was that my big brother? No in-depth lecture? No excuses for how he can't get together with us soon? Who is this man?

For a moment I'm tempted to ask him to bring me to pick up my car after work, but in the end that stick is still somewhere up his ass. I don't want to deal with it. I text Amy instead.

Me: Hey B, are you free tonight? Need a ride to pick up my car.

Ames: Yeah for sure, what time?

Me: Pick me up around 4:30? They're open til six but I don't want to push my luck.

Ames: You got it, see ya later

Thank God Amy is always willing to step up and give me a hand. I should get her something. I file that away for "things to ponder on" and head back into my home office to finish up the day.

Ames shows up at 4:30 on the dot, and waltzes into the house. I'm just powering down my computer when I hear the door close.

"Just turned off my computer," I call out.

"Okay, ready when you are!"

I use the bathroom, slide on some shoes, and we're off. She pulls onto the street, and I put the shop into her GPS, so we don't have to stop talking to navigate. Lazy, I know.

"So is *the guy* going to be there tonight?" she asks, heavily emphasizing "the guy".

"Well, it *is* his shop," I reply.

"I'm coming in with you. I need to see this." She doesn't even ask.

"You can't embarrass me," I warn her.

"I won't…" she says, and I don't believe her for one second.

"Ames, I'm serious. Don't make this weird."

"What? Weird? Me? I never make things weird," she insists, not looking at me.

"I mean it. Don't come in if you're gonna be all awkward."

"Okay, I promise. I'll just wait by the door or something. I won't even come up to the counter."

"Pinky?" I challenge.

"Pinky," she replies.

She holds up her right hand, pinky out, and I loop mine with hers. We awkwardly kiss our thumbs while also trying to keep her on the road. We giggle and she puts her hand back. I was serious in my request. She has no shame and will embarrass the shit out of me if I don't make her pinky promise.

We pull into the parking lot and grab a spot near the door.

"Princess parking!" Amy calls in a singsong voice.

I laugh and pop the door open. As soon as I close the door, the nerves come back. I give myself an internal shake.

Come on, I can do this. He's nice, he's not pulling one over on me. I'm sure my car will work when I drive out of here.

I take a deep breath and start walking around the car.

"Liv wouldn't recommend this place if it was crap," Amy reminds me gently. "It'll be fine."

I give her a grateful smile and open the door to the office. It's empty this time, but the "someone's here" chime goes off when the door closes. Amy, as promised, hangs out over by the door while I approach the counter, beating the nerves back and placing my hands on the counter, folded and waiting. I see movement in the shop and glance over to see a blonde god looking at me.

He's got long hair that's tied back into a low ponytail and green eyes that see straight through me. He's staring at me like I'm his next lunch and I can feel my breath quickening from his gaze.

Is there some rule in this shop that only hot guys can work here?

He starts to walk toward the office before I see Jax pass by the window and give him a wave. Jax opens the door and walks into the waiting area, grinning the minute he sees me. My heart picks up the pace when I see him and I'm pretty sure I'm a goner. Something about him just draws me in and I can't resist.

He looks just as good as I remember. Tall, broad, piercing blue eyes and that smile. His hair isn't so long that it's in his face, but it's not super short either. Just enough to run my hands through and maybe grab a little. My fingers want to touch it.

"Hey there Sunshine," he greets me. "Fancy seeing you here."

I smile back at him. "Well, you do have my car…"

"Too true, and it should be all better now," he says.

"Well, what's the damage?" I ask him.

"So, your subframe bushings were worn out and needed to be replaced, like I had mentioned. Normally I would have gone through several options with you regarding parts we can use, but on this one there's only one level of part. I'm sure I could dig up some super fancy labeled part, but it would have been a waste of money."

"I appreciate the honesty," I tell him. "I mean, assuming you're being honest."

I can't help teasing a little and I hope he picks up on it and gives it back some. I love some good banter.

"I guess you'll just have to drive it and find out," he replies. "Thankfully, I'm good at what I do, so I know you're in good hands." He pulls out the paperwork and lays it on the counter, grabbing a pen. "The total is gonna be $250," he tells me, pointing out each line and what the cost covers.

I follow along and I actually understand what he's saying. I'm pleasantly surprised and I'm seriously hopeful that maybe this is a shop I can actually rely on. It would be nice to have somewhere I know I can go to any time.

"Wow, this is, like, super easy to understand. I really appreciate you explaining it all," I tell him, looking up as I talk.

I realize we were both bent over the paper and now our faces are super close. We look at each other for a moment and I see him glance down to my lips and back to my eyes. My eyes do the same before I stand up straight, clearing my throat a little. He keeps his eyes on me, and a slow smile comes over his face.

"No problem at all. Always happy to help you out."

I give him my card and he hands me my keys. Easy peasy. I fiddle with my keys a little, knowing I should go but not really wanting to leave. I glance back at Amy, and she nods towards him, quickly raising her eyebrows up and down a few times. I turn back with a smile.

"Okay, well, thanks again," I tell him.

"Of course, like I said, any time. Hey, uh, I wanted to ask you something but, I don't wanna come off wrong or like make you uncomfortable."

"Okay…"

He clears his throat twice and I'm surprised to see a small blush spread across his cheeks. "Could, I, uh, call you sometime? I'd love to get to know you more over drinks or something?"

I smile. "Yeah, I'd like that."

"Here, I have a pen, so you can write your number down."

I start backing up slowly, and his face falls a little. "You already have it," I tell him, and sashay out with Amy silently chuckling behind me.

We're not two steps into the parking lot when I hear my phone ding with a text. I grab it out of my pocket and unlock my phone.

Unknown: Hey, it's Jax, wanted to make sure you have my number too

I bite my lip and smile, saving his contact information. I look back at the shop and my gaze passes by the open bay doors as I turn. They catch on the blonde god again and I'm pretty sure I stop breathing. He gives me a knowing smirk and nods at me. Amy is watching with a smile on her face and an eyebrow raised.

"What?" I ask.

"Oh he *likes* you. You have hit the hottie jackpot my dear, and we are *not* gonna let you pass this up."

I smile and shake my head at her. I'm grateful she doesn't seem to notice the other guy; I think that's more attention than I can handle.

"I'm getting in my car now," I tell her and walk away.

"I'm gonna text you later about Mr. Hottie!" she yells.

I turn back and look at her, horrified. Everyone in that building has to have heard that.

Shut up I mouth at her and quickly walk the rest of the way to my car. Looking down at my phone, I send a text back before I forget.

Me: Thanks, got it saved so I remember you're not a stalker.

Jax: Oh good, wouldn't want to mix myself up with any existing stalkers you have *winky face*

Me: Good plan *smiley face*

Jax: I'll text you to make plans soon, Sunshine. Looking forward to it.

I smile again and get in my car to head home, where I can officially girl out and squeal.

 # Chapter 8

Roman

It's the end of my lease and I finally got all my shit moved yesterday. Today after work I'm turning in my keys to my old landlord, then going to Jax's house. I guess my house too now. I really don't want to lean on Jax like this, but I know he'll offer me cheaper rent and he wouldn't want me to get into any more financial trouble just because of my pride.

Dan has closing duties today, so I wave at him as I leave the shop. He waves back and I think again about how glad I am to have another reliable person in the shop. Jax put a lot of sweat and tears into this place, and I sacrificed a lot of hours to help make it happen, even if it's on Jax's dime. He deserves for this to go well; he's worked hard for it.

My keys get turned in and I walk into Jax's house, officially at my new home. I leave my shoes at the door with all the other shoes and make my way to my bedroom. I can hear Jax doing something in the kitchen, so I'll have to go see what he's up to later. For now, I need to shower and change. I'm covered in oil and grime.

Once I'm clean, I head into the kitchen. Jax is attempting to, emphasis on attempting, make pizzas from scratch. I lean against the wall, watching him struggle. The dough is too sticky, and I bet he didn't let it rise enough. I'm not a pro at making pizza dough, but I've made it once or twice just to see if I could, and even I can tell this dough is not quite right. I could step in, but Jax will never learn to do it himself. When he tries to pull his hands off the dough for the fifth time and they come away sticky, I figure I should step in. He's done enough swearing.

"Need some help?" I ask, not moving.

Jax jumps. "DAMN IT ROMAN!"

I can't help it, I laugh. Laughing isn't something I do super often, but when Jax gets startled, it never fails to get me laughing.

"Been standing here for five minutes," I inform him.

"This is getting to be a weird pattern," he throws back.

"You should pay more attention," I say, walking toward the dough.

"You should make more noise."

"Where's the fun in that? You baking me something good?"

"I was attempting pizzas," he confesses.

"I know."

"Then why did you ask?"

"To see if *you* knew what you were trying to do." I smirk.

"Fuck off," he says, smiling.

I push him to the sink to have him wash his hands and take a peek at the dough.

Too sticky, didn't rise enough. This isn't gonna work.

"How about I buy you pizza?" I offer. "This dough is no good and I don't think we have two hours for another batch to rise."

Jax sighs. "Fine, let's do that."

"Thanks for trying, honey," I say in a falsetto voice.

"Again, fuck off," he says, laughing.

I put in the pizza order and use my card to pay. Least I could do for the first night of living here. When the pizza arrives, we set it on the dining table, take our shares, and promptly flop onto the couch. Jax throws on *Top Gear* and we sit and eat for a few moments. I can feel myself get antsy and I can't help but ask.

"So, how's things with Charlotte?" I ask.

"We haven't been on a date yet, but the texting has been fun," he says.

"When's the first date?"

"Next weekend. Figured give it a bit before I take her out. Trying not to come across as a creeper."

"Nah, you're good. It's not like you're breathing heavily into the phone, right?"

"Oh, am I not supposed to do that?"

I roll my eyes as he laughs at his own joke. "Where are you taking her?" I ask.

"We're gonna go axe throwing. I figure I'm not good at it, so it won't be intimidating if she's not either." He shrugs.

"That's an understatement."

Jax chuckles. "Shut up."

I give him a small smile. "Well, let me know how it goes. She seems awesome."

Jax gives me a thoughtful look and nods. "Yeah, will do."

 # Chapter 9

Jax

The kitchen is a mess, and while I'll help clean it, I'm sure glad it's not my kitchen this year. Bethany and I finally get all the batter mixed together, but with the girls helping, it's taken us twice as long as usual. I couldn't say "no" to them helping though.

What kind of uncle would I be if I denied them anything? Probably one my sister would appreciate more. Whatever. My nieces, my rules.

We scrape the batter into some pans, and my sister pops them into the oven. While she isn't looking, I swipe my finger through the remaining batter on the sides of the bowl and stick it in my mouth. The girls giggle and I quickly take my finger out and put it to my lips, silently telling them to shush.

"What's all the giggling about, hmm?" Bethany asks as she turns back around.

I set my chin on my hands, leaning on the island, attempting the picture of innocence. "You know girls, always giggling over something. Maybe they were laughing at your butt. Butts are funny."

The girls erupt in laughter. They are definitely at the "butts are funny" stage of life. Honestly, I'm not sure that stage ever really ends.

Butts are always funny, unless you're talking about a hot woman. If you disagree, you're a liar.

My sister gives me the side eye.

"What?" I ask. "They are."

"Whenever you feel guilty, you immediately deflect to humor, especially butt humor. What'd you do?"

I put my hand to my chest, affronted. "I can't believe you don't believe me!"

She rolls her eyes. "Jax, I know you better than you know yourself, I swear. Girls, go take a potty break and play for a bit. We'll call you when the cake is ready to be frosted."

The girls whine a bit, but do as their mom asks, leaving us in a little peace as we tidy a little and grab ingredients for frosting. I walk past the oven as I cross to the fridge, subtly turning the oven to broil instead of bake.

"You gonna help me clean over here?" she asks.

"Not my house, you clean it up," I quip as I grab out the butter.

"Don't put it on broil, you're gonna ruin it!"

"It'll cook faster. I'm just trying to help," I protest, internally gleeful that the button pushing worked so quickly.

"I can't believe you own your own business, but you're still so stupid."

"Aww you really do love me," I tell her, giving her a light noogie on my way past. I hit the dial for broil again.

"Oh my God, stop!" she yells.

I chuckle and start mixing ingredients for chocolate frosting. Bethany starts cleaning up and when she isn't looking, I change the oven again.

"Do you understand it beeps when you do that? I can hear it."

"I was hoping you were deaf to it by now," I say with a smile.

She smiles back, switches the oven to bake, and walks over to where I'm standing at the island. I stop stirring and look over at her.

Her standing right next to me doesn't feel like a good thing.

My guard is instantly up, and I'm trying to work out what she's doing.

"You know I love you, Jax, right?"

"Um, yeah, I love you too. Why?" I ask warily.

"Just making sure you know," she says sweetly.

I give her one more look and slowly go back to the frosting. Then I feel it. The hard shell slamming on my head, cold goo running down through my shaggy hair, dripping down my neck and sliding down my shirt.

She could have at least used a room-temp egg.

"I WILL KILL YOU!" I roar through my smile, and Bethany yelps and runs.

I take a second to dump the yolk off my head and take after her. We circle the counter, laughing and breathing hard, not willing to take this out of the kitchen with the egg still dripping off me. I finally nab her and proceed to pull her into a headlock. She might be in better shape than me from her job, but I still have muscle from mine and my arms are longer.

At that moment, Trevor, her boyfriend, walks into the room, having come up from the basement, empty glass and bowl in hand. He was clearly intent on refilling his snack but stops and looks at us. We're frozen, Bethany's head still locked by my arms, so she has to strain to look up to see why I stopped moving. Trevor walks to the island, sets his dishes down and starts walking away.

"You don't want a snack?" I ask him.

Trevor looks back over his shoulder. "I'm not getting in the middle of that shit. You're both on your own."

"I thought you loved me!" Bethany yells after him, laughter in her voice.

"Not that much, honey," Trevor replies as he walks toward the basement door.

I hold her there for another moment, just to prove I can, and let her up. We're both grinning and breathing hard, but it's time to get the frosting finished. While the cake bakes, we finish making the frosting and chat.

"Do you remember the first time we did this?" Bethany asks, getting out the cake stands.

"Barely. What I was like nine and you were twelve?"

"Yeah, somewhere in there. I still remember we got that stupid powdered mix all over the kitchen and had to go borrow some from the neighbors."

"That's right! We ended up with like, a weird chocolate strawberry mix," I say, chuckling.

Bethany laughs. "It was so awful; Mom was such a champ to pretend it was good."

I grin at her. "This has been a good tradition."

"Yeah, it has."

"I still maintain we should add candles for each birthday."

She slaps me lightly on the arm. "You know Mom doesn't want candles on the cake. She says the wax makes it taste funny."

"I cannot understand that logic. It's not like the wax actually absorbs into the cake."

"Yeah, well, that's Mom for you," Bethany says.

The oven beeps, and she pulls the cakes out to check them. They're good to go, so she pops them in the fridge to cool faster.

"Hey, grab me a beer while you're in there," I tell her.

"Grab your own!" She shoots back and grabs one from the top shelf.

I hold out my hand, waiting for her to deposit it in, but right as she is about to hand it over, she yanks it back, pops it open, and takes a long pull.

"Mmmmm, so refreshing," she taunts.

"Beer makes you fat, you know," I tell her.

"Whatever. Have you seen these abs?" She pulls her shirt up.

"You painted those on, don't try to deny it."

"You wish. You're just jealous you have to paint yours on," she shoots back as she grabs another beer.

I glance down at my belly. I mean, I'm not chiseled, you can't see my ab muscles, but they're there. I'm strong, just not gym fit. More like an average guy with lots of strength from using my hands all day.

"It's ok guys, we don't need her judgement, we're beautiful the way we are," I whisper to my hidden muscles.

Bethany chuckles. "Did you name them too?"

I take the new beer from her outstretched hand. "We don't feel the need to divulge that information to you," I tell her and look down at my stomach again. "Do we, guys?"

She laughs and sets her beer down. "I'm gonna go get the girls. By the time they get their little butts in gear and get down here, we should be good to start frosting."

"Heh, butts," I tell her.

She rolls her eyes at me. I'm surprised she hasn't sprained a muscle yet.

"Kinsley! Abigail! We're getting ready to do frosting," she calls as she walks away.

A few moments later, I hear the thunder of tiny feet. I still don't understand how a five- and six-year-old can make as much noise as these two, but somehow, it's a thing. I move to stand in front of the kitchen entrance as they come racing across the living room.

"Halt!" I say loudly and they come to a stop a couple of feet from me, bouncing with excitement.

"Uncle Jax, move!" Kinsley, the older one, demands.

"Yeah, move!" Abigail echoes.

"Not until I get my uncle hug. You two skipped right over that when I got here, and I have been trying not to cry all day!"

The girls roll their eyes and groan.

Seriously, why is there so much eye rolling in this house?

"Uncle Jax, we DID hug you!" they protest.

"Well, I don't remember, so I demand new ones!"

Abigail is the first to break since she's always been the snuggle bug of the two. I grab her and swing her up and around, holding her tight at the end.

"Love you, bug," I tell her.

"Love you, Uncle Jax," she replies softly.

My heart swells. These damn kids get me every time.

"I'll only hug you if you promise to let me swipe some frosting!" Kinsley tries to negotiate.

"That's up to your mom, squirt, but I won't force you if you don't want."

She smiles a little and comes racing over, slamming into me before I can get her airborne. I hug her as best I can while she's latched onto my leg.

She looks up at me. "Frosting?"

"Frosting!" I cheer, throwing my hands in the air.

Bethany is setting the cakes on the island, testing their temperature. She looks a bit uncertain. "I'm not sure these are quite ready. They still feel a bit warm."

I walk over and slide my hand under the cake pan carefully. If it is still hot, I don't need my fingers burned. It's warm, but not hot.

"Eh, it's borderline," I hedge. "Girls, what should we do?"

Kinsley and Abigail look at each other and then back at the cake. My personal opinion is just taking the damn things out since they'll be covered in frosting anyway, but it's not just my project.

"Let's frost!" Abigail chirps up.

Bethany nods and grabs the plastic scraper to loosen the sides of the cake. With some gentle finagling, she manages to get it out mostly intact. There's a small circle of cake in the middle of the pan, but nothing that will detract from frosting it.

She attacks the second, and this one isn't quite as lucky. It comes out, but only about half of it does. It comes free at the bottom on one side and the cake tears as gravity takes over, so it's almost a diagonal half that comes out.

"We can work with this. It's fine," Bethany says in what I'm sure she thinks is a calm tone. It's not.

She takes a breath and gently scrapes the rest of it out of the pan, so it lays together, flat side down.

Definitely not gonna be sturdy enough to support the other one.

"Top layer?" I suggest.

"Top layer," she confirms, and starts leveling out the cake that stayed intact.

Once she's satisfied with the flatness of that cake, she sets it on the cake stand. She pulls out two small spatulas and hands one to each girl.

"Okay girls, let's put just a little on to start," she instructs. "And NO swiping frosting to eat. We don't need the extra calories."

Each girl grabs a little from their designated frosting supply bowls and slowly applies the frosting to the flat-topped cake. The cake starts to pull apart as they go, and Bethany stops them. There's only so much her control freak nature will allow.

"Ok, let's wait, they're not quite ready. We can't pull the cake apart more than it already is with frosting," she says, gently taking their frosting bowls back.

She didn't take mine.

As she moves to put the cakes to the side, I grab my frosting, make the silent "shush" gesture, and quickly apply it to their faces. One swipe under each eye and a swipe down their noses and chins. War frosting. The girls are grinning and trying not to laugh out loud, and Kinsley reaches for my frosting. I hand it over and close my eyes. She swipes the same pattern, one line under each eye and a line down the nose and chin. I open my eyes and grin back at them.

Bethany's gonna freak. I'm so excited.

We all turn and pretend nothing has happened as Bethany turns back around.

"What is on your faces??" she loudly demands.

I look at her, feigning confusion. "What do you mean? Did my nose disappear?"

"You put chocolate EVERYWHERE!" she yells.

"I didn't, but I could." I shrug.

"Mommy, I think your face is missing something," Kinsley says. "It looks weird."

Bethany sputters. "MY face looks weird?!"

Abigail nods solemnly, but I can see her trying not to crack. I've been working on keeping straight faces with these two. They're coming along well and I'm a proud uncle. Someday they'll fully grow into their mischievous ways, especially since they come by it honestly. Bethany's more tricky than she leads one to believe.

"Seriously, Jax, you can't give me ONE minute of peace?" She's still yelling.

"I feel pretty peaceful," I say calmly.

I hear the basement door open from the other side of the house and smile to myself. The cavalry has arrived. Trevor walks in and surveys the scene, slowly moving toward the kitchen.

"Who are we fighting?" he asks casually, swiping some frosting off Kinsley's face and popping his finger in his mouth.

"What? Fighting?" Bethany looks confused.

"Yeah, the girls and Jax have their war frosting on. Where's the battle?"

Bethany pinches her nose. "You are not helping."

He grins and asks, "Was I supposed to?"

Bethany finally breaks and starts giggling. "I hate all of you."

"No, you don't!" Kinsley chimes in.

"Yeah, you love us Mommy," Abigail adds.

"Come on, my little warriors," I say. "Let's see if we can get that first layer of frosting on now."

It's still a little warm but the girls are able to get the first thin layer applied without more cake breakage. After that, Trevor grabs them to get them cleaned up.

There's frosting on their faces, in their hair, and who knows where else with these two? They'll need a quick bath.

Bethany and I tackle the rest of the cake together. It's fun to include the girls in our tradition, but there's something about doing it, just the two of us, that makes me happy. It's a reminder that no matter what, we're always here for each other, even if it's just making a cake for our mom. I lean against the island as Bethany pipes on her fancy frosting blobs. I swipe one and pop it in my mouth.

"You are gonna get fat and get diabetes eating all my frosting like that," she scolds as she replaces it.

"At least it'll be delicious as I get closer to losing my foot," I quip.

"Yeah, well, can I call you PegFoot if you lose it?"

"Doesn't have the same ring as Pegleg, keep workin' on it."

She chuckles. "So how is the shop going? You mentioned it was going well. Is that still the case?"

"Yeah, I wish we had a little more business, but Roman has been busting his ass trying to get our social media out there to drum up some business. We've been asking for reviews and encouraging people to send referrals if they're happy with their service, all that shit."

"Sounds like you're doing things right, then. It'll take time to get that customer base up. I know you guys will get there. You work hard, and it shows," Bethany reassures me as she adds the last finishing swirl of deliciousness.

"That was nice and now I feel awkward," I tell her.

She replies by squishing the last of the frosting in her piping bag at my face. I open my mouth, trying to catch some just to see if I can. Bethany laughs and obliges by changing her aim into my mouth, except she doesn't stop when it's clear my mouth is full.

"Yield! I yield!" I try to say, except with the frosting, it's all muffled and garbled.

She laughs and grabs a washcloth for me to clean up with. I lean over the trash and dump most of the frosting out from my mouth, keeping just a little.

Life tip: don't waste chocolate, it's bad karma or some shit.

As I finish wiping my face, the front door opens, and our parents walk in. I lightly jog over to greet them and stop when I see my mom carrying four bags filled with takeout containers.

Shit.

"Aw mom, I'm so sorry," I tell her as I reach to take the bags.

"Why, did you forget my cake?" she asks, handing over her bags.

One of the things I love most about my mom is she never refuses help. She's always taught us that taking offered help is not a weakness, and we should make a point to help others. My desire to help others is one of the reasons I started my garage. I got sick of seeing over-priced repair shops absolutely extorting people for their money. You have to turn a profit, but ripping people off isn't the way to do it.

"No, I forgot to make any dinner!" I tell her, "I'm sorry you had to go get the food. You shouldn't have had to today."

"Nonsense. I know you get laser focused on that cake every year, so I figured I'd do my part and just grab the food on the way," she says.

"What if I cooked, Mom?" Bethany asks as she walks into the foyer.

"Then I'd ask you who you were and what did you do with my daughter? I don't even think you know what seasoning means," Dad quips.

She sticks her tongue out at him, and he chuckles as he gives her a hug in greeting. I take the bags over to the kitchen, laying out what I can on the counters, leaving the cake as center stage on the island. I know Bethany wants that baby to shine in the spotlight. As I start to take the first container out, the squealing starts.

"Grammy! Grampy!"

The girls shriek as they power into my parents' legs, begging for hugs. My dad lifts Abigail, pretending she's immensely heavy, and my mom leans down to bear hug Kinsley. My sister chuckles as she puts plates on the opposite counter from the food as we make an improvised buffet line.

Our mom got all the classic Italian food one could hope for. It's always a crowd pleaser and who doesn't love the gooey cheese the restaurant always adds to the top of manicotti? If you say you don't, you're a liar.

"The cake looks wonderful, you two!" Mom exclaims as she gets closer.

"I made all the decorative bits. Bethany kept trying to sabotage me. It was really rude."

As predicted, Bethany scoffs in outrage. "You little son of a..."

I grin as my mom reassures her she's well aware that Bethany is the one who always does the fancy piping. In my defense, the one year I was allowed to try, our mom thought that Kinsley, who was three at the time, had attacked the cake. She told Kinsley how much she loved it before I finally confessed that I was the disaster in that situation. We load up our plates, Bethany ensuring the girls at least have one green piece of food present and sit down at the dining table.

"Jax, honey, how is the garage?" Mom asks.

I give her the same rundown I had given Bethany and my parents both nod along and reaffirm what Bethany already said.

"You and Roman make a good team, you'll get there," Dad comments.

"What about you, Bethany? Whip anyone new into shape this week?" Mom asks.

"We had a couple of new people show up to classes this week. One was new to the gym entirely, and the other decided to start classes in addition to their typical workout. It was really encouraging. I spent a little time showing the new person around the facility a bit, so she hopefully feels more comfortable as she gets familiar with us."

"That's great!" Mom gushes. "Seeing any progress?"

"Well, some people are definitely starting to look better, but it's a journey. I don't expect overnight results."

"Good thing they have an excellent instructor for their classes as they lose that extra weight," Mom comments.

We finish up our food, filling time with small talk here and there, nothing of real substance, and then break into the cake. We slice and serve at the table and the girls immediately whine that their pieces are too small. Bethany gives them the side eye.

"We don't need to eat a lot of junk girls, you know this. We don't want extra weight on our bodies."

I wait until she's not looking and deposit the two blobs of decorative frosting on the girls' plates. One for each. I wink and they both mime zipping their lips. A small smile lifts one side of my mouth and I'm reminded, yet again, about how much I love these two little whirlwinds.

"Oh my goodness," Mom exclaims after her first bite. "This is so delicious! I'll have to do an extra workout this week to offset these calories."

I shift in my seat. Talking about weight and food always makes me a little uncomfortable. It's like women don't know how to talk about anything else, and I really don't care to hear about their bodies all the time.

Why can't we talk about cars? There's a new Corvette C8 out with a mid-engine. Man, what I wouldn't give to see how that handles with all that weight right in the center point of the car. I need more rich friends.

"So Jax," my mom starts and I'm immediately on guard. "Have you met any pretty girls lately?"

My mind flashes to Charlotte, but I'm not ready to share that yet, so deflection it is. "Mooooom," I whine like the thirty-year-old man child I am.

"Honey, you aren't getting any younger, and I just want to see you happy."

"I promise when I meet someone, you'll be the first to know," I lie to her.

I would honestly promise that except Roman's already seen her.

She eyes me. "Even before Roman?"

"Can't guarantee, but will try."

Too late, sorry mom.

"Good enough for me!" She claps her hands together excitedly.

"Thanks mom, you're good enough for me too," I quip, holding back a smile.

She gave me The Look and I just chuckle. I stand and start taking plates without asking. This way they'll remember me doing something nice and want to see me again.

There's a system… annoy, aggravate, then do something nice. Works every time.

 # Chapter 10

Charlotte

I've had my car back for about a week now, and we finally have solid plans for some sibling time. Trying to get Graham and Thomas on the same schedule is headache-inducing. Thankfully, Courtney runs on Thomas' schedule, so it's not like we have to make any additional accommodations. She might not be blood family, but she's chosen family for sure, so she gets included in these plans.

The only thing that's saved me from my annoyance at making plans this week is the consistent texts from Jax. I was surprised when he kept texting me the day after I picked my car up, but I'm glad he did. I'm loving our conversations. There's fun banter, some light flirting, but a bit of introspection too. It's a nice mix.

My phone dings on the couch next to me and I smile. It's after work and I'm enjoying bad reality TV by myself. It's a guilty pleasure; I can't help it. I pick up the phone and my smile gets wider.

Jax: How was your day?

Me: Uneventful, which is how I like my workdays. *smiley face* how was yours? Is Dan still pulling his weight?

Jax: Yeah, he's finally on to me, though. It makes the harassment not as fun.

Jax explained to me over text they had hired a new guy a few weeks before I brought my car in. The day I went in, he had been razzing him to see if he would get rattled. After our texts, though, I suspect he also finds fun in it. He seems like that kind of guy.

Me: I guess you're going to have to get creative now!

Jax: Work, work, work, it's hard being me

Me: SO hard

Jax: You're not wrong there, it's definitely hard over here

Me: Hmmm I bet you're stiff too…. after your long day I mean

Jax: Definitely stiff, it's a little uncomfortable. Wonder if I could get some help to massage the stiffness… out of my muscles *winky face*

Me: Yeah, sure, muscles. I totally believe you on that one. Too bad I'm too far away to help you with that.

My face flames after I send that. We've been getting a little more suggestive with our texts lately, but I haven't been quite that forward yet. Part of me is a little embarrassed, but the bigger part of me is hopeful he responds in kind. Banter is easy for me. Flirty banter and borderline sexting? That's harder. This man has had me in a chokehold all week with his flirting and banter. I can't wait to see him again and go on an actual date.

Jax: I'll just have to imagine you're here with me while I… massage… until I get to see you again

I grin outright and giggle a little, and I can feel my body responding to our texts. My low belly tingles and there's a slickness between my legs that wasn't there earlier. The blonde god from the shop flashes in my mind again, and I wonder what it would be like to have both of them. I think Jax said his name is Roman, and for a moment, I do feel a bit guilty, but my mind doesn't care. I shouldn't get greedy. Not only do I not know if Roman would be interested, I want to see where it goes with Jax. I really enjoy his company. I position my hands to reply and my phone rings.

My parents. Talk about a lady-boner killer.

I clear my throat before I pick up. "Hey!" I answer, not sure which is actually calling.

My parents share one cell phone as the "house line". If one of them has to leave, then they pull out the backup phone with pre-loaded minutes. They claim it saves money. I claim it's ridiculous.

"Hey there, sweetie, how are you?" My mom's voice comes through, and I relax a smidge. My dad can always read me better than my mom, so I'm less worried about her hearing something odd in my voice.

"I'm good. How are you doin'?" I ask my mom.

"Hey kiddo!" My dad chirps in.

My tension comes right back.

Oh God. I'm on speakerphone and my dad is there. Shit, I hope he doesn't hear how nervous I am.

"Hey Dad!" I say brightly.

"We just wanted to call and see how things are going. Graham mentioned you had to get your car fixed up," my dad explains.

Fuck, Graham, can't you keep your mouth shut? I wanted to wait until the next family dinner to let them know about the car thing.

I roll my eyes. "Yeah, it was making a weird clunking noise and Liv said she had a good mechanic to recommend. It worked out pretty well!"

"What was wrong with it?" My dad starts grilling me.

"Um, he said the bushings in the subframe were bad," I tell him, trying to remember if there was another detail I forgot. "I think that was it, but it wasn't very expensive so that was nice."

He grunts, and I can hear him thinking, even over the phone, about what he's going to ask next.

"Well, honey, your father and I were hoping to do family dinner soon. Do you have any weekend that would work better than others?" My mom chimes in.

That's cute. She thinks I have a life.

"Really, any weekend is fine," I tell her. Jax and I have plans this weekend, but I doubt they will want to do dinner so soon.

"Great! I'll check with your brothers, too," she says.

"Ok, cool, anything else going on?" I ask, trying to be polite but move the conversation on. I want to reply to Jax and maybe visit my nightstand drawer.

"Were the shop guys nice to ya? I know you've had some doozies in the past," Dad asks.

"Yeah, they were really nice. They explained everything and showed me how the cost was broken down," I tell him.

"Oh? How nice?" Dad latches on to something in my voice. "You know how those blue-collar guys can be."

Shit. I thought I played it cool.

"I mean, I was their customer so, like, normal nice? They talked to me like I'm a person," I tell him.

He just grunts again. Nobody says anything for a moment.

"Ok, well, love you guys," I say into the quiet.

"Love you too honey, we'll see you soon," Mom replies.

"Wait—" Dad starts but I've already hung up.

I sigh. I don't understand the big deal about blue collar vs white collar, but it is a THING to my parents. They seem to think their children are too good to be with someone who works with their hands. I've never had to worry about it before, but I'm sure they'll get past it when they meet Jax. I push the phone call from my head and revisit my last text.

He's texted again.

Jax: Sorry, did I overstep?

Me: No! Not at all, my parents called. Sorry about that.

Jax: Oh good. I don't want to make you uncomfortable but I'm also having a hard time getting you out of my head.

Me: Yeah, you mentioned a *hard* time already… I'm excited about our date too.

Jax: Is there anything you really hate? I want to surprise you but not in a bad way.

Me: Um…. I really hate shopping. I know, not very "girly" of me.

Jax: Well thankfully, that's not what I had in mind. You're safe with me. Night Sunshine.

Me: Night *heart emoji*

I sigh and look at the clock. It's close to 9 pm, time for some self-love. I turn off the TV and sashay to my bedroom, turning off lights as I go. My nightstand and all my toys are calling me.

#

I'm looking forward to tonight and tomorrow. It's Thursday, and I'm heading out the door to meet my brothers and Courtney. It's been months since the four of us have hung out, so here's hoping we have fun and avoid any spats. Tomorrow night, I'm going out with Jax for our first date.

Since Monday evening our texts haven't gotten more heated, but we are definitely toeing the line of sexting. I'm 100% here for it while also feeling incredibly awkward. He's also insisted on keeping what we're doing for our date a secret, and I'm looking forward to the surprise. He's so relaxed that I think whatever we do will be fun, even if it doesn't go according to plan.

I hop in my car, get my karaoke going, and head for Jerry's, the local pub where I'm meeting everyone. As I go, I listen for any clunking, but so far so good. I think he really did fix the problem. I've had zero issues since getting the car back, and I'm really pleased with that.

After reaching the bar, I pull into the first spot I see and slide out of my car. This parking lot is always a bit tight, but I can get out without much of a problem. Of course, once I'm cleared of the car, that's what I hear the snickers from whoever was in it. I didn't even realize someone was sitting in it.

"OMG, I can't believe she fit," the first voice says.

Definitely a girl, but at least she's not shouting the words out of the car. I just happen to be close enough to hear.

"What the hell is she wearing?" a different girl's voice says.

Great, mean girls enjoying the view.

I keep walking. I don't need to hear more of that. It's already hit its mark though and I'm suddenly unsure of my outfit.

I have a fitted tank top on, with embroidery along the collar, and a tea length gauzy skirt. My blue hair is piled on top of my head, and I've got my favorite sandals on. I was happy when I walked out the door, but now I'm not so sure.

Maybe I should have worn a looser shirt, or some jeans. I could have at least worn a cardigan. What was I thinking?

The thoughts swirl in my head as I walk in, and I bite my lip uncertainly as I look around the high-top tables and actual bar for my family. I spot Graham at a table beyond the bar area.

I walk over and take a seat next to him. "Hey bro," I greet him.

He gives me a warm smile. "Hey sis."

We do the awkward half hug thing you do when you're sitting down. "Whatcha drinkin'?" I ask, looking around a bit.

"The other two aren't here yet. I just got Fat Tire on tap."

"Ooo sounds good. Maybe I'll do a beer tonight."

He smiles a little, a teasing note in his eyes. "Always trying to be as cool as big brother, eh?"

"Oh, you wish." I laugh at him.

A server stops by, and I order a local on tap and a basket of tortilla chips. We're going to need something to soak up the alcohol. I fidget with my skirt, making sure it fits where I want it to, the voices from the car outside living rent free in my head.

"How's your car?" he asks.

"Good! Seems like the mechanic knew what he was doing. Hasn't made a peep. I have a place to go for car stuff too, now."

"Glad to hear it. Now maybe you won't wait five weeks to get your car fixed?"

"It was only three."

He shakes his head and chuckles. "Stubborn."

"Just like big bro," I tease back.

As the server comes back with my beer, Thomas and Courtney arrive. I'm always stunned at how much Thomas and Graham look alike. There's six years between them, but they could almost be twins, I swear. They're the same height, same hair color, same brown eyes, similar build. The only real difference is the facial hair. Graham sports a neat goatee and Thomas is fresh-shaven.

"Hey guys!" I greet them, standing to get hugs.

I hug Courtney first, then Thomas. Graham does the "bro hug" and Courtney gets a real hug. We all sit down, and I fidget with my clothing without thinking, moving the top a little and making sure the bottom covers everything. Thomas looks a little too closely at me.

"What?" I ask, hoping my insecurity isn't showing.

"What happened?" he asks.

"Um, I got a beer?"

He just looks at me, eyebrows raised. I'm saved by the waitress who seems to be on point with her timing tonight. She drops the tortilla chips and gets more drink orders.

"How have you been?" I ask Courtney.

"Good, nothing too crazy, which I'm ok with. Other than dealing with Thomas' crazy ass," she says.

"Hey, you love my crazy ass," he defends.

"Sure, honey," she placates him and pats his shoulder. I glance over and see Graham lasered in on her hand, and now I'm wondering what the hell his problem is.

Why is he staring at her hand like that?

"Seriously though, Charli. What happened?"

Thomas is a dog with a bone.

I sigh and take a sip of my beer. All three of them are looking now. Apparently, my clothing fidgets were not as subtle as I hoped.

"There were just some people in the car I parked next to that were assholes, that's all," I say, hoping against hope that he'll let it drop.

"What did they say?" Graham asks, a little forcefully.

Oh cool, we're doing the overprotective brother thing tonight. Should be fun.

"Just the usual shit people say," I deflect.

"Goddamn it," Thomas starts. "It's not okay for people to say anything to you. Why don't you say anything?"

"What am I gonna say? 'Hey sorry my fat offends you?' Nothing I say is gonna make them stop."

"You gotta stick up for yourself more. Everyone deserves basic respect, and those girls were just petty assholes," says Graham.

"Truth," Courtney chimes in and holds her non-existent drink up to cheers.

Graham's lips twitch in a quick smile and he invisible cheers with her, pretending along with her.

"You *have* a real drink to cheers with," I tell him, trying to change the subject. I hate it when they get like this.

I could stand up for myself, I really could. I've spent so long doing it though, with nothing to show for it, that I've given up on it. Why waste my energy when people are going to dismiss me consistently? Better to change the subject than argue.

"Yeah, but I'm not gonna real cheers a pretend one. That's rude," Graham tells me.

"Rude? There are no rules about it!"

"Sure there are," Thomas adds in.

"What are they?" I challenge.

"First, you don't drink a real drink if the other person doesn't have one," Graham says.

"Second, there has to be a reason for the cheers. You can't just randomly do it," Thomas adds.

I squint my eyes at him. *How dare he gang up on me with Graham? They are definitely making this shit up as they go.*

"Third, if the reason is weak, you have to do a ridiculous saying with it," Courtney adds.

My mouth pops open. *What the hell is happening? How am I the odd one out?*

"Fourth?" Graham looks at me.

I laugh a little and think for a moment. It always makes me a little warm and fuzzy when they make a point to hear what I have to say. Even if it's for a stupid cheers rule.

"Fourth, it has to be between people who we love in our lives, friends or family. No cheers-ing with strangers."

Courtney puts her finger on her nose and points to me. "Perfect!" she says.

The waitress comes back with Thomas and Courtney's drinks, and they promptly hold them up.

"A real cheers, to the rules of cheers and to a siblings' night," Thomas says.

"Siblings' Night!" I echo.

Graham puts his drink in the middle, and we all clink and drink. I set my beer down and hear my phone buzzing against the table. I pick it up and see Jax has messaged.

Jax: Are you enjoying your night out?

Me: Yeah, and Graham doesn't even seem to have a stick up his ass. Well, it's a short stick at least.

Jax: Glad to hear it, sunshine. Hopefully tomorrow is just as fun for you.

Me: It's with you, of course it will be fun!

I smile as I send that, and I hear someone clear their throat.

"Who's that?" Thomas asks, a teasing and knowing note in his voice.

My eyes snap up to him, and I silently try to tell him to shut it. He just grins and waggles his eyebrows. "Uh, nobody, just the girls," I lie.

"Lie," Graham says.

"What? How do you know?" I challenge.

"You're sitting next to me. I can clearly see the name of the person you're texting. Who the hell is Jax, and what are you doing tomorrow?"

Graham tries to swipe my phone, but I hold it away from him and tuck it in my pocket.

Yes, my skirt has pockets. Suck it.

I sigh and take another drink of my beer before answering. "He's the mechanic from the shop I went to this week, and he's taking me on a date tomorrow," I say primly, trying not to let embarrassment overtake me.

Whenever my brothers start drilling into my life, it feels weird, and I don't like it. It's like we're kids again and they're trying to be in my business 24/7 and annoying the shit out of me. Plus, it always feels like they're judging, even if they're not. Amy and Olivia would point out that it's actually my anxiety acting up, not them judging me, but they're not here, so I'm going with my story.

"You sure that's smart? You don't even know this guy," Graham points out.

"It's not like we're going to be in private. We're going somewhere public."

"Okay, so where are you going?"

"Um, it's a surprise. I told him he could pick."

"How do you know he's actually gonna take you somewhere safe?" Graham challenges, his voice rising a little.

"Oh my God, Graham, it's fine. We're both adults and I'm meeting him there. He's gonna text me the address right tomorrow before we need to be there, and both Liv and Ames are on standby in case I need help."

"Oh cool, Complacent and Crazy, good choices. They're definitely the right people for backup."

I roll my eyes. This was what I was expecting from him. Lectures and a bad attitude. One day, I'm going to actually shine a flashlight up his ass and see if there's a stick in there. Then I think about that too hard and shudder.

Don't need to see Graham's butt. Nope. Hard pass.

"I'm sure it'll be fine," Courtney tries to intervene. "It's not like Charli is helpless. She knows how to take care of herself, and I'm sure she'd call if she was in trouble."

"THANK YOU!" I exclaim. "At least someone at this table understands I'm an adult."

Graham shoots Courtney a look, and she looks away, uncomfortable. Honestly? I don't blame her; his looks can be intense.

We sit there in the relative, semi-awkward quiet for a moment, not that a bar can get super quiet. Courtney stands and excuses herself to the restroom, and not two minutes later Graham follows her.

"The fuck is that about?" I ask Thomas.

He shakes his head. "I'm staying out of that one."

"Fair."

"Seriously, though, you'll let us know if he ends up being a creeper, right? All three of us are here for you and Graham would come get you in a heartbeat," Thomas says more gently than Graham did.

"Of course, I promise. Cross my heart and all."

He smiles at me. "I hope he's a good one."

"Me too." I smile back.

My last relationship in my early 20s ended horribly and all my dates since then have been busts. My ex isn't a bad person, but we just couldn't find that happy place unless it was sex and when he couldn't offer more, it got nasty. Since then, every guy I've seen has either been an asshole or has issues with my weight.

"To hope." He holds his glass up.

"To dick," I add, making him snort laugh.

Chapter 11

Jax

This has simultaneously been the longest and shortest week of my life. Texting with Charlotte has been amazing, but it also means I've jacked off every night this week. God, her humor. I love that she throws it back at me and I just keep picturing those blue eyes. I can't wait to take her out.

It's finally Friday evening, and I leave Roman to lock up the shop while I go home and get cleaned up. I texted Charlotte earlier to give her the address and told her to arrive at seven. Thankfully, I remembered to make reservations earlier this week, so we should be good to go. My phone chimes with a text.

Roman: Have fun tonight, bro. I wanna hear about it tomorrow.

Me: I don't kiss and tell, asshole

Roman: Bold of you to assume she'll kiss you.

Me: Fuck off

Roman: Ha - good luck man

I shake my head at my best friend's antics. He's honestly the best friend I could ask for. Once I'm showered and my hands are as clean as they're going to get today, I head to the closet and pull out a basic T-shirt and some jeans. The weather is calling for some chill, so I grab my leather jacket too.

I won't need the jacket. I run hot, but if Charlotte gets chilly, I'll want something to keep her warm. Presumptuous? Maybe. I like to prepare for the best. I make a sandwich and chow down since we're not including food on the date. As soon as I'm done eating, it's time to leave the house, so I grab my keys and head for the garage.

It's a short drive to our destination and after I park, I stand next to my car, waiting for her. I make a point to be ten minutes early, so she doesn't have to wait around, wondering what to do. I might also be too antsy to stay home, but I'm going to go with me being a gentleman. As I wait, I keep an eye out for her car, since I already know what she drives, and I don't have to wait long. She pulls in a few spots down from me and I can see her mouth moving and hear just a touch of some music. I grin.

Can she get any cuter? Car karaoke, I can't wait to do it with her sometime.

Maybe I'm getting ahead of myself, but I don't think so. The crisp fall air sweeps through, adding a slight chill, and I see Charlotte pull her scarf a little tighter as she closes the car door and looks up. She sees me standing near my car and the smile on her face is heart-stopping. There's a reason I call her Sunshine; she is absolutely radiant, and I want to bask in her.

"Hey, you," she says as soon as she's close enough.

"Hey yourself, did you have a good day?" I ask.

"Yeah, been looking forward to this, so it made the day drag a little, but we're here now." She grins.

I lean in for a hug, hoping I'm not overstepping, and she leans in as well. We do the short and polite hug instead of the long one I want, but baby steps.

"So, you come here often?" she asks and waggles her eyebrows.

I bark out a laugh. "I've been known to come here a time or two. I'm happy to *come* here with you."

She giggles. "Well, let's go then. I still have no idea what we're doing. I didn't want to spoil the surprise, so I just put the address in and hit go on the GPS without looking at the destination name."

We turn towards the door. There are some windows on this side of the building, but not on the doors, so she can't really see inside very well. I step in front of her and open the door, and we're assaulted by the noise of people chatting with the occasional *THWACK* noise. She looks at me, then walks past into the building. I step in behind her, closer than I normally would be because she's stopped and is looking around.

"Like what you see?" I say softly into her ear.

"Axe throwing?" she asks, a smile slowly spreading across her face.

"Ever been?"

"No! I've been interested but haven't tried it yet!" Her excitement is showing now.

This particular axe throwing venue recently moved from their prior location in a strip mall, so everything looks a little shiny and new still. The owner added a bar area for patrons to wait, or to get bar patrons to throw. There's a path behind the building as well that people can walk while waiting their turn to throw if the weather is nice enough.

"Well, we have reservations so we can skip by the bar and check in over there by the throwing area." I tell her.

I take her hand without thinking and we start forward. She doesn't pull away and I do a mental fist pump.

Off to a good start.

I give the host of the axe throwing area my name and we're escorted to our lane, and right after we finish getting coats and scarves off, an employee comes over with three small axes in each hand.

"Hey folks, I'm Jeff and I'm here to give you an overview. Have either of you been throwing before?"

"I have, but she hasn't," I tell him.

He nods and gives us a friendly smile. "Let's go over some basics, then. It's always good to review these, even if you've been before."

Jeff goes over safety rules, the mechanics of throwing, and demonstrates a one-handed and two-handed throw. His entire time with us is about five minutes before he tells us to have fun and call if we need help.

"Okay, okay. I'm so nervous I'm going to be terrible!" Charlotte says.

"You'll be fine! I'm not very good at this, but it's fun to do."

"Do you want to go first?" she asks, looking a bit nervous.

"Totally up to you, Sunshine. I'm happy to go first if you're more comfortable with that."

Her face relaxes in relief. "Yes, please!"

She sits on the stool in our lane behind the throwing line and I can feel her eyes on me. I turn and give her a wink before throwing. It hits the wood but nowhere near the target. I can hear her giggle.

I make a show of swinging my arms and flexing. "I'm just warmin' up!"

"Sure okay," she says with a teasing note.

Each target is made up of a few strips of wood, pressed tightly together, the target area taking up the center of the combined boards. My axes all hit the wood boards, but only one hits within the target. I pull them all out and walk back to where Charlotte is now standing, looking a bit nervous, but also a bit more relaxed.

"Let's' see it, killer," I tell her.

She looks at me with a smile, then turns back and makes her first throw. She's as bad as I am, and I can't help but enjoy that a little. It's nice to not get shown up, but I want her to have fun. It would be cool if she got some bullseyes as well, though. I would only be a little jealous.

We throw back and forth for about thirty minutes and chat between throws. Every now and again I catch a little uncertainty creep into her, but she always comes back with a smile. She's wonderful and her laugh is completely infectious. We hand our axes back at the main desk, and I don't want the evening to end yet.

"Um, do you have anything else planned…?" Charlotte asks tentatively.

"No, I figured after we were done, we could grab a drink or maybe go take a walk? There's a nice trail behind the building. It's one of the reasons they moved to this location, plus it's a nice way to pass the time while waiting for a turn at the axe throwing."

"A walk sounds wonderful," she tells me with a smile.

We take each other's hand this time and walk out of the main door. I feel her stiffen a bit, then start to move a little more quickly. I keep my pace up with her, but when I look over, she glances at me and has a small blush on her face. Seems odd, but maybe she's just excited to get outside. We get to the main trail and start to walk.

The trail is pretty well lit, either with some string lights or a few streetlamps that have been placed along the path. It makes things a little less spooky since it gets darker faster this time of the year, but we still have a little daylight. Our hands stay clasped, fingers interlaced as we go.

Our conversation comes easily, and Charlotte is an open book. She tells me about her anxiety, her family, her friends, all the shenanigans she and her brothers used to get up to. She's so vibrant and honest, and the pull keeps getting stronger. I open up about my own family and friends and tell her about my nieces like they're my own girls.

"Your nieces sound amazing. They must really love you," she says.

"Oh man, they are just a blast. I can't wait to keep watching them grow. Hopefully, you can meet them sometime."

"I'd really like that."

We get back to her car, and stand by her driver's door, still holding hands. Neither of us is in a hurry to say goodnight, but our walk took a while and it's pretty dark now.

"Thanks for a great time," Charlotte says, changing the topic. "This was an amazing date."

"I'm glad you liked it," I tell her, feeling light and buoyant. "Maybe next time we can chop down some trees with our axes."

She laughs. "I'm not much of a lumberjack, but if it's with you, then I'm in."

We stand by her door, looking at each other and grinning, and I can't resist her. The pull to her is too damn strong and her body has been tempting me all night. It's too soon to go far, but if I don't get my lips on her soon, I might go crazy.

I swallow. "May I kiss you?"

Part of me feels ridiculous asking, but with two nieces and a big sister, I am big on consent.

Her smile gets even bigger, if possible. "I'd like that."

I step closer, our bodies almost touching, and I love that she's tall. I don't have to bend down to reach her, and I can stare straight into her eyes. Her smile falls as we look at each other, replaced with a hunger that I can feel. I raise my hand, brushing her hair back behind her ear. My hand cups her cheek and she meets me as I lean in.

Our lips touch, featherlight at first, exploring each other tentatively. I press a little harder and she responds in kind. I pull her closer to me, placing my other hand on the other side of her face, desperate to touch her. I give her lips a small lick and she moans and responds immediately, allowing my tongue access to her.

She strokes my tongue with hers, and I can't get enough. Her hands are on my waist, and she holds on to me like she'll fall over if she lets go. Her lips are soft and I'm looking forward to exploring how soft she is all over. I lick her tongue a few more times and pull the kiss back. As if neither of us can stop, we add one, two, three more small kisses and finally breathe. I rest my forehead against hers and just breathe. I'm pretty sure my whole body is Jello after that.

"Fuck," I whisper.

"Yeah," she whispers back.

"I cannot wait to explore you more. I want to feel how soft you are everywhere," I confess.

She whimpers a little. "I like that idea."

"Soon, Sunshine, but let's get you home for tonight. I'm trying to be a gentleman on our first date."

She pulls back and gives me a small smile. "Okay," she says softly, almost unsure.

"You better believe I'm gonna text you tonight, and tomorrow, and all next week."

She smiles, and it's confident this time. "Good."

I open her door for her and sneak in one more quick kiss. She giggles and gets in, waving after the door closes. I watch her drive off and my heart is still pounding.

This woman is something else.

 # Chapter 12

Charlotte

It's a beautiful day out today, so the girls and I decide we should enjoy nature and do a small hike. We're not exactly backpacking or going into the mountains or anything, but it's moving, and we get some fresh air. Of course, now that we're actually doing the hiking, Olivia is officially crabby and I'm grateful that there aren't many bugs in the fall. Ragweed is another story.

I'm pretty sure Amy isn't actually human. She's been chipper and almost skipping along down the local trail we went to. It's a local nature trail that gets decent traffic but isn't overly crowded. We've passed a few people with dogs and joggers have passed us too. Part of me is suspicious Amy is trying to find someone for Olivia to take home, but she'd never admit it. Olivia is happy single, but I know she gets lonely sometimes even with the "friends with benefits" situations.

"OK, so recap everything for us," Amy finally says, turning to me.

So far, we've been talking about her family and the shenanigans her brother has been getting up to with their mom. Apparently, he really was leaving stains on their mom's counter to poke at her. Oliva perks up at the change in subject. She enjoys Amy's family, but sibling relationships aren't something she can relate to, being an only child.

"Yes, we need to hear about the date in person," she chimes in.

"I've already told you guys everything in texts this week," I remind them.

Olivia waves her hand in the air. "Doesn't count. It's different in person."

"Exactly!" Amy agrees.

I sigh, both pleased to have something to tell them and annoyed that I'm having to rehash what I told them. Then again, reliving that kiss is worth it.

"Alright, fine!" I give in. "So, he had me meet him at this random building. There wasn't much of a sign. It just said 'Al's' but not what Al was doing with the building. Could have been a country dance hall for all I knew."

"Oh my god, can you picture our Charli doing a line dance?" Amy says to Olivia, laughter barely held back.

Olivia has no such qualms and belly laughs at the image.

"Shut up!" I can't help but laugh, too. I'm so far from country it's ridiculous. "So anyway, we went inside and as we started walking, he took my hand, and it was so natural, like we've been doing it for years. No clammy palms, just comforting, you know?"

Olivia nods. "Yeah, that's how you know they're a keeper. It's all in the hands."

I laugh and continue. "Turns out it's an axe throwing place along with a small bar/food area that wasn't, like, packed, but definitely busy. It was a little awkward though, 'cuz I could see people just sizing us up as we walked through the building to where they had the throwing lanes."

I didn't tell them about the self-consciousness over text. It's better for me to talk it out with them instead of texting. I tend to start spiraling if I say something over text like that and they can't respond right away.

"They were totally jealous," Amy insists. "He's a looker."

"He's pretty fuckin hot," I confess, though I don't really believe that people were looking because they were jealous.

Olivia pouts. "Man, when we went there, he wasn't working and now I'm sad I don't know what he looks like. I did see the other guy, long blonde hair and doesn't smile much? He was definitely some hot stuff."

I chuckle. "I'm sure you'll meet Jax soon enough. Also, yes on that other guy being crazy hot. Anyway, it was a lot easier to block people out when we were throwing. The guy showing us how was super nice and helpful. It was actually a lot of fun! We're both terrible, so it was zero pressure to try to be good, you know?"

They both are smiling now, and I can tell I am as well. This man has me twisted up, that's for sure.

"So, after we finished, we decide to go for a walk, but we had to go back through the bar area," I tell them.

"What happened?" Olivia asks, like she knows something happened before I even have to say it.

I sigh. "It's stupid, but it's been bugging me."

"Just tell us," says Olivia.

"We were walking past a table with some people who looked like they were on a double date or something, and I heard someone say, 'can't believe someone like him is with *her*' and then the snickers that always come with that shit. I glanced over and they were all staring at us."

"I hate people," Amy says.

"Seriously, people suck," I agree.

"What did he say?" Olivia asks.

"Nothing. It's like he didn't even notice."

"Did you mention it?" Olivia asks.

"No, it seemed like it would ruin the vibe we had going, so I just kept walking," I confess.

"I guess maybe it's a little early to talk about that stuff," Amy tries to reason. "Don't let it become a habit though, that shit will fester."

"Yeah, I know, he's just so easygoing I figured take a page from his book. We ended up walking a small trail that was behind the building and just talking about our lives and getting to know each other a bit."

"And theeeeeen?" Ames prompts.

"He kissed me goodnight," I say, blushing a little.

As I tell them that, a trio of guys are passing us, going the opposite direction and decide they need to chime in.

"Who's kissing YOU?" one asks with a sneer.

The others laugh and high five as they keep going.

"Fuck off, I bet you can't get a girl to even give you her number!" Olivia shouts at their backs.

I slow down, not fully stopping, but my brain is officially swirling.

The kiss was great, and he seemed interested in more, but maybe he was just being nice. He's probably gonna change his mind. Who wants to be saddled with my shit, anyway?

Anxiety sits on my shoulder and takes over the second I falter. He doesn't need to be a part of my anxiety. I should just tell him I don't want to see him again. That's the easiest thing to do. I don't want to do it, but it feels like what I should be doing.

Fingers snap in my face. "Hey!" Olivia shouts at me.

I startle at the interruption to my thoughts and look around. "Shit, sorry."

"You okay?" Amy asks.

"Yeah, just spiraled for a minute there."

"We could tell," Olivia said, a wry smile on her face.

"Need to talk it out?" Amy offers.

"Yes, but I don't want to."

Honesty sucks.

"Do it," Olivia insists, and gets us moving again.

"I started thinking they're right. Who wants to be saddled with me and all my shit, anyway? He was probably just being nice, right? Probably changed his mind by now, so I should just like give him an out."

"FIRST of all," Amy starts. "*We* want to be saddled with your shit. We love you and all your shit. So, knock that out of your head. He would be *lucky* to have to deal with your shit."

"SECOND," Olivia picks up. "Guys don't say shit they don't mean. Usually. He might get super nervous and say the wrong thing or whatever, but if he's stone cold sober and telling you he wants more? He's interested babe, he's not just being nice."

"You guys think so?" I ask, my eyes stinging a little as they tear up.

"Absolutely," Amy says, and loops her arm through mine.

Olivia takes the other arm, and we keep going down the path together, arm in arm.

"Thanks for always talking me down, guys. I don't know what I'd do without you," I confess.

"Same, girl," Olivia says.

"Same." Amy echoes.

 # Chapter 13

Roman

It's actually a decent fall day today, which is surprising for mid-October. So, I decide to hit one of the local trails and do a jog. I don't have a rigid exercise routine, but sometimes it's nice to get things moving, and it helps clear my head. I had debt collectors calling again this week to check payment plans and make sure I'm still able to keep up my end. It's fucking exhausting.

I've made a lap around the trail once, and on my second time through, I hear some asshole 'bro' type guys ask someone who would want to kiss them and then high five each other. I round the corner, slowing down, and see their high five as they walk away. There's a girl turning to face them, and she yells at their retreating backs.

"Fuck off, I bet you can't get a girl to even give you her number!"

I smirk at the fire.

Atta girl.

I take a closer look at the group she's with and I see that shock of blue hair and a tall figure. Charlotte's back is to me, like she couldn't bring herself to turn and see the assholes taunting her group, and her shoulders are rigid and straight. She's taking small steps as she slowly progresses down the trail, but doesn't seem to be looking at anything, her head facing forward and stiff. I decide to slow my jog a little and follow at a distance to see what I can hear.

Does this make me a creep? Probably. Do I care? Nope. Okay, a maybe little, but I want to see how this plays out before I step in.

I see the same girl snap her fingers in Charlotte's face, and she startles. Their conversation isn't so loud that everyone can hear, but I'm able to stay close enough to catch it. She's managed to convince herself that Jax is just being nice to her and thank god she has good friends to talk her out of it. The three of them obviously have a strong bond, and I'm glad to see she has good support. I resume my jog and pass them without a word.

Should I say something? Probably.

I'd rather have Charlotte to myself, though, so at the end of the trail, I head to the parking lot and hang out by my truck. The three girls emerge about twenty minutes later and Charlotte's smiling, having forgotten the whole thing, it seems. They part ways and I decide to step in and take a small shot.

"Hey," I say, walking towards her.

She turns, startled, and looks at me with wide eyes.

"Mind if I walk you to your car?" I ask, keeping a respectful distance between us.

"Well, I don't really know you, so that seems kind of odd," she says, wary of me.

Good, she doesn't trust random men. She shouldn't.

"Sorry, I'm Roman. I work with Jax. I remember your blue hair from when you picked your car up and Jax has been talking about you," I explain.

She smiles, relieved. "Oh, okay then. Oh! I think I saw you in the bay when I picked my car up."

"You good, girl?" I hear one of her friends call out.

I guess I wasn't as stealthy as I'd hoped.

"Yeah, I'm fine. He's Jax's friend. See you bitches later!" she yells back.

We walk toward her car, and I sidle slightly closer to her as we go.

"That would be me. Is your car still behaving?" I ask her, trying to figure out how to get my in.

"Yeah, you guys did a great job on it," she says, beaming. "Usually when I go to mechanics, they talk down to me, leer at me, and/or overcharge me. You guys have a good shop you're running."

"Glad to hear it. It's important to have reliable transportation."

She smiles at me and I'm pretty sure I melt a little from her radiance. No wonder Jax is head over heels for this girl. This is going to happen, the three of us. I can feel it in my bones. Jax is home to me, and looking at Charlotte, I get the same feeling. The three of us will be good together; I just need to get them to see it.

"I hope this doesn't come across wrong," I start.

She giggles. "Always a good start to a conversation."

I huff a small laugh. "Yeah, you're right. I, uh, heard those guys on the trail and some of your conversation after. I wanted to make sure you were alright but not crowd you or anything. Before you say it, I am also aware that it makes me just a bit of a creeper."

She stops at her car door and leans her back against it and frowns a little. "Well, I can see why you were concerned about saying something. That *is* a little creepy."

I rub the back of my neck. "Yeah, I'm sorry about that."

She cocks her head and meets my eyes. "I appreciate that you care, though."

I can't pull my eyes from hers as we stand there, face to face. Her face is warming up to me as we look at each other, a small smile starting. To prevent myself from doing something stupid, I put my hands in my pockets. She doesn't need me trying to grab her and kiss her when we just acknowledged my creeper move.

"I want you to know they're wrong."

"Yeah, Liv and Ames tried to tell me that too," she says.

"No, I mean, those guys were completely wrong. There are guys who want to kiss you. Jax wouldn't do it if he wasn't into you." I glance down at my shoes and then back up through my lashes, unexpected nerves hitting me. "I'd kiss you too."

My heart is in my throat a bit. I don't have a problem telling a girl if I want her, but I don't normally say it to someone who has started seeing my best friend, either. If I didn't intend to share her, I wouldn't approach her, but knowing Jax has already taken her on a date does make it a bit harder.

"Oh." She looks flustered. "Well, thanks, I guess?"

"You're an attractive woman. Don't let some asshole jocks tell you otherwise."

She gives me a smile this time. "I'll do my best. I'm sure you heard me talk about my anxiety, so the reminder is nice."

I take one hand out of my pocket and lean it against the car, next to her shoulder, bringing us a little closer, but hopefully not invading her space too much. We're the same height, Jax a little taller than both of us by an inch or two. I can stare right into her eyes and her pupils widen a bit and her breathing picks up. I don't want her to feel bad.

"I know this is forward of me, and I know you and Jax just started dating, but, well, I was hoping maybe I could be a part of this," I tell her.

"How so?" she breathes.

"Have you ever been shared?"

She gives a self-depreciating laugh. "As if."

My other hand finds its way to her chin and grasps it firmly. "Don't do that, don't talk yourself down," I say gently.

She nods, staring into my eyes like I'm a savior she never expected. "Okay then, no, I haven't been," she says softly.

"I'll talk to Jax. I don't want you to ever feel torn or awkward. I want to share you with him and since it's me approaching you with the idea, I can take the responsibility to ask."

She nods, her chin still in my grasp. "Okay, yeah."

"Would you be okay with that?" I ask her, wanting to hear a yes from her before I do anything.

"I've never tried something like this, but I think so. Yes. It could be worth trying," she says, her eyes flicking to my lips and back.

I smile at her, pleased to hear she's interested. I start to move in and give her plenty of time to shove me off. Slowly, I bring my mouth to hers, and she doesn't ask me to stop or push me away. My lips meet hers in a soft touch, and she responds beautifully. Her mouth meets mine and our lips explore each other in broad daylight. I hope those douchebags can see this. I press in a little more and she moans slightly as she meets the pressure, her hand grasping at my forearm while I hold her chin. Knowing I can't push this, I pull back and look into her eyes.

"I cannot wait to do that again," I tell her, my breathing quicker than it was.

She bites her lip and smiles. "I'd like that."

I kiss her forehead and help her get into her car. Before I close the door, I lean in to tell her one more thing. "Don't worry about this, okay? I'll tell Jax about the kiss and talk to him. I don't want your anxiety telling you the wrong thing, okay?"

She nods and gives me one last smile. I give her a small smirk back and close her door gently. After she pulls out of the parking space, I walk over to my truck and hop in.

Now I just gotta figure out how to get my best friend to be okay sharing his new girl. I'm sure it'll be fine. Right? Right.

#

When I get home from my jog, Jax is home and I'm not sure if it's good or not. I want to talk to him about Charlotte, but it feels soon. Then again, I don't want to wait, so I'm torn about it. Probably better to do this sooner rather than later, I guess. Rip the band aid off and all.

After I get showered off, I find Jax in the living room, grabbing his keys to head to the shop. Shit, I forgot about the shop. I didn't have a shift today, so it didn't cross my mind that he'd be going in.

"Hey man, how was the run?" he asks.

"It was good, felt nice to get my heart pumping a bit."

In more ways than one.

"Nice, I'm headed to the shop. It's a light day on the schedule, but I don't want Dan to have to hold the fort down on his own. It's only a couple hours."

"Hey, uh, can I talk to you about something before you go?" I ask.

Maybe not the best time, but if this pisses him off, at least he'll have time away from me to simmer down.

Jax nods. "Yeah, always. What's up?"

"I'm gonna just rip the band-aid off on this," I tell him and see him get immediately wary. "I want to share Charlotte."

He stares at me for a minute, blank-faced, and I can't tell what he's thinking. Finally, his eyes start to focus back in on me, and I can see multiple emotions flicker across his face. Anger, amusement, anger again, then curiosity.

There it is. That's the one I'm looking for.

"Are you kidding?" he asks.

"No, man, I saw her that day she picked up her car and couldn't stop thinking about her. Didn't realize who she was until she left with the Lexus. Then I saw her on my run this morning with her friends and I feel hooked. I made a point to talk to her and mention this."

"So, you're just gonna move in on her?" Jax asks, starting to get mad.

I hold up my hands. "No, man, I would never without your permission. I don't want to take her away from you. I want to be a part of it. You don't have to decide now, but I wanted to bring it up now to show I have nothing to hide and I'm not trying to push you out. I admit I did kiss her before leaving the trail."

"The fuck?" He's mad now and takes a step toward me.

"I promise, it wasn't like a big thing, and I told her I would tell you, so she didn't feel caught in between us. I don't want to drive a wedge."

He finally nods, his anger starting to fade as he reasons through the situation. This isn't something the two of us have ever really tried before, and I've never gone for a girl that he's been into. Of course, he was dating Morgan for a long time, and she never interested me, but a few girls he took home caught my eye. I never moved in though. He made the move, so I stepped back.

Not this time.

"Just- just think about it, okay?" I ask him. "You don't have to respond now, but think it over."

He nods slowly and eyes me up. "Is this why you wanted to move in?" he questions me.

"NO! I swear to God, NO, that is not why I asked," I tell him, starting to speak faster by the end.

Jax chuckles. "I'm just fuckin' with ya. I'll think about it."

"You dick," I tell him without heat.

Chuckling, he pauses before asking, "What did she say?"

"She seemed open to it, but she didn't want to betray you, and neither do I. It's in your court, man."

He laughs. "Alright, you're lucky you're basically my brother, or I'd punch you."

"Fair man, fair," I tell him.

Jax nods at me before walking out of the house to his truck. I blow out a long breath.

That could have gone worse. Could have gone better too, but at least I didn't get punched.

 # Chapter 14

Charlotte

I am going to pee myself.

"Stop!" I tell Jax, laughing hard enough that there's a serious threat to my bladder control right now.

"No, seriously! My dumb eighteen-year-old ass starts mouthing off to the new teacher at our trade school like she's just an admin or something. Roman's trying to wave me off, but I was like 'I got this', and told the teacher if she's looking for baking classes, that they're in the next building over."

"Oh my god, I'm sure that went over well." I giggle.

"I thought she was gonna wipe the damn floor with me." He chuckles. "She looked me up and down, looked at the class, and goes 'here's your example for what happens when you're an asshole', and suddenly I was not so confident."

"I bet not!"

"She made me go look in the spare tires for a specific make that didn't even exist. Of course, I wasn't about to admit defeat, or admit I didn't know the brand, so I spent the entire first hour of the day searching for this damn tire while the rest of the class got to actually learn from her and put their hands on a car."

"When did she tell you the tire didn't exist?" I ask, taking a sip of my water.

He picks up a mozzarella stick. "On graduation day."

"I want to meet her," I say, laughing. "She sounds awesome."

"I gained an entirely new outlook on women in trade jobs, that's for sure. Forced me to face that prejudice fast," he says after chewing.

The local diner we were at was a staple for the town, but there wasn't usually much of a crowd after 6 pm on a Wednesday. Jax had texted me today asking if we could do a random date tonight, just something simple, and I agreed without any coercion. I picked the restaurant, or diner in this case, and he picked the time. It worked seamlessly.

"So, how's the new guy?" I ask him, grabbing a mozzarella stick for myself.

"Dan? He's good. Finally caught on that I was just giving him shit and has started throwing it back." He chuckles. "I think he'll be alright."

"I'm glad to hear it," I tell him.

"Yeah, I hate the hiring process, and it can be tricky to find the right fit. They have to be able to roll with the punches, ya know?"

I'm not super familiar with how the culture is in a mechanic's world, but I at least understand making sure people fit into whatever the culture is.

"Yeah, finding the right fit can be tricky for sure," I agree.

He bites his lip, trying not to laugh. I look at him and then look around a bit.

"What?" I ask.

"I want to make so many dirty jokes," he confesses.

I giggle and grab my water. "Hit me with them then."

"I can show you how I fit in," he says, waggling his eyebrows.

I almost spit out my water and can't help the chuckles that start rolling out of me.

"Hopefully, the fit is good, otherwise you might have to put it somewhere else," I tell him with a wink.

He chuckles. "Well played."

I smile at him, grateful to my friends for helping me out of my anxiety spiral after our date last weekend. The number of whispers and stares that I heard in the building really threw me, so I'm glad it's a little quieter here. Jax looks at me, suddenly more serious than before. I look at him and cock my head, waiting for him to speak. I can see something is rattling around in his mind.

"So, I talked with Roman," he starts, and I can feel the blood drain from my face.

Oh shit, this is it. He's going to end things now.

"Don't be worried," he says, a little panicked at my face. "I'm not mad and we're not done because of it."

I take a deep breath and sigh. "Okay, good to know."

"I wanted to ask how you feel about it. Roman said the ball is in my court with him and I, but this involves you too, so I'd like to hear what you have to say."

It's hard not to laugh a little at his nerves. He doesn't come across as insecure to me, so when his speech picks up and he talks fast, it's hard not to be amused. My eyes wander as I think.

I told Roman I was interested, but do I want to pursue both of them? Is that fair to them? It feels selfish to have two guys at once. Roman caught my eye from a distance and his kiss was like lightning in my body. Jax drew me in with his eyes, makes me laugh, and kisses like sin. Of course, I want both, but should I?

"I mean, it feels selfish," I tell him.

"Don't worry about that. Just focus on what you want."

"Then, yes, I am interested in both of you," I say quietly. "But I don't want to come between you guys and your friendship."

Huffing a laugh, he replies, "That's exactly what Roman said to me about you and me. I'm willing to try if it's what you want. Roman and I have been friends for years, and with him living at the house, it makes communication easier."

I nod. "Yeah, my friend Ames is in a polycule, and they make communication a necessity. So, if you're okay with it, let's try?"

"Let's do it, but tonight is just you and me still."

We smile at each other, and Jax nudges my foot with his.

I gasp in mock affront. "Sir, are you playing footsie? In this esteemed establishment?"

"Oh I am, I won't let anything get in the way of something I want," he says, leaning forward with a mixture of humor and seduction.

"Well," I start, hoping this isn't too forward, but I don't want the evening to end. "We could play footsie in a more appropriate venue. My couch isn't too far from here."

His smile widens. "I'd really love that."

He waves the waitress down for the bill and I give him basic directions in case we get separated. We make it with no problems, and I lead him inside. My house isn't anything fancy, two bedrooms and a bath, but it's cozy and I make an effort to keep things as up to date as I can. I show him where he can put his shoes and coat, and I sit on the couch, reaching for the remote. I'm not sure how close he really wants to get, so I sit on one end, so he can sit on the other or in the middle. He walks over and pretends to trip and fall, landing almost on top of me, but not quite.

"Oh no! I'm so sorry!" he says with absolutely no apology in his voice.

I laugh. "Oh, are you now?"

He places a hand on his heart. "Deeply sorry, I could have landed further away and how tragic would that have been?"

He grins at me as I laugh and puts his arm behind me on the back of the couch. I remember he's big on consent from our texts and our kiss, so I try to dig up the courage to tell him I don't mind snuggling, but the words stick in my throat.

What if he doesn't want to? What if I sound stupid?

"What do we want to watch?" He interrupts my thoughts, trying for a bright tone. It's like he can tell I started to spiral.

"Um, have you ever watched *Whalewolf vs Sharktopus*?" I ask.

His eyes get unbelievably wide. "No, but I think I need to."

I giggle again and lean into him some as I pull the movie up. "Um, so, I feel awkward saying this…"

His eyes cut to me sharply. "What is it?"

"If you… want to cuddle, I'mokaywiththat," I rush out at the end.

He grins. "Yeah, I would love to. It means a lot that you told me what you're comfortable with."

I smile, relieved, and he puts his arm around me fully, pulling me a bit closer. The feel of his body next to mine is heavenly, and I find myself relaxing more into him. I can feel his solid muscle from his manual labor, but it's not uncomfortable. It's soothing, and his chin tickles the top of my hair with his close-cropped beard. I start the movie and tilt my head back against his arm, looking up at him. Our faces are close as he looks back.

"This is nice," I tell him softly.

"It is," he agrees.

He starts to lean in, and I meet him halfway. Our lips meet and it's as amazing as I remember. His lips are soft but strong, and I push for more almost immediately. He obliges and meets my intensity, each of us kissing the other like it's the air we need. I don't know who instigates, but our tongues touch and I moan.

God, the feeling of his tongue on mine, strong and controlling, does things to me.

I flick his tongue with mine and raise a hand to the back of his head, hoping to hold him there longer. I hear a groan come from him and he breaks the kiss to trail his lips across my jaw. His mouth explores the back of my jaw where my ear meets my neck and he kisses and licks his way around my neck, like he's learning about how my body feels.

I'm on fire. I can feel my panties becoming damp and a tingle started in my lower belly. All I can think of is mounting him on the couch, but things are still early, and I know we should take things at least a little slow. I pull his head back to slam my mouth back onto his, wanting more of him, not being able to get enough. The hand that's around my body brushes the sides of my rib, barely missing my breast, and I whimper, wanting to feel the touch. My nipples are begging for attention and my body is a live-wire, ready to explode. He pulls back and a disappointed noise leaves me involuntarily.

"I want to devour you," he confesses, breathing hard.

"I want you to."

He groans. "We probably should wait just a bit, right?"

"That *would* be the responsible thing to do," I agree.

He exhales hard through his nose. The hand not resting behind me comes up to tuck a piece of hair behind my ear.

"Soon, Sunshine, if you're okay with it, very soon," he promises.

"Okay," I tell him, a little disappointed but also knowing this is for the best. I do want us to build our relationship a little more before taking that step.

I sigh. "Well, we wouldn't want you to miss this cinematic genius."

He huffs a laugh. "I suppose not."

We readjust to look at the TV, and he's still holding me close. I feel a kiss press to the top of my head and my stomach swoops.

I am gone for this man.

 Chapter 15

Jax

Charlotte and I have been on a grand total of two dates over three weeks. We just haven't seemed to be able to sync up much and I'm pretty sure I'm dying. Roman says I'm being dramatic, but it feels like death is imminent. I've seen him texting her with a smile on his face, so I would be surprised if he wasn't feeling dramatic, too.

I drop my wrench on my foot for the third time today. "FUCK!"

Roman starts laughing. Really, it's a low chuckle, but it may as well be riotous since it's coming from him.

"What?" I snap.

"That's the fourth time you've dropped something today," he teases.

"I only dropped the wrench three times!"

"Yeah, but you dropped your hand earlier when you were tightening a bolt with a wrench and slammed it into the car."

"Doesn't count, hand is still attached to my body."

Roman smirks. "Okay, whatever you say, man. You got it bad."

I groan. "Like you don't? I see you texting her."

Roman's smirk just turns into a smile as a response. I hear Dan yelling out from the office suddenly.

"Hey! Stop dropping the tools and get to work! I don't pay you to drop shit!"

Roman's full out smiling now.

"You don't pay me at all, asshole!" I yell back with a grin.

Dan tosses his head back in a laugh and closes the window to the reception area.

"What are you doing tonight?" Roman asks, starting to pack up his stuff.

I look over at him. "Why the hell are you packing up? It's not closing time yet."

"Uh, yeah, it is."

"The fuck?" I look at my watch. Shit. It's 6 pm, closing time.

"That's what happens when you daydream all day instead of working. Dan's over there cashing out the register, doin' your job for you."

I toss a towel at him. "Fuck off."

"So, what are you doing tonight?" he repeats.

"Don't have plans. What are you thinking?"

"I need to get out for a beer. Wanna go hit the pub?"

"Sounds awesome, man."

We finish packing up and help Dan close and lock all the doors.

"Great job today, man. Appreciate your hard work," I tell Dan.

"Thanks, good to hear," he says as he starts getting into his car. "Catch you tomorrow."

"Bye," Roman and I respond.

Roman and I climb into my truck. We've been taking turns driving when our shifts align to keep things simple. We have a few

127

options for where to grab some beer, but Jerry's Pub is a local staple and people go for the atmosphere. Food's not bad, but it's not the reason people go. We grab a couple of spots by the bar and order two beers. He clinks his glass against mine in an impromptu cheers.

"To friends," he says.

"To friends," I agree.

We start drinking and Roman turns to me. I stop with my beer halfway back down to the counter.

"Should I put this up and keep drinking?" I ask him.

He chuffs a laugh. "Nah, I do feel like we should talk about Charlotte."

"I'll never complain about talking about Charlotte," I confess.

"I haven't taken her out yet, and I'd like to, but everything's so tight with these damn bills," he confesses, frustration lacing his tone.

"Maybe you guys can do something at the house?" I suggest.

"Would that be weird with you home?"

I think for a moment. "I don't think so, but if I start to feel awkward, I can always duck out somewhere."

"You're the best, man. I appreciate it. I was hoping to bounce ideas, but having her over seems like the easiest option."

"Anything for you two. I know this can easily get twisted if we're not talking and compromising."

He tips his head toward me. "Here I thought I would be the mature one in this relationship."

I slap him lightly upside the back of his head in retaliation. "Maybe after we can do a group date, see if the three of us can all spend time together?" I ask.

"Yeah, I think that's a great idea," he says with as much enthusiasm as I would expect from his stoic ass.

My phone buzzes in my pocket and I pull it out, anxious to see what Charlotte has to say. I am grossly disappointed by what I see.

Mom: Hey honey, we're doing family dinner this weekend. We're going to do it at our house this time.

Me: New phone, who dis?

Mom: Very funny, mister. I mean it, you will be there this weekend.

Me: Isn't Thanksgiving next weekend? Why do I have to come over twice?

Mom: Thanksgiving is in a couple weeks.

Damn, I need to look at a calendar. I try a different excuse.

Me: What if I already have plans? I love you guys, but I do have a life.

Mom: Ohhhh are you going out with that girl? Bring her along. I'd love to meet her.

Me: What girl?

Mom: Don't try to pull one over on me. Roman spilled the beans

Asshole. I try for a new tactic to throw my mom off *this* trail.

Me: Isn't it a bit soon to meet the parents?

Mom: Nonsense, I'll love her. Bring her. Stop making excuses.

How the fuck does she always do that?

Me: I'll ask, no guarantees.

Mom: Fine, fine, looking forward to seeing her!

Me: What about me?

Mom: I guess you too, my baby boy

Me: Gross, sorry I asked

Mom: *laughing emoji*

"Fuck," I say to Roman before taking a long drink.

"Not Charlotte, I take it?" he asks.

"No, it was my mom. She wants me to bring Charlotte to dinner. You're an asshole for spilling the beans, by the way."

Roman cringes. "Good luck with that one. Didn't mean to tell her. It came out when she called to say hi the other day. Does that mean this weekend is out for me?"

My family is great, they really are. It's really soon though and I know my mom can be overbearing when meeting someone new. I don't know if I want Charlotte to be busy or not.

"Nah, there's Friday and Saturday. You take one, I'll take the other. Besides, next week is Thanksgiving and I won't subject you to them twice in two weeks," I tell him.

He snorts and nods in acceptance, then we wrap up our beers and head home. Once I'm in my room for the night, I pull out my phone and open the text thread I have with Charlotte.

Me: Hey beautiful girl, how was your day?

Sunshine: Hey yourself! It was nice, no work drama, so that makes the day go smooth.

Me: Did you get that drama from earlier this week figured out?

Sunshine: Yeah, we got things back on track and the stakeholders are happy now. How was your day?

Me: It was fine, the shop had steady business and Roman and I went for drinks after.

Sunshine: You didn't invite me?? *winking emoji*

Me: I'm not sharing you until this weekend. You're all mine to devour right now.

Sunshine: Oh? You planning to eat me up?

I groan. I can see where this is going, but I need to get the awkward question out of the way.

Me: I want to tell you all about how I plan to eat you out, but first I have a question.

Sunshine: Ugh, you got me all worked up! What's the question?

Me: I know it's awkward to ask after that message... but my family is doing a family dinner this weekend and my mom asked for you to join.

I see the three dots appear and disappear a few times while she works to reply.

Shit, I hope this hasn't caused any spirals.

Her reply finally comes through.

Sunshine: Are you sure? Is it too early? I mean, I don't mind, but...

I decide to call her at this point. I'm worried she's spiraling.

"Hey," she answers softly.

"Hey, I was worried you started to spiral," I reply just as softly.

She huffs a laugh. "Yeah, I guess I started to there. It just feels early, you know? Plus, with having Roman involved with things, will it make it weirder? I don't mind meeting them, but I don't want them to feel like they have to invite me."

"Hang on, I'm gonna get the three of us on the same page," I tell her, throwing my covers off and walking to my bedroom door.

She's asking what I'm doing as I knock on Roman's door. I tell her to hang on, and a minute later, Roman finally opens the door. I put the phone on speaker.

"Hey beautiful, I have Roman here too," I tell her.

"Oh. Hey Roman," she says, a little shyly.

"Hey baby girl," he replies, a smile on his face.

"Charlotte's not sure about coming to my parents' house since the three of us are involved," I explain.

Roman frowns slightly. "Are you worried they'll chase you out of the house?"

She giggles. "No, I guess I just feel like they're going to judge us for it, and I don't know about you, but I don't really appreciate being judged."

"That's understandable, Sunshine," I tell her.

"If you don't want to say anything yet, I'm okay with that. I know it's hard to open up to new people and I don't want you to be uncomfortable," Roman says to her.

"I don't want you to feel like you're a dirty secret," she says.

"I'll be dirty for you," he says, lowering his voice.

"Roman!" she scolds, but we can both hear her smile.

"Honestly, I don't feel like a dirty secret. This is all new and I think we're all just trying to find our feet. I don't mind keeping to ourselves right now," Roman assures her.

"Does that help?" I ask her.

"Yeah, that does. Look at us all communicating already," she says, teasing.

"I'll communicate with you some more later. We have a date to plan," Roman says. "Goodnight gorgeous."

"Night Roman," she says.

I take her back into my room and off speaker phone.

"So about my family... my mom can be overbearing. She wants you to come, but I'm more than happy to tell her you're busy. She means well, but she doesn't always think."

"Oh, okay then, um, do you want me to come?" she asks.

"Baby, I always want you to come," I tell her, my voice dropping a little. I hear a hitch in her breathing after I say that. "For family dinner, though? I'd love you to join us for that," I tell her.

"Okay, then," she says, and I can hear her smile.

 # Chapter 16

Roman

Charlotte and I have been texting almost nonstop, and I'm looking forward to spending time with her. Jax decided it would be best for us to have space, so he went into the shop to work on some stuff there. He told me what projects he was going to do, but I'd be lying if I said I listened. I couldn't stop thinking about Charlotte being here. I made pizza dough so we could make our own pizzas together and then maybe watch a movie if she's interested in that.

I've looked around the house about five times now and cleaned every surface I can think of. My nerves are clearly getting the better of me and I should care, but I don't. I wonder if I should have put on something less in the "lounge" category of clothing, but it's pretty hard to resist sweatpants at home with a T-shirt. Hopefully, she doesn't mind. I told her to dress comfortably.

The doorbell rings and I have to keep myself from running to answer it. I manage a speed walk. Charlotte's standing on the other side, in leggings and a long tunic shirt. Her blue hair is up in a ponytail and she's carrying a six pack of beer.

Be still, my beating heart.

"People say the way to a man's heart is food, but I figured beer couldn't hurt either," she says with a grin, holding it up.

"You are a miracle," I tell her, standing aside so she can come in.

She takes off her shoes and looks around. "So, this is you and Jax's place, huh?" she asks.

"Yup, home sweet home," I tell her, putting the beer away. "I figured you would want to eat during dinnertime. Do you like pizza?"

"Is that a serious question?" she asks, teasing.

"Good! I made us some pizza dough, figured we could make our own pizzas tonight."

"Oh man, I don't think I've done this on homemade dough before. If we made our own, it was usually on pre-made crust. This is cool!"

"Let's get some toppings on," I say to her, pulling the cheese out of the fridge.

She grins and rubs her hands together as I pull out the toppings I've gathered. We end up with pepperoni, fresh mushrooms, black olives, peppers, ham, and green olives. She eyes the spread critically and hums.

"This is a good spread. I don't know what to choose!" she says.

"Well, we've got enough dough for a couple of personal size pizzas, or we could make four minis."

"OH! We should each make two and the other has to try what we made," she says excitedly.

"I'm game," I tell her.

I split the dough into four pieces and set two balls in front of her. She watches carefully as I show her how to spread the dough into a circle. We both add sauce to our pizzas, but after that, she turns hers away from me. I try to sneak a peek, and she bats me away.

"No stealing my ideas!" she scolds with a smile on her face.

A small smile appears on my face as well and I pull my own pizza to the side to add toppings. I finish up and place them on the baking sheet.

"How's this gonna work if I'm not supposed to see them?" I ask her. "I'll see them when you put them on the pan."

"Oh, it's fine at that point. I just didn't want you to steal my ideas before that."

"Well, then, I see how it is."

She cackles and moves back from her creations, working with laser focus. When she's ready to put them on the pan, I swoop in before she can get them and do it for her.

"I could have done that!" she exclaims.

"Yeah, but I like doing things for you," I tell her, sneaking a kiss on her temple without thinking.

"You haven't done much for me yet. How can you know?"

As I close the oven door, I set a timer, so we don't burn the food. "I can just tell." I smirk at her.

She smiles and rolls her eyes. "What should we do while we wait?" she asks.

"Do you like games?" I ask her, surprising myself.

"What kind?"

"I've got some old board games we could go through and see what sounds fun."

"Okay! Let's do it."

She is almost bouncing with excitement. That earns her a smile, and I sneak a kiss onto her cheek as I exit the room. Apparently, I can't keep my lips off her. As I walk away, I can feel her eyes on me.

"Stop staring at my ass," I tell her, taking a guess.

"What? I was not!" she objects.

I turn to see her face bright right and her eyes determinedly looking elsewhere. "Uh-huh."

"Well, if you didn't wear grey sweatpants, this wouldn't be a problem," she mutters.

Chuckling under my breath, I'm now pleased with my choice of clothing for the evening. Looking in my storage box, I find Monopoly, Checkers, Life, Clue, and Settlers of Catan. I'd forgotten about that last one. I think we got it right before my sister left for college. Charlotte is waiting patiently at the kitchen table when I return. I place the pile next to her and tell her to pick what looks good.

She critically eyes each game, and I can tell she's taking the task seriously. I would love to know what's going on in that head of hers. Finally, she pulls out Monopoly, confidence all over her face.

"Your funeral," I tell her.

She laughs at me and opens the box to pull out all the pieces. Honestly, I'm not actually great at this game, but I can hold my own most of the time. At least, I could when I was younger. Charlotte sets herself up as the banker but lets me choose my piece first. I choose the dog. Obviously.

If you don't choose the dog, there's something wrong with you.

We set out on the game and chat about our lives, smack talking to each other as we go. About ten minutes in, I've realized my mistake. Charlotte played me for a fool when I was being nice at the start. She is a Monopoly shark.

"Are you sure you don't play professional Monopoly?" I ask her as I fork over more money.

Cackling, she counts the bills. "Not quite, but I'm sorry your ego has been bruised."

"It may never recover," I tell her, keeping a straight face.

She looks up, suddenly alarmed. I can see her trying to decide if I'm serious or not, so I throw her a wink. Smiling, she takes her turn. Halfway through the game, our pizzas are ready, but we're not ready to eat yet. I put the oven as low as it will go and leave the pizzas in to stay warm.

We wrap up the game a bit later, Charlotte winning by a landslide. Now we're both starving, so Charlotte grabs beer while I grab the pizzas. We sit side by side and try the pizzas. She has one completely covered in olives, black and green. I'm not even sure there's cheese on it. Her other pizza is a smiley face made with pepperoni for eyes, a folded piece of ham for the nose, and peppers for the smile.

I just threw some meat and mushrooms on mine. She took this way more seriously than I did.

"I don't think you used enough olives," I tell her, poking at the olive pizza.

"Want to hear a secret?" she says, smiling.

"Always," I tell her.

"I hate olives."

A full belly laugh bursts out of me. "Why did you even make it?" I ask her.

She shrugs. "I wanted to see if you'd eat it."

I laugh again. "Well, joke's on you cuz I loooove olives."

She hums. "We might have to end this now. I don't know if I can be with someone who likes olives."

"It works out perfectly. I'll eat them for you, so you don't have to. Match made in heaven."

Laughing, we eat our pizzas and sit back in contentment with full bellies and almost empty beers.

"Tell me something about you," she says.

I think for a moment. "When I was a kid, I played soccer all through high school and hated every minute of it."

"Why did you do it?" she asks with a small laugh.

"It made my mom happy, and I loved seeing her happy," I tell her softly.

She reaches over and grabs my hand. "Did she know?"

"She suspected," I tell her, threading our fingers together. "She always told me I could quit whenever I wanted to, but I just loved the joy on her face when she watched me play. It was worth playing when I hated it to see that. It was one of the few times she smiled."

"You're sweet," she tells me.

"Back at you, tell me something," I prompt her.

She thinks for a moment, chewing on her lip.

"If we're talking about stuff we don't like, I guess I'd confess that I get harassed a lot when I go out because of my weight."

"That's a big thing to tell me," I say gently. "I'm sorry that happens to you."

She shrugs. "Sometimes it really bothers me, and sometimes I can let it slide. You know about my anxiety, so when that kicks in and I hear the comments, that's when I have real problems."

"Want to tell me about it? You don't have to."

"I suppose there's not much to tell. I *am* okay with my body, I'm just not okay with how others think it's something they have permission to talk about or harass me about. My anxiety usually kicks in when I hear it and it's hard not to believe them in that moment."

"Nobody deserves to be harassed. Basic respect should apply to everyone. I'm sorry that you don't get that when you go out."

Her eyes look like she's tearing up a bit as I talk. "Thanks. Most guys I tell that to brush me off, like I'm being dramatic or unreasonable."

I turn my body toward her and swivel her chair to face me. My legs bracket hers on the outside of her chair and I lean in close to her, still holding one hand as I grab the other.

"You are not dramatic, and you are not unreasonable. You matter, your experiences matter, and they are valid."

Without any warning, she leans forward and slams her lips into mine. I don't hesitate to bring my hand to the back of her head and hold her there. The kiss starts out aggressive but turns into exploration. I scoot my body closer to her and lick her lips, wanting to explore how her tongue feels against mine. She obliges and moans when my tongue touches hers. Our kiss turns intense, neither of us battling for control, but both excited to explore and see where things go.

Our breathing grows heavy, and I tilt her head where I want it to get a deeper angle. My mouth moves from her mouth, and I press kisses along her jaw and down her neck. Charlotte's hands grasp my shoulders, like she's trying to anchor herself to me. Our lips meet again; my body is on fire and my cock stiffens the longer my mouth is on her.

She whimpers in protest as I break the kiss and stare into her eyes. She leans forward and I oblige a few more soft, more chaste kisses. As much as I want to keep going, I know it's really our first date and I don't want to assume anything.

"I could kiss you all damn day."

"Same," she says breathlessly. "I'm sorry for just attacking you."

"Attack me any time, baby girl."

She laughs a little and reaches down to squeeze my hand that's not holding her head. "I've never had a guy take my side so quickly and willingly on this topic," she confesses.

"Jax didn't say anything?" I ask.

"Well, I didn't really tell him about it. There hasn't been much of a chance to tell him, honestly. It's happened a little with us, but I didn't want to ruin our evening by bringing it up with him."

"I'm honored you shared it with me. It's yours to share with him, but I'm sure he'll support you if you do tell him," I encourage her. "Do you want to go sit on the couch and watch a movie?"

"That sounds awesome, but it's gonna depend on what kind of movie you want to watch," she says.

"What's acceptable?" I question her.

"Bad horror, action, comedy, suspense, mind-fucks," she lists off.

"What? No Rom-Com?" I ask her, teasing, as we take our places on the couch.

"Excuse ME, sir, I have *some* self-respect! Those are for when I'm super down about life. Thank you very much."

A laugh escapes me, and I open my arm, inviting her to snuggle in. She pounces at the opening and snuggles in as close as she can get. We put on a suspense movie and settle in. A few minutes later, the door opens and shuts loudly.

"Shit! Sorry!" Jax says softly.

My eyes open and I realize it hasn't been a few minutes; it's been like an hour. Charlotte is knocked out, head on my shoulder. Pretty sure she's drooling, actually.

Jax smiles. "Fuck, you guys are cute."

I roll my eyes at him, and he just laughs.

Charlotte stirs, and when her eyes open, she immediately spots Jax. She gives a sleepy smile before really registering it's Jax. When she figures it out, she shoots upright with wide eyes.

"Jax! I, uh, I fell asleep on your couch. With your friend. My date? How do we do this?"

Her speech picks up pace as she talks and Jax moves to sit on her other side. He grabs her hands and guides her through a deep breath.

"Hey, there's no problem, okay? We talked about this and at some point, I imagine we'll all spend time together. I'm sorry I spoiled the end of your date."

"Oh. Are you sure? It feels kind of awkward to me," she says.

"I don't feel awkward, so I hope that soon you won't feel like that either," I assure her.

She nods and shoots me a quick smile, relieved. "Okay, then, I'll do my best."

She gives Jax a quick kiss, then turns and does the same to me. All three of us are now smiling like idiots on the couch. Charlotte glances at her watch and sighs.

"I probably should go soon," she says.

"Looks like we still have forty-five minutes left in the movie. Do you want to stay and finish it?" I ask.

"Is it okay if Jax stays?" she asks.

"Sure, if he wants to."

She looks at Jax, who is already taking his boots off and making himself comfortable. Charlotte is set snugly between us, her body slightly twisted so her head is on my shoulder, but her feet are in Jax's lap. It feels right; I hope they feel it too. This is how our evenings should be, the three of us sitting together, just existing.

 # Chapter 17

Jax

My nerves are higher than I thought they'd be today. Charlotte is going to meet my family, and I'm really hoping they like her. If they don't, that doesn't really change things, but it sure makes my life easier if they do. I hop into my car and drive to Charlotte's house. She offered to drive herself, but I want her near me. Our couch snuggle wasn't nearly enough, and I want to spend as much time with her as I can. She opens the door quickly after I arrive, and I step into her house.

"Just one more minute. I need to pin my hair back real quick," she tells me as she walks away.

Her blue hair is loosely curled and falls softly down her back. She's got on a casual fall dress, gray on top and plaid fall colored skirt that seems at odds with bright blue hair, but it works. Anything she wears works for me, honestly. I stare at her ass as she walks away.

"Uh, what?" I snap back to reality when she walks out of sight. "Yeah, okay, no problem!"

I hear her laughter from the bathroom. "Maybe you should spend more time listening and less time staring at my ass," she taunts.

I walk toward the bathroom and lean against the door, watching her put some pins in her hair to hold it to one side. "Yeah, but where's the fun in that?" I ask.

She turns and grins at me. "Okay, I think I'm ready to go."

I walk closer to her and place my arms on the bathroom counter, on either side of her, pinning her in place. "I think you missed something," I tell her softly.

"What's that?" she whispers.

Leaning down, I put my mouth on hers. I will never get over how soft her lips are. I give her a gentle kiss, which she reciprocates. When I pull away, she chases me keeping me locked in with her. The kiss heats up, and she runs her hands up my torso, clasping them around my neck. The feel of her hands as she moves them up my body sets fire to my skin.

I want to feel her hands directly on me, not over this fucking sweater.

I take one hand from the counter and grab the side of her head, avoiding the side her hair is pinned to. I hold her mouth to mine and our tongues start to dance. She whimpers in my hold, and I can't stop a small groan from bubbling up my throat. I give her tongue one more caress and pull back from her, more quickly this time, so I don't get sucked back in.

"We should probably go, otherwise we're gonna completely miss dinner."

She bites her lip. "I want to ask if that would really be a bad thing, but I suppose you want to see your family."

"Oh, trust me, I would rather be here with you, but I'll never hear the end of it if we miss it." I push my body into hers. "I'm hoping you can feel how much I want to stay here, though."

She gasps lightly when she feels my hardness against her, and she moves her body against it just enough to tease. "Soon?" she asks.

I can see the desire in her face. Her pupils are wide and her eyelids heavy. "Soon, baby, so soon," I assure her.

We pull back and I take her hand as we leave the bathroom and the house. I'm praying this boner goes down before we get to my parents' house or it's going to be really embarrassing for me. I open and close her car door before sliding in behind the wheel to start the car. She turns on the radio and the last rock station I had on starts blaring through the speakers. She jumps a little, then laughs at herself, turning the volume down.

"I don't know why I didn't expect that, but I didn't." She laughs.

I chuckle. "You can change it if you want to. I don't mind."

"You say that, but do you mean it? I'm big on songs you can sing to, not necessarily good music," she confesses.

I turn the radio to Bluetooth and hand her my phone with Spotify open. "Okay, do your worst, ma'am."

She grins at me, and I hear a classic rock riff start. When I hear Pat Benatar's voice start, I laugh out loud.

"This is appropriate."

"You said to hit you with my best shot." She's laughing too.

"I don't think that's what I said, but I'm gonna let you win this one because well played, Sunshine. Well played."

She laughs and starts dancing in her seat as we drive. The drive to my parents' house isn't too bad, about twenty minutes, just on the other side of town. The closer we get, the quieter Charlotte gets. First, she stopped the dancing, choosing to just bob her head along to whatever was on, and now she's still. I pull up and park in the driveway and I see she's now wringing her fingers. I reach over and put my hand on hers, lacing our fingers together.

"You still okay?" I ask her.

"Yeah, just nervous." She smiles quickly, and it fades.

"Hey, just remember, if the food is terrible, just lie and you'll be fine."

She snorts a laugh, "Okay, I'll keep that in mind."

I grin at her and undo my seatbelt. "Let's go hot stuff."

I grab her hand as we walk up to the door. I squeeze it in reassurance and open the main door. We're assaulted by the noise of two little girls, and a smile immediately lights up Charlotte's face at the sound. We step inside and said little girls are immediately barreling toward us.

"UNCLE JAX!" they shriek in tandem.

I bend down and open my arms, bracing myself for impact. They barrel into me, and I wrap my arms around them, squeezing tightly.

"There are my favorite nieces," I say to them.

They giggle and look up, noticing Charlotte for the first time. They let go and stand back a little, staring at her. She waves at them, a smile on her face.

"Hi there," she says to them, her voice kind and soft.

"Who are you?" Kinsley asks with all the tact of a six-year-old.

I stand up and put my arm around Charlotte.

"She's my girl," I tell them.

"Uncle Jax, we asked *her,* not *you.* You can't talk over people like that," Abigail chastises me.

"Okay, my bad," I say, holding my hands up while leaving my arm around Charlotte.

"My name is Charlotte. I'm friends with your Uncle Jax."

"That means we're friends too!" Kinsley says, excited.

She grabs Charlotte's hand and drags her down the hallway toward their overstuffed playroom. My parents decided that there was a need to spoil the girls silly the moment they were born, including their own playroom at grandma and grandpa's. Charlotte giggles and allows herself to be pulled away, turning to flash me a smile.

I smile back, pleased that she's comfortable enough to play with the girls. I walk further into the house and find my mom and sister in the kitchen. Bethany sees me first and smiles, nudging Mom. I roll my eyes, bracing myself for the onslaught.

I'm gonna need a beer for this.

Mom turns and sees me digging in the fridge. "Jax! You made it!" she exclaims.

"Well, you kind of threatened me to show up," I joke. "I'd rather not have you running me down in a tragic 'accident'."

She walks over and smacks my arm lightly before planting a kiss on my cheek. She and Bethany are trying to look around the corners of the kitchen to see if they can spot Charlotte.

"Where is she?" Mom asks, craning her next so much it must be uncomfortable.

"The girls got to her."

Bethany chuckles. "Poor girl."

"She was smiling when they dragged her, so I think she'll be alright," I tell her, taking a pull from the bottle.

"Well, go get her! Food will be ready in just a couple of minutes," Mom instructs.

I tip my beer bottle in her direction and head out of the kitchen. I traverse the hallway, following the sounds of giggles to the playroom, where I poke my head around the corner. Not only did they get Charlotte, but they also took my dad hostage as well. They're all seated around the play table, cups and saucers in front of each of them and the rest of the matching set in the center of the table. Charlotte and my dad both have plastic jewelry on them, and they are politely sipping their pretend tea.

"Well, it looks like I missed all the fun," I tell them.

"Of course! Don't you know tea parties are the best?" Charlotte says.

"We like Charlotte. She plays tea party properly. Can we keep her?" asks Kinsley.

"Well, *I* want to keep her, so maybe I can share her sometimes. How does that sound?" I offer.

"I guess that's okay, you did find her first and finders keepers," Abigail says seriously.

Abigail has been big into finders keepers lately. It's caused quite a few arguments, according to my sister.

"Grammy says dinner is done and we need to head to the table. I don't want to make Grammy mad, do you?"

My mom doesn't get mad often, but when she does, you better look out.

"Well, we better listen, eh, girls?" Charlotte says, starting to take her play jewelry off. "Wouldn't want to make Grammy upset my first time meeting her!"

"I guess not." Kinsley pouts. "Grampy, we better make sure Grammy doesn't yell for Charlotte's first time here."

My dad chuckles. "Alright girls, I guess we better go."

He stands up, removing his jewelry and starts to help the girls take off some of theirs. They protest over the crowns, though, and those stay on. I hold my hand out for Charlotte, and she grabs on, letting me pull her up. I catch her with a quick kiss on the cheek as she settles on her feet. We walk into the dining room, and Bethany is putting food on the table. She looks up and sees us walking in.

"Girls, did you wash your hands?" she asks.

"Yes!" Abigail responds.

"Liars, go wash your hands," Bethany says.

"How does she always know?" Kinsley mutters.

"Come on girls, let's go get those hands washed," my dad says, shooing them towards the kitchen.

Bethany looks up at Charlotte and pauses a minute, her smile still on her face. Charlotte smiles back, and I can see her shuffle her feet in place a bit as nerves set in.

"Bethany, this is Charlotte," I introduce them. "Charlotte, this is my big sister, Bethany."

"Nice to meet you," Charlotte tells her.

"Uh, yeah, I'm glad you were able to come. I need to grab some more food from the kitchen. I'll be back in just a moment," replies Bethany.

"Hey where's Trevor?" I call after her.

"Oh, he had some software thing with work happening tonight." She waves me off.

I look over at Charlotte. "Are you doing okay?'

She looks at me and smiles briefly. "Yeah, fine."

"Okay, are you good if I go help bring food out? My mom will never let me hear the end of it if I don't at least offer."

"Sure," she says. "Can I just pick anywhere to sit?"

"Yup! Go for it," I tell her.

I walk toward the kitchen and lean in the doorway. The kitchen shares a wall with the dining room, but it's not an open concept, so you can't really see what's going on while at the table.

"—going to need more food. I mean, I'm not sure if we have enough, if you catch my drift," says Bethany.

"Hey, need any help?" I ask.

Bethany jumps and turns, eyes shooting to mine.

"Okay weirdo, why you so jumpy?" I ask.

She glances at mom and then grabs the biscuits off the counter. I raise my eyebrow at her as she scoots past me. Her cheeks are faintly red. I turn to mom.

"What's wrong with her?" I ask.

She waves me off. "She's just worried about making sure we have enough food for everyone. You know how she gets. Grab that plate of vegetables and bring it to the dining room, would you?"

Bethany doesn't usually care that much, but maybe she's making an effort. Charlotte is the first girl I've brought home since Morgan and I broke up. I grab the vegetables and bring them to the table, setting them in the middle with the rest of the food. I walk around to the other side of the table and put my hand on Charlotte's shoulder.

"You want something to drink, Sunshine?" I ask her.

"Um, water is fine," she says.

"Are you sure? We have beer and wine too," I offer.

"I guess a beer would be nice," she relents.

I kiss her on top of her head. "You got it."

My dad and the girls come back in as I'm headed to the kitchen and the girls immediately start arguing over who is going to sit next to Charlotte. I chuckle, grab two beers from the fridge, and head back. My mom follows me into the dining room and we're all finally ready to eat.

Sure enough, Kinsley and Abigail are sitting on either side of Charlotte, beaming.

"Girls, one of you has gotta move," I tell them.

"Awww Uncle Jax! You always get to see her, and we just met her!" Abigail whines.

"Sorry, thems the rules toots. Beat it," I tell her.

She huffs with the professional ease of a teenager and gets up to go sit by my mom.

Good luck when she is an actual teenager, Bethany.

I slide in next to Charlotte and place the beer by her plate.

"Thanks," she says with a smile.

"Any time," I tell her.

My dad, not one to stand on pretense, grabs the nearest serving dish and starts loading his plate. Bethany takes his lead and grabs the dish closest to her. Soon we're all scooping and passing the food until everyone's plates are full. I suddenly realize I didn't do proper introductions.

"So, Charlotte, this is my mom, Susan, and my dad, Tucker. You've met Bethany and the girls. Mom, Dad, this is Charlotte."

Charlotte waves from her seat and says a quiet hello.

"We met already, we bonded over torture–I mean tea," my dad says.

The girls giggle. "Grampy! You're so silly."

He chuckles and scoops some food into his mouth.

"Girls, make sure you take plenty of vegetables," Bethany encourages the girls as they eat.

"You know, you are what you eat," I taunt the girls. "So pretty sure you're gonna turn orange, just like those carrots."

More giggles.

"So, Charlotte, What do you do?" asks my mom.

"Oh, um, I work as a project manager," she says.

"Oh, so a desk job? That makes sense, since…" She drifts off and waves her hand around at Charlotte.

"Mom, plenty of employers are fine with crazy hair colors, doesn't just have to be for jobs where you're at a desk," I say.

Charlotte's looking down at her plate now, cheeks a bit flushed. There's a semi-awkward pause to the conversation now.

"Well, I've considering dying my hair," I say to lighten the mood. "What do you think of neon green?"

"You look more like a purple guy," my dad chimes in between bites.

I laugh and my mom and Bethany let out small chuckles as well.

"Mommy, can I dye my hair like Charlotte?" Kinsley asks.

"No baby," she says.

"But why?" Kinsley whines.

"You're too young, sweetheart."

"My mom didn't let me dye my hair when I was little either. I had to wait until I was all grown up," says Charlotte.

Bethany mutters something under her breath that I miss, but Charlotte's cheeks redden again, and she looks down at her plate. The rest of dinner goes similarly. I do my best to keep the conversation light and I can tell Charlotte goes from awkward to comfortable and back again. I knew it was a bit soon to meet the parents, but I was hoping she would have warmed up by now.

After the meal, we say our goodbyes, and Charlotte promises the girls she'll play with them again the next time she sees them. We get into the car and start back to her place. She sighs in her seat and relaxes with her face to the window. I reach over and place my hand on her thigh.

"You made it through," I tell her, smiling.

She clears her throat. "Yeah, I made it."

"I'm glad you and the girls got along so well. That means a lot to me."

"They are wonderful little girls."

I check in with her. "You okay? You sound kind of off."

She clears her throat again and turns to face me. "Yeah, I'm okay." She tries to reassure me. It doesn't work.

There's a definite sheen to her eyes, like she's holding back tears. My heart constricts at that, and I wish I could fix whatever it is right now. Since we're stuck in the car right now, I grab her hand and squeeze, not wanting to push her too far. Maybe she'll be more comfortable talking at her place.

 # Chapter 18

Charlotte

I'm not sure if I'm angry, sad, or just shocked from dinner at Jax's house. His dad and the girls were great. The girls were so freaking adorable, and I love how sweet they are. Jax's dad was super nice and seemed very welcoming. His mom and sister are a different story. The second his sister saw me; I knew it was going to be awkward or downright miserable.

She had that look on her face that skinny people get when they see someone in a larger body. It starts with "I assumed you'd be skinny", then moves to "holy shit you're really not skinny" and ends with "need to keep my mouth shut about her not being skinny even though it's all I can think of". I've seen those same thoughts play over the faces of plenty of people in my life, so I'm not sure why I thought his family would be any different. Wishful thinking, I guess.

I heard some of the things Bethany whispered to her mom, and when Susan came out to the table, she got those same emotions on her face before she composed herself. Jax completely missed her slight about my weight, but I'm not sure I'm surprised about that. I don't think he's had to deal with that ever. The nail in the coffin for me was when I heard Bethany mutter, "She grew up big alright". I'm sure she thinks nobody heard her, but I'm so used to noticing stuff like that, that it blared in my ears like she was using a loudspeaker.

Jax asks me a few times on the car ride if I'm okay, and I don't really want to lie to him, but I don't know if he would hear the truth. If we get into a fight about it, we'll be trapped in the car. So, I tell him I'm fine, but I think he knows I'm not.

Maybe I should just open up to him like I did for Roman. For some reason, it was easier to talk to Roman. Something about the way he lasered his focus in on me made me feel seen and heard. I know Jax sees me, but it's different, and I'm not sure I'm ready to open up to him like that.

We pull into my driveway, and he parks the car before looking over at me.

"Do you want to call it a night? I don't want to invite myself in, but I also don't want to leave you if I don't have to," he says.

"Yeah, why don't you come in for a few?" I tell him, needing some snuggles.

He doesn't hesitate to turn off the car and hop out. He tries to open my door but I'm too quick for him, so he settles for closing it for me and takes my hand, threading our fingers together. I'm hoping that he's open to talking about his mom and sister, but I suppose we'll see where the night goes. I just know I don't want him to leave yet, despite my apprehension about this conversation.

We get inside and take our shoes off, flopping on the couch next to each other. He puts his arm around my shoulders, and I tip my head back to look up at him.

"What's going on in that beautiful head?" he asks.

"I'm a little afraid to tell you. I'm worried you'll get upset," I confess.

"How about this? I can't promise not to get mad, but if I start to feel upset, I'll tell you and we can keep talking. Deal?"

I smile. "Deal."

He kisses my forehead and then leans back a bit. He always knows how to get my anxiety to slow down. It's intuitive for him.

"So," I start, and my hands immediately start fidgeting. "I'm not sure how to say it, but I think your mom and sister were bothered by the fact that I'm fat."

"What?" he says, sounding confused. "What makes you say that?"

"Well, they both got *that* look on their faces when they saw me. Your sister made a comment to your mom about not having enough food, your mom insinuated my weight was because I'm at a desk job, and then your sister used my story of not dying my hair until I was grown to point out how big I got."

It all spills out of me and I pause, looking at him anxiously.

I hope he's not mad. God, I'll feel horrible if I upset him.

He's quiet for a moment, and I can see him processing.

"Well, I am gonna tell you that what you feel matters, okay? Your feelings are yours and they are important. I don't agree with you on what you think you saw or heard, but I know it upset you and I'm sorry that happened."

My heart drops a little. I didn't expect him to rally a mob to my cause or anything, but hearing he doesn't agree with what I experienced is a bit of a stab to the heart.

What I think *I experienced? Is he kidding right now? I was the one who experienced it, not him. Who is he to say that what I experienced didn't happen?*

"I'm upset that you said, 'what you think you saw or heard'. I've experienced this behavior before, Jax, and it's always the same."

I know it's not the same as confessing it to Roman, but I'm trying to hint at how often I encounter it and that it does hurt. I'm hoping he'll understand at least a little.

He nods his head. "Okay, I'll openly admit that I haven't experienced what you're talking about. At least, if I have, then I've forgotten about it. What other people think of me isn't something I consider often, if at all. So, I can't say I understand. I just don't pay attention to what other people say about me."

I sigh a little. "Do you believe me, though?"

"I truly don't think they meant what they said in the way you took it, but I believe you're upset. I also believe that they said something to make you think they don't like you."

That's probably the best I'm going to get out of him right now. I know I'm feeling emotional and if I keep going, then I'm going to spiral.

Maybe I can talk with Roman about how to approach Jax with this.

I put my head on his shoulder, looking away for a moment. He puts a hand underneath my chin and forces me to look at him.

"Hey, I really like you, and I don't give a fuck if my family does," he says.

I look into his eyes and I can tell he means it. This man clearly has not experienced bias against him, but maybe I can help him learn about what I've been through. I can't change him, but I can give him information to learn from.

I smile at him. "I really like you too."

He grins and brings his mouth to mine. I didn't specifically invite him in to make out, but I definitely hoped the evening would end this way. I just wish his mom and sister hadn't been so shitty.

I kiss him back, and we're gentle at first. A bit of a reconnecting after a rocky talk and evening. When he swipes his tongue against mine, that starts things moving faster and my hands grip the back of his head, his hair threading through my fingers. He places a hand underneath one thigh and swings me from sitting next to him, to sitting on his lap.

I let out a small sound of surprise. I didn't expect him to literally manhandle me, but I'm not complaining. I lean further in, pressing my body close to his. Jax's hands are on my hips, and I feel him pushing at my body, encouraging me to rock against him. It doesn't take much encouragement before I'm grinding my hot core on his hard length. Thank goodness he's not scary large, but he's not small either. I've read novels before where the guy is described as massive, and I'm not interested in that level of big. It sounds too painful. Hard pass.

He pulls back from my mouth, one hand still on my hip and the other sliding up my side, finding my breasts with ease. He trails kisses across my jaw and suckles that spot where my ear and jaw connect again. I moan in ecstasy, that spot making me wetter, and my breathing gets faster.

"You are so fucking perfect. I can't wait to feel all of you," he whispers near my ear.

I whimper in response as his grip on my breast narrows to fingers teasing and pinching my nipple. I can feel my body come alive at his ministrations, and my head tips back in pleasure. He pulls the fabric of my wrap dress to the side, his mouth finding my nipple through my bra. I'm sure it was easy to see by how hard it is right now.

"Fuck, yes, keep going just like that," he says huskily, his breathing getting heavier.

"God, Jax," I whine, feeling my orgasm start to build as I continue to rock against him.

He hums low, pulls my bra aside and latches directly on to me. The suction of his mouth feels amazing, and when his tongue flicks my hardened bud, I lose it. My pussy clenches, and on the next swipe of my clit against his cock, I feel the contractions start and tingles spread over my body. My body gushes more wetness on to him, and I cry out in bliss. He rocks me through the orgasm, wringing as much as he can out of me before letting me fall forward onto him.

"God, you're gorgeous," he says, his face buried in my hair and neck.

"Mmmmm." is all I'm capable of replying with, my head on his shoulder and face nuzzling his neck. After a moment or two of sitting in peace, I suddenly sit up.

"What about you?" I ask, unsure if he came or not. Seems selfish to only worry about myself.

"I'm perfect, babe, don't worry about me," he assures me with a smile.

"Are you sure?"

"Positive. I could live off the noises you make and never come again." I giggle and he smiles at me, giving me a kiss, almost reverently. "I can't believe how lucky I am that you took a chance on me," he says.

"Pretty sure I'm the lucky one," I tell him.

"Guess we're both lucky then."

"Absolutely."

 # Chapter 19

Charlotte

It's girls' night again and we're back at Amy's house for the evening. We're settled in her living area, with me on the beanbag this time around. *Toxic Shark* lined up for tonight and is playing in the background. We recycle so many of these that I'm not sure when the last time we saw a new one was. Maybe we'll have to find one soon. I settle back with my small plate of chips and a brownie and start munching.

"Soooo how did first date with Roman and meeting Jax's parents go?" Amy asks.

I didn't text them about either evening, other than saying they both went well. Which was mostly true. Just not the dinner part at Jax's. The after festivities were the fun part.

"Oh my god you guys, the night with Roman was awesome. We made our own pizzas, I whooped his ass at Monopoly, I got a good make-out session in, and we had couch snuggles. It was so nice, and he's so easy to talk to. Jax came home while Roman and I were snuggling and joined us... and it felt right." I tell them.

"I'm so glad! If you ever have questions about navigating more than one person, I'm your girl, okay?" says Amy.

"That sounds perfect," Olivia adds.

"It was really wonderful. I'm surprised at how much I opened up to him, but he made me feel seen. He understood the frustration of not feeling like you matter. I feel connected to him because of it."

"Oh God, that's adorable and nauseating all at once," Olivia groans.

I chuck a chip at her while laughing.

"Tell us about dinner now," Amy insists.

"Well, I guess it was okay," I say.

Olivia looks at me with her usual laser eyes. "That means it didn't go very well."

"I mean, dinner itself didn't go great, honestly, but before and after was actually good," I admit.

Playing with Kinsley and Abigail was a blast, and those girls were so freaking cute. Plus, his dad was great.

"So, give us all the details!" Amy exclaims impatiently.

I clear my throat. "So. Obviously, I was nervous at first, but when we walked in and Jax's nieces grabbed my hands to go play, I felt a lot more relaxed. They were just the sweetest and had Jax's dad already set up for their tea party, so I sat down and joined them. His dad was great, and I'm amazed at how little the girls fought and bickered, but that's probably 'cuz I was there."

Amy nods sagely. "Yeah, kids are always more well behaved with someone new."

"Dinner itself was… not as great. There was the awkward meeting of Jax's sister where she clearly disapproved of my weight. Then I heard her whispering to her mom about it. Jax's mom *also* was not a fan of my weight and actually referenced it in a generic way, so that was fun. His sister also made comments I'm not sure I was supposed to hear, but I did."

"God, what assholes. Did Jax call them out?" asks Olivia with disgust in her voice.

"Weeelll… that's the thing. He didn't see it. I mean, he was there, but he didn't see that it was happening. He thought they were maybe talking about my hair."

"What the fuck?" Olivia exclaims.

Amy looks furious.

"We talked about it after, he tried to in the car, but I was just trying not to spiral and cry so I didn't say anything. I couldn't focus enough for that, plus I didn't want to fight in the car. When we got back to my place, I did bring it up."

"And?" Amy prompts.

"Well, Jax has a lot of great qualities, but I'm not as comfortable opening up to him as I am with Roman. Like I said, he brought up that he thought they were referencing my hair, so he doesn't believe that it was about my weight. He didn't belittle me at all, which I appreciated. Though he acknowledged they did upset me and that my feelings were valid, he disagreed with what the topic was."

"I mean, what kind of an asshole dismisses that?" Amy asks.

"The kind that has probably never faced any biases or discrimination," I point out. "I'm hoping if I can educate him on some of the stuff we go through as fat girls, he might understand. I know I can't get him to change. I see that look on your faces, but I can at least educate him and see what happens."

"Yeah, I guess so. I still feel like this isn't a good start. Maybe you should ditch Jax and just go with Roman. He seems better," Olivia grumbles.

I throw a pillow at her. "Stop it! I agree, it's not great, but if he shows the capacity to understand and educate himself and change, it's worth trying, I think. He's funny, he's smart, he's already picked up on my spiraling and is super intuitive about helping me through it. I really like him *and* Roman, you guys."

"Just… be careful, okay?" Amy adds. "I don't want to see you get too deep and have things fall apart. Especially with two guys to juggle who are friends."

"Seriously, for once this bitch is right," Olivia chimes in.

I crack a smile as Amy throws a chip at her. "You asshole! I'm always right!" She laughs.

Olivia chuckles and eats the offending chip. "You guys keep throwing stuff at me like it's bad, but now I've had two chips and an extra pillow! So, what happened after dinner that made it so good? Doesn't sound very nice so far."

"Ummm." I blush.

"Oh my God, you did NOT!" Amy shouts excitedly. "Tell me you DID!"

I laugh at her contradictions and shrug, taking a drink from my water. "A lady doesn't kiss and tell."

"There's a lady in here?" Olivia asks, looking around.

"I hate you," I say with a laugh.

She grins. "Give us the deets, then."

"I'll give you SOME," I tell them begrudgingly. "Clothes mostly stayed on, but there was a definite orgasm. He is an amazing kisser, you guys, and he focused solely on me. Didn't ask about himself at all. I tried to offer to reciprocate, but he wanted to cuddle instead."

"Ugh, someone giving," Amy says wistfully. "That's a definitely point in his favor."

"*That* is a good sign. You want someone who makes sure you get pleasure and doesn't demand anything," Olivia adds.

As she says this, my phone vibrates with a notification. I pick it up from beside my leg and take a look at whatever is trying to get my attention. It's from Jax, and I start smiling without realizing it.

"Ooooo, someone's ears are ringing," Amy teases. "What's Lover Boy got to say?"

I roll my eyes, but my smile doesn't leave. I unlock my phone and open messages. The girls stare at me and I look up.

"You guys are being creepy," I tell them.

"You say that like it's news," Olivia counters.

Jax: How's it goin Sunshine?

Me: Good. Girls' night is in full swing and the girls are being as nosy as ever.

Jax: You gonna tell them how amazing I am in bed?

Me: I haven't been in bed with you, so I can't tell them anything.

Jax: Touché, I'll let you win this round

Me: How benevolent lol

Jax: I'll leave you to your evening, I guess, but I'm dying to see you again. Plans soon?

Me: Absolutely *kissing emoji*

"Sooooo…." Amy starts.

"He was just saying hi, but wants to get together soon," I explain.

"We need to meet both of them, so you guys should plan a group thing with us! You guys all get to see each other, and we get to meet. We can kill two birds with one stone!" Amy says excitedly.

"Yeah, but then I don't get to make out with him," I pout.

"Gross, just make out later," Olivia says with a smile.

I roll my eyes. "Fine!"

Amy and Olivia start chatting while I start a group chat and make plans with Jax and Roman. We decide on a group date this weekend, and once we've got that squared away with the girls, I refocus on our night together. We watch the *Toxic Shark* kill the townspeople as the hero tries to save the day and chat the night away.

#

As Jax, Roman, and I drive to the bar for our group night, I can't help but look at them during the drive. Jax's hair is messy styled, and I love how neat and trim he keeps his beard. I want to rub my hands on it all day long. His subtle muscles fill out his T-shirt that I can glimpse under his leather jacket and his jeans do something to me.

Roman's blond hair is brushed back neatly into a low ponytail. It's not very long, but it's long enough that he doesn't like to leave it down all the time. His face is clean shaven, as always, and the man is wearing a damn Henley with the sleeves rolled up. That shit should be illegal.

"You're staring," Jax comments, his lip twitching up into a small smile.

"I can't help it," I confess. "You both just look so good."

His full smile appears, a small dimple peeking through the hair on his face, and a small smirk shows up on Roman's face. Jax glances at me and gives me a once over.

"You're always looking like a goddess. It's so fuckin' hard to keep my hands off you," he tells me.

I flush a little and when he puts his hand on my thigh, I wrap my fingers with his.

If he keeps touching my thigh, I might combust.

Roman, sitting behind me, wraps his hand around the seat to brush my hair back from my face a little.

Okay, I'm going to combust, it's inevitable.

We arrive at the Jerry's Pub, and I hold hands with Jax as we walk in. Olivia and Amy aren't here yet, but Jax heads over to a table that has open seats with plenty of room.

I snag a seat and sit, an open spot on either side of me. There's a silent battle happening behind me for where Roman and Jax are going to sit. I'm sure there's a guy strategy that they're using, but Roman ends up next to me with Jax across from Roman.

I'm not sure why they aren't just sitting on either side of me, but whatever floats their boats.

"So how did you guys meet?" I ask. "I know you were in shop class together, but I don't think I've ever asked either of you how you met."

"That was actually the first day we met. We both got lost looking for the shop room and just kind of stuck together," Roman confesses.

"Yeah, he's had my back since hour one, especially with that teacher I told you about," Jax adds.

"Oh man, I wish I had been there," I tell them. "That was hilarious."

Roman's lips pull in a small smirk. Which means he's basically laughing, I've learned.

The waitress comes by to take drink orders. I add an order of appetizers as well, knowing Amy and Olivia will be here soon, and the waitress gives me a once over before pasting a semi-polite smile on her face and walking away.

Well shit, I didn't want to deal with this tonight. I wanted a fun, worry-free evening.

Roman notices and puts his arm around my chair protectively.

"You okay?" Jax asks, noticing Roman's shift and my tension.

"Yeah, I'm good."

Before Jax or Roman can push the subject, I hear someone loud behind me. "Hey bitch!"

I recognize the voice and smile, turning in my seat to see Olivia and Amy approaching. "About time, bitches!" I reply.

Amy cackles, and Olivia smiles in amusement. "We're only like five minutes late. That's an achievement!" Olivia comments.

They arrange themselves at the table, Amy next to me and Olivia across from her, leaving a seat between herself and Jax. The waitress returns with our drinks and gets Olivia's and Amy's orders. She gives them the same once over as she leaves, and I see Olivia's eyebrow raise. I shoot her a look, silently saying 'I know', and she shakes her head.

"Liv, Ames, this is Jax and Roman," I start introductions. "Jax and Roman, this is Liv and Ames."

I gesture to everyone to put a person to a name, and they exchange the usual polite greetings. Amy puts her hands under her chin, fisted, and looks directly at Jax.

"So. What are you doin' with our girl?" she asks.

"Ames!" I scold her, "At least give him some lube before you start."

Olivia cackles as Jax laughs and Roman cracks a small smile. Amy looks at me, trying to look innocent.

"What? I'm looking out for you," she insists. "Okay fine, what caught your eye first about Charli?"

"Charli, huh?" Jax says, looking at me, "Well, when she walked into the shop and I saw those green eyes, I was done for. Then the blue hair came into focus, and I just kept seeing more beauty the longer I looked."

"Yeah, with your jaw hanging open." I laugh at the memory.

"Pretty sure I drooled," Jax jokes.

"It was cute," I insist.

Amy makes an exaggerated gagging noise and I elbow her in the ribs. She turns her attention to Roman.

"What about you?" Amy asks him.

"Saw her in the parking lot and could just tell she was special. Overheard you guys on the trail that day and it was confirmed, so these two let me join the party."

"Succinct, I like it," Olivia comments.

The girls are laughing when the waitress comes back, two drinks and our appetizers in tow. She sets everything down and looks at the guys.

"You fellas need anything else?" she asks.

Well, shit. Did I say that already? I double down. Shit. This is gonna be an interesting evening.

Amy and Olivia exchange a look while the guys decline anything else and turn to us to check. The waitress has already started walking away.

Roman leans down to ask quietly in my ear. "Is that waitress going to be a problem?"

I shrug. "Maybe. She's got some solid Resting Bitch Face, and she's definitely judging."

Roman nods, taking in the situation.

"We're fine too. Don't worry!" Amy shouts after the waitress.

"Ames, stop," I plead with her, not wanting a scene.

"Well, if she wasn't being a bitch, I wouldn't have to yell," she reasons, picking up a chip loaded with cheesy goodness.

"It's a valid point," Roman states.

"I knew I liked you better," says Amy.

Jax looks over with his hands spread open in a "what about me?" gesture.

"So, what's your story?" Olivia asks Roman.

He looks over at her, a bit surprised. "Didn't I already answer this?"

Amy is like a shark with blood in the water. She turns to Roman with THAT look on her face. She's going in for the kill.

"Oh, I'm sure a blond beauty like you has a backstory we should know about," she says sweetly.

"Who doesn't have one?" he counters.

"Some are better than others," she says.

"True, maybe someday you'll hear a good one."

"I bet you have a good one."

"Guess you'll have to keep wondering," Roman says, nonplussed.

"Maybe I'll have to pry it out of Charli," she threatens.

"Hey, keep me out of this! I'm just here for the kisses and orgasms," I tell her, holding my hands up in surrender.

"So Jax," Olivia interrupts. "I hear your nieces stole Charli away during your dinner for a tea party. How old are they again?"

"Five and six," he responds with an easy smile. "They're the best. I love spending time with them. Abigail was extremely unplanned, but now the two of them are thick as thieves."

"That's awesome, I love when siblings are close," Olivia says.

"Do you have any siblings?" Jax asks.

"No, just me and my parents. It was a bit lonely sometimes but Charli more than made up for it when we were kids."

"Aw, I love you too," I say as I fist bump her across the table.

Jax looks at Amy. "How about you?"

"I have a little brother. He's in high school right now. Extremely unplanned like Abigail, but in the opposite direction." She laughs.

Jax gives a chuckle. "Sometimes the unplanned is the best way to get something."

"Agreed!" Amy shouts. "We need a cheers!"

I smile and shake my head, but hold my glass up. Everyone else joins, Roman a little more straight faced than the rest of us. He definitely reserves his full smiles for me and it makes my heart warm.

"To the unexpected," Amy declares. "May we always find joy in it."

"Cheers!" We echo and drink.

We've barely set our glasses down before we hear someone yelling at us from not too far. "Jax!" The voice calls out. "Hey!"

He turns toward the voice and immediately grins. "Morgan! Hey!" He gets up and gives a short hug to the girl who has walked over to our table.

"Shit," I hear Roman mutter.

She's shorter than I am, not really skinny, but not fat either. She's got long black hair and dark blue eyes. I can't tell if her hair is natural or not, but she wears it with confidence either way.

"What are you up to?" she asks, a friendly smile on her face.

"Out with my girl and our friends," he says and then turns to me. "Charlotte, this is Morgan, Morgan, this is Charlotte."

I stand and hold out my hand. "It's nice to meet you," I tell her.

"You too! I'm glad to see Jax has someone. He hasn't really found anyone since we dated," she says.

Well, shit. Again. Tripling down on the shits of the evening now. Maybe it's quadruple down on it since Roman just said it too.

Of course Jax's last girlfriend is here, of course she is gorgeous and *of course* she's nice to boot. They look like they would fit together nicely, and I can start to feel the spiral coming.

Maybe dating both of them was a bad idea. Maybe I should have just picked Roman. Wait, does HE have any former girlfriends in town?

The waitress chooses that moment to swing by. "Any refills?" she asks the table.

The guys order refills, and as the girls and I are ordering ours, the waitress' RBF takes over. She looks at each of us in turn. Jax resumes his conversation with Morgan after his order and isn't paying much attention to us. Roman is watching the entire interaction.

"You sure you want all those carbs?" she asks.

Oh God, she probably sees Morgan as belonging to Jax more than I do, and that's why she's pulling this shit. There's no way she'd think Roman is actually with me. Morgan's smaller, prettier, and fits nicer with Jax. Maybe I shouldn't have anything else, water's fine right?

I change my drink order and the waitress walks away, a smug smile on her face.

"What the fuck was that?" Amy starts in on me.

"Baby girl—" Roman starts too.

"I need to use the bathroom," I interrupt and walk away.

Thank God they're all getting along, but I think I might explode.

I'm so overwhelmed, Ames and Roman starting in on me, the waitress' face, Morgan showing up. My brain is on overload. I shut myself into a stall and just sit and breathe on the toilet. My head is between my knees, and I can feel tears threatening. My heart is racing, and I feel like a piece of dirt. I shouldn't have come out tonight.

Seeing Morgan, the judgy waitress, me giving into the judgement; it all feels like too much. My brain is telling me to just give up and be alone. It's not worth this trouble.

I'm not going to spiral. I'm not going to spiral. I'm not going to spiral. Maybe if I chant it enough times in my head, it will come true. I need to leave. How am I supposed to get out of here? I rode with the guys and neither need to see me like this. Fuck, why didn't I drive myself? I could just avoid this whole mess and go home. This is why I don't date; it always goes wrong one way or another. And now I have two guys to think about! I'm not cut out for this.

Jax and Roman are going to realize I'm not cut out for this and take off. Why would they stick around for this? I kept telling the girls that, but they wouldn't listen. They're both better off with someone who isn't judged by everyone for their weight. They're definitely better off with someone who's not riddled with anxiety. I'm sure they can do better. I don't deserve romance, anyway; all I do is ruin things.

The thoughts swirl in my head, and I can feel my chest start to ache.

As I spiral, while simultaneously pretending I'm not spiraling, I hear the bathroom door open and close. Footsteps come closer to my stall, and I hear a soft knock. Someone's shoes are now in my line of sight.

"Charlotte?" I hear a voice call out. It's not Olivia or Amy.

I clear my throat. "I just need a moment."

"I totally understand. Would it be ok if I talked to you for a moment?" Morgan asks.

Why the fuck does she want to talk to me? What could she possibly have to say? How I should stay away from Jax? Fine, I'll do it. Just let me wallow in peace.

"Sure. I guess," I say and pull my head out from between my knees, just leaning forward now, forearms on my knees.

"I heard what that waitress said and saw her face," she says softly.

"Okay."

"She had no right, Charlotte. She doesn't get to say what you put in your body. I'm sorry I didn't catch her in time to say anything. Olivia and Amy both started after you, but I asked if I could come first."

"Why did you?" I ask, my voice flat, trying to figure out her angle.

"Sometimes it's easier to hear from someone you don't know well. I've been where you are," she confesses. "I used to weigh a lot more and I would get that kind of treatment a lot."

There it is. I am not hearing this. She's going to tell me to "just lose weight" as if it's the easiest thing in the world. As if I don't already eat healthily. As if it should be the primary force in my life and the one thing that will fix all my problems.

Anger pushes the anxiety out of the way, and I quickly stand and unlock the stall door.

"Good for you. I don't need to hear about how you got skinny and now your life is roses and sunshine. Keep it to yourself."

I storm out of the bathroom before she can respond and walk back to the table.

I am over this night. I'm leaving.

I grab my purse at the table and look at Amy and Olivia.

"Can one of you take me home? I'm not feeling well," I tell them.

"Uh, sure, yeah, we can do that," Amy stammers.

Olivia pulls out $40 in cash and places it on the table. "Nice to meet you guys," she says politely as she stands.

"Wait, Charlotte, what's wrong?" Jax asks.

"Charlotte, please, can we talk?" Roman adds.

"Just not feeling well. I'll text you both later."

Jax frowns, concerned, and Roman looks resigned, but neither pushes the issue. I walk out, Amy and Olivia trailing behind me. I get into the backseat and Amy hops in the driver's seat.

"Let's get you home," she says gently.

"Do you want us to stay?" Olivia asks.

"No. I need to be alone," I tell them.

We ride in silence, and Ames drops me at my house. I walk inside and close the door. After removing my shoes, I plop on the couch and promptly start crying.

 # Chapter 20

Jax

Charlotte left the bar like a hurricane, and I'm left with my jaw on the floor wondering what the fuck happened. I look over at Roman, unsure what to make of this. His face isn't exactly pleased either, but he looks upset rather than the confusion I feel.

I thought the night was going fine. What set her off?

"Um, that was interesting," I tell Roman.

"I wish she would have talked to us," he says, sounding more sad than angry.

"I've never seen her just run off like that," I admit.

Morgan comes back to the table, an awkward look on her face. "Sorry, that might be my fault."

"What did you say?" I ask, a little more sharply than I probably should have.

"I just tried to talk to her about how the waitress was treating her, but maybe I should have let her friends talk to her," she says. She looks from Roman back to me and sighs. "I'll go back to my group. Sorry I threw a wrench in the evening. Nice to see you both. Hopefully, we can hang out again, but on purpose next time."

"If Charlotte's okay with it," Roman says.

"Sure, thanks for trying tonight. I'm not sure Charlotte would have listened to anyone. Sometimes she spirals and it's hard to get to her," I tell Morgan.

I get up to give her another hug and debate if Roman and I should stay or go. Roman looks at me and makes an executive decision. He drops another $20 on the table, and we walk out.

By the time we get home, Roman's completely shut down and in his head and I'm starting to worry a little more about Charlotte. I'm hoping she's with the girls and they can help her through whatever is happening in her head. My phone shows no new messages from her in our chat *or* the group chat.

"Any messages?" I ask Roman.

"None," he replies before walking into his room and closing the door.

The next morning, I call her. It's Sunday morning, so no shop time to worry about. I've resigned myself to voicemail when it finally picks up.

"Hello?" Her voice sounds hoarse, and she sounds exhausted.

"Hey Sunshine. How are you?"

She sighs. "I've been better, I guess."

"Would you be opposed to a coffee delivery? I'd love to see that beautiful face. I didn't get enough of it last night."

"Oh. Sorry about that." Her voice softens.

Crap, that came out badly, didn't it?

"No, I just mean I missed you is all. I'm sorry I didn't text you. You seemed like you wanted space. Did I mess it up?"

"No, I needed the space, but I missed you, too. I should have texted or called. I said I would and then I didn't. You and Roman are probably both upset with me."

"Of course we're not. How about you let me bring you coffee?"

She sighs. "That sounds heavenly. Will Roman be with you?"

"I'm not sure. He hasn't gotten out of bed yet. He's usually a late sleeper unless there's a big need for him to get up."

"Oh, okay." She sounds a little disappointed, but I'm hoping she perks up when I get there.

I take her order and promise to be there in fifteen minutes. I debate on waking Roman, but if I wake him, he'll be unbearable, so I leave him to sleep. I make it to Charlotte's in ten. I'm not saying I want to catch her in her underwear. But I want to catch her in her underwear. That body gets me every time. I ring the doorbell and wait a moment. She opens the door and is wrapped in a robe.

"Damn," I say, disappointed.

"What?" she asks, confused and a little upset.

"I was hoping you'd be in your underwear," I confess.

She barks a laugh and I want to listen to that laugh forever.

Forever? Yeah, I have it bad.

She steps back and I come into the house, handing her the large to-go coffee cup.

"You have major brownie points for doing this," she tells me and tilts her head toward me.

I take the cue and bend down to kiss her in greeting. We keep it light, but still more than just a casual peck.

"Anything for you," I tell her.

She looks at the bag in my hand. "What's in that?" she asks, taking a seat on the couch with her legs curled under her.

"I saw some muffins, and they were calling our names. I wasn't sure what flavor you like, so I got one of each. You can pick first," I tell her, pulling the three muffins out of the bag. She looks over the variety, finally choosing lemon poppyseed. "Solid choice. I knew I liked you."

She grins and takes a bite out of the top. "The muffin top is the best part," she says, smiling.

"Totally agree," I tell her, grabbing the blueberry muffin and taking my own bite.

We smile at each other as we eat our muffins in comfortable quiet. At least I'm comfortable; I hope she is too. I take a sip of my coffee and look at my girl. She looks exhausted, and all I want is to see a smile on her face. We probably should clear the air about last night, though.

"So, do you want to talk about last night?" I ask tentatively.

She sighs and sips her coffee. "Not really," she admits. "I suppose we should be adults and do the adult thing, though. Should we call Roman too?"

"I can think of an adult thing I'd love to do with you." She rolls her eyes but smiles while she's doing it. "Okay, I'll be serious. Mostly. I think Roman would want to talk to you in person, so I'm thinking after we talk, we can text him to let him know?"

Her smile gets a little bigger before fading.

"Okay, we can do that." She takes a large breath. "So last night, there were a few things that set me off. The waitress kept giving me and the girls looks when we asked for food or drinks, and when I tried to order a second round, she basically told me to lay off the carbs. Morgan showed up by then and I was trying really hard not to do the crazy girlfriend thing and be all weird and jealous. All I could think of was that she looked better than me. You guys just looked like you would be so cute together and that, coupled with the carbs comment from the waitress, set me off."

"Oh, babe, I promise you have nothing to feel jealous of," I assure her, scooching closer and taking her hand in mine.

She gives a little smile. "Thanks, I was working on convincing myself of that, so I really appreciate the validation. I was spiraling pretty bad and trying to convince myself that I should just break it off with you and Roman. At the same time, I was trying not to do that, so it was pretty stressful."

"Hey, I promise that neither Roman nor I want that. We like you and we both want to see this thing through. Besides, you already said that you're my girlfriend, so you're stuck now."

A small laugh escapes her, and she shakes her head, then hesitates for a moment.

"Was there something else?" I ask gently.

"Well, Morgan said something in the bathroom that wasn't helpful and was actually a bit hurtful. I don't know if she meant it to be, but that's how it came across."

Morgan is the nicest person I've met. She and I split amicably because we just kind of fizzled out, but we've been good friends ever since. I can't imagine what she would have said to Charlotte, but it must have been bad for her to get so upset.

"What did she say?" I ask, trying not to come across as aggressive.

Charlotte sighs. "She heard what the waitress said and tried to come help me through the feelings and started talking about how she *used* to be in my shoes. I didn't want to hear about how she's miraculously skinny now, like that's what I should do to get basic respect."

It's true, Morgan was heavier before we dated. She showed me pictures when we were together. I never really thought to ask why she lost weight, though. I just figured she was happier that way. Was there another reason behind it? Why would she suggest that to Charlotte? It doesn't add up, but I wasn't there for the conversation either.

"You're right. You shouldn't have to lose weight to get basic respect. I never want you to change your body because someone else says you need to. If you want to change your body because it's what *you* want, I support that. I don't ever want you to change for anyone. Okay?"

She sets her coffee down and throws her arms around me. I manage to get my coffee on the table instead of spilling it and hold her close. I feel her shoulders shaking a little and my shirt is now a little damp.

"Hey, hey, it's okay," I tell her.

"No guy I've ever–dated has–said something so nice. Now both you–and–Roman–are being so–amazing," she cries, hiccuping through some of her words.

I plan to erase all those previous assholes who made her think she wasn't worthy. They were the unworthy ones. I hold her as long as she lets me, and when she pulls back, it's sudden.

"Oh God. I got your shirt all wet and I'm sitting here sobbing when we should be enjoying each other's company," she says, mortified.

"I don't mind, but I suppose now we might as well go eat worms." She looks at me, her brow furrowing. "You know the rhyme, right?" I ask.

She shakes her head.

"Nobody likes me, everybody hates me, might as well go and eat worms? So, like, anytime you feel like something bad happens, you just say might as well go eat worms?" I explain.

She looks at me, mouth open and disbelief on her face. Then the first laugh comes out, and she's suddenly laughing so hard that more tears roll down her face.

"That is NOT a thing!" she says through her laughter.

"It's totally a thing!" I tell her, grinning.

We dissolve into more laughter, and I'm so glad I got her to smile and laugh a little. When we settle a bit, I take her hand again.

"Want to do something this morning? Maybe see if Roman wants to join in?" I ask her.

"Yeah, that would be nice. Let me go change and try to do something with my hair."

She leaves me in the living room and gets ready to go. I stand up when she comes out and walk over to her, grabbing her face in my hands and bringing my lips to hers. She sighs softly into my lips, and I take the opportunity to deepen the kiss.

Her mouth is heaven, and I never want to leave.

I pull back and look into her eyes. "Ready?"

"Yeah, let's go. Mind if I drive?" she asks.

"Yeah, that's cool."

I pull my phone out and dial Roman, putting it on speaker so Charlotte can hear too.

"Hello?"

He doesn't sound too groggy, that's good.

"Hey man, I'm at Charlotte's and we are gonna go find something to do. Want us to swing by and grab you?" I ask.

"Sure, it would be nice to see her," he says, sounding a little more awake.

"We'll be there in a few minutes then," Charlotte chimes in before I end the call.

Once we're in the car, she turns it on and immediately it dings with a warning. She groans and throws her head back on the headrest.

"Really?" she says.

"What's the alert say?" I ask her.

"Something about tires, it just says 'check tires'," she tells me.

"Well, good thing you have the world's best mechanic in your car." I wink at her. "Let me take a look."

"We could just take your car," she protests.

"Sunshine, we may as well see what's wrong before we try to change plans. I don't want to leave your car here if there's something wrong with it," I tell her.

She relents and I hop out of the car, walking around each tire to see if there is anything visually obvious going on. Sure enough, when I look at the front driver's side tire, I can tell the air is low. Probably not super noticeable to most, but I'm used to seeing it.

I open her car door. "Looks like a tire pressure issue. Turn off the car and I'll pump it up. Do you have an air compressor?"

She hesitates. "Ummm… maybe? My dad put a bunch of tools in the garage when I moved here."

"Let's go look and see what we got," I say, keeping my voice upbeat.

She opens the double car garage, and one side is packed with stuff. Some looks like extended storage and some looks like tools and basic house care items. I start to look through things and find an older air compressor. It should do, assuming it still runs.

"Got an outlet in here?" I ask.

She brightens. "I know that one!"

She walks toward the astragal and does a Vanna White flourish to display the outlet that resides there. I smile and walk over, pulling the air compressor behind me.

"So fancy," I tell her.

"Classy with a capital 'K'," she says, grinning.

I lean down, grab the cord where it's wrapped up neatly around the designated holder hooks, and plug in the machine.

Immediately, a large buzzing noise starts, and I stand up. I nod my head and gesture for Charlotte to walk outside the garage with me.

"Well, it turns on, but no way to know if it actually holds the compressed air until we let it run a bit and see if it shuts off when the air is compressed. So we can just chill until we know if it's gonna shut off."

"Okay, well, we can go sit on the swing in the backyard. Maybe we should call Roman, too," she offers.

"Let's go," I tell her, grabbing her hand.

She pulls her phone out this time and dials Roman up, putting it on speaker like I did before.

"Hey baby girl, what's up?"

He's definitely awake now.

"So apparently my car tires are out of air? We have to fill them up before we can leave," she says.

"One tire," I interrupt before Roman can ask anything. "One tire is a little low. We've fired up her air compressor to see if it will actually hold air for us."

"Oh, okay, do you want me to swing by there? I can bring a tire gauge and a backup compressor," he offers.

"Yeah, sure. Doesn't hurt to be prepared."

"Like the Boy Scouts," Charlotte adds.

"Pretty sure that's Lion King, baby girl," Roman says.

"You and Ames, you're both wrong, I swear it." She sniffs.

We laugh and hang up as we reach her porch swing. The backyard isn't huge, but it's not tiny either. Just enough room to have people sit outside around a fire, and a cute, worn porch swing out on the patio area. We sit, and I'm surprised to find it's comfortable.

"The swing was my parents'. I think they had it about five years before they moved, so it's worn in but not worn out."

"It's surprisingly comfortable," I confess, and wrap my arm around her.

She leans into me and gets comfortable. I drop a kiss to the top of her head, and we swing gently together. The silence is comfortable, and I find myself a little annoyed when the compressor shuts off.

"Good news, the compressor did its job. Bad news, we gotta get up and go put air in that tire."

"I don't think I'll complain about getting to watch you work," she tells me, a smile on her face.

I kiss her nose, and we head back toward the garage. I unplug the compressor and cart it over to the car. I put the chuck on the tire valve and, sure enough, it works like a charm. I eyeball it so it looks inflated a bit more, but I don't go too far with it.

"There, that should do it until Roman gets here with a pressure gauge to make sure it's in range."

She looks at me and bites her lip. My eyes are immediately drawn to her mouth.

"What's goin' on, pretty girl?" I ask her, walking closer to her.

"You just look good doing your thing," she tells me.

"All I did was pump up a tire, but I'm gonna take the compliment. Wait until you see me really work," I tell her, raising an eyebrow.

She steps into me and puts her arms around my neck. "What do you say we spend the morning in?"

I put my hands on her hips and start walking her backwards towards her house's back door.

See, I was specific there, the house's back door. Hers will be later.

Roman decides to pull up at that moment and hops out of his truck, his eyes zoned in on our bodies. "I almost missed the good part," he says, his voice pitched lower.

Charlotte looks between us, realizing where this could go. "Are you guys okay with this? It seems soon to be all together like this. I guess I'm also assuming where this is going, which I probably shouldn't do…"

"Sunshine, I don't mind if you don't. Roman and I haven't done this together before, so we can talk through it as we go if needed."

"If it's what you want, baby girl," Roman assures her. "I'll go if you want me to, though, my feelings won't be hurt."

"NO!" she says, almost shouts it actually.

I grin and my mouth descends on her as we walk awkwardly through her house. Roman following us and closing the door behind us.

"I have no idea where your room is," I confess, my mouth kissing up and down her neck.

She looks to her left and points to the door we're about to pass. Roman slides around us and opens the door, brushing his hands over Charlotte's body as he goes. I gently push her back on the bed and climb on, hovering over her. My lips descend on hers and there's no hesitation or warm up. We go for it full force, kissing hard, tongues tangling, breathing heavy. Her hands wind back around my neck, keeping me close as I press my hips into hers. The bed dips on the other side, and I can tell Roman's making himself comfortable.

"I've been dying to feel you again," I tell her, pushing further into her despite our clothes in the way.

She moans with the pressure and her hips grind up into mine. I move to kneel and my hands explore her body from her hips to her breasts. They fit perfectly in my hand, with some to spare. The best breasts overflow your hand, and give you more to touch, and hers don't disappoint. I experiment with them for a moment, exploring what gets her moaning louder, while Roman watches his gaze consumed by Charlotte. My fingers find her hardened nipples and begin to flick them lightly back and forth. Her breathing increases with the constant, subtle attention to her nipples, and a whining sound starts to come from her.

"Please Jax, oh God...." she moans.

"You gonna come already, baby?" I ask her, breathless from how gorgeous she is like this.

She cries out. I tweak her nipples between my forefinger and thumb, and sure enough, I feel a rush of heat from her cum as she writhes beneath me.

Fuck, she is gorgeous.

"Roman, make sure those pretty nipples don't get neglected?"

"My pleasure," he says, descending onto her.

My hands run down her body to her jeans, and I unfasten them, pulling them off her body. She puts her hands on mine, and I look up.

"Do you want to stop?" I ask, wanting to ensure I haven't overlooked her mental space.

Roman pulls back and we both look at her, waiting.

 Chapter 21

Charlotte

Roman's mouth is hot around my nipples even through the fabric of my shirt and the slight drag of his teeth makes me shiver with pleasure while his fingers tease my other breast. Jax's hands run down my body and start to unbutton my jeans, and on reflex, my hands shoot out to stop him. I'm not really sure why I'm stopping him. It just kind of happened. Roman and Jax both immediately stop and look at me.

"Do you want to stop?" Jax asks.

Do I? Part of me thinks this is soon for any relationship, let alone with two of them for our first time, but it doesn't take me long to decide. I don't know where this relationship is going to go, but our physical chemistry is off the charts and if there's anything I know from the first two orgasms Jax has given me, it's that I want more. I want to feel Roman too and see how he feels.

"No," I tell Jax, looking from him to Roman so they both know I'm in.

Jax grins at me and I move my hands off his wrists and wiggle my hips to help him shimmy my pants off. Roman takes the opportunity to grab my hands and hold them above my head. My jeans slide down my legs and Jax leaves them in a heap on the floor, pulling my socks off with them.

Thank God he did that. It's always so awkward trying to decide if you should leave socks on or off. I mean, it's not very sexy leaving them on, but there's never like a great time to take them off.

I'm ripped from my sock thoughts by Jax's warm mouth inching slowly up my legs and Roman's free hand moving my shirt up so he can get to my breasts. He slips his hand into each of my bra cups and flips my breasts out before putting his mouth on one of my hardened nipples. Roman uses his teeth lightly to drag on them, pulling gasps of pleasure out of me as he does. Jax places open-mouthed kisses past my knee, nipping at my thighs.

"God, your body is gorgeous," Jax tells me as his lips keep moving higher.

Roman hums in agreement and takes my mouth captive with his. Our tongues tangle together, exploring more slowly than we did before, but with more passion and excitement for what's building.

Jax trails his tongue up my leg, replacing his lips with a slow trail of warmth. I feel his hands come up the backs of my legs to pull them apart further before grabbing my ass. He's finally reached my soaked core and my breath quickens in anticipation. Roman's hand reaches down and flicks my nipples, and I gasp when I feel Jax's tongue lick up my slit, lingering to tease my clit for a moment before he backs away. Roman pulls away to look, and a low groan of pleasure at the sight of Jax between my legs rumbles from him.

"You taste amazing," Jax growls and his thumbs come around to pull my waxed lips apart, giving him better access.

He attacks my pussy like a man starved, tongue drawing circles around my clit only to flick it roughly. Roman's breathing picks up at the sight, but he keeps my hands firmly placed above me as his mouth focuses back on my nipples, alternating between one, then the other. I throw my head back on a moan as Jax's tongue spears into me. He mouth fucks my pussy for a moment, his tongue spearing in and out of me fiercely, before sealing his lips around my clit and *sucks*.

My body explodes, tingles spreading over my limbs, my pussy clenches on air, and cum flows out of me.

"Yes," Roman groans. "God, you're fucking beautiful when you come."

Jax moans in pleasure as he continues to suck and lick me through my orgasm. Finally, I can't take anymore and try to put my hands on his head, failing when Roman keeps them firmly trapped.

"Too sensitive," I gasp.

He chuckles darkly, rising from between my legs and slamming his mouth against mine, forcing me to taste myself. Roman releases my hands and moves his body around to take his turn between my legs. He lazily pumps two fingers in and out of my pussy, and it feels amazing. My hands clasp Jax's head to mine, keeping him there as I explore his mouth with my tongue. Slowly, I let my hands drift down his body and pull at his shirt, encouraging him to take it off.

Jax looks at me, then over to Roman, and gives me a dark smirk before doing that thing where guys remove their shirt with one hand. Roman pulls his fingers out, steps to the side, and copies the action.

Why is that so hot? I think I just melted more, maybe even self-combusted with both of them doing it.

Based on the look on their faces, they are well aware of what that did to me.

"You are gorgeous," I whisper to them, sitting up to start removing my shirt.

Roman steps around the bed to stop me, putting his body behind mine. He slowly pulls my shirt off and drifts his hands down to my bra, freeing my breasts fully.

"Fuck, your body is amazing," Jax says, staring at my naked body.

I smile at him, and in an effort to be efficient, I work at his pants, pulling the zipper and shoving them down his hips. Roman pulls away with my bra in hand and drags his own pants off his body.

I am not one to waste time, so I curl my fingers into the top of Jax's boxer-briefs and look up through my lashes at him. I smile slowly as he puts his hands over mine and pushes them down his body. His cock springs free and smacks me in the nose. I'm not even mad. I'll let him smack me with that masterpiece all day long.

"Oh! Are you okay?" Jax asks, pausing.

I curl my lips in, trying not to laugh at the fact that his dick just attacked me. He catches the action and starts chuckling, making quick work of the rest of his clothing. Roman takes advantage of the moment and grabs me, pulling me back into him. He's moved from between my legs and is now resting with his body against the headboard and he has me leaning back into him.

Roman's hard cock is resting between my ass cheeks, just waiting to be put into my body. I can feel him flexing his hips ever so slightly, seeking out the friction he desperately wants. I try to rock back into him a little more and am rewarded with a low grumble of pleasure from his throat. His mouth caresses my shoulders, neck, and any other piece of skin he can find. Jax stares for a moment, gently caressing his own hard length.

"Jax, Roman," I moan in pleasure.

Jax leans in close and lavishes each nipple in turn, while Roman's fingers reach down to rub circles on my clit. Starting soft, he circles around it, not directly adding pressure. He soon increases the pressure and starts to rub it more quickly before thrusting his fingers inside me. I tilt my hips, encouraging him to explore my dripping pussy, making a point to rock back on him. Jax's mouth comes up from my nipples and he studies my face.

"You gonna come for Roman, pretty girl?" he asks.

I whine. "Yes, I'm gonna come."

"Yesss," he hisses, his face intent on mine, watching my every reaction. "Give it to us, Charlotte. We want everything you have."

Jax grabs my hair and tilts my head to the side so he can nip at my exposed neck.

"Let go baby girl, give us your pleasure," Roman growls into my ear.

"Fuck!" I whine, feeling my body give into Roman's thrusting fingers, the taps my clit receives from him, and both of their dirty words.

"I could watch you come undone every day," Jax groans. "You're so fuckin sexy."

"Good girl," Roman whispers into my ear.

Starting to come down, I realize we're missing something. "Condom?" I ask, breathless.

"Got it covered, baby," Jax says, reaching to his left for the small packet.

I notice he grabbed two of them, and my heart swells for my goofy, considerate guy. The foil rips as Jax opens it with his teeth and rolls the condom down his cock. My mouth salivates as I watch, and I promise myself that next time I'm putting my mouth all over that masterpiece.

"He's gonna fuck you now. Do you want that?" Roman says softly, but loud enough for Jax to hear.

"Yes, I want that," I whine.

"Are you sure? You sure you can take him and then take me? If you let him fuck you, I don't know if I can hold back," he threatens, nipping my ear.

"Put your money where your mouth is," I breathe to him.

Roman chuckles darkly in my ear, while Jax grins and enters me. Slowly at first, but as my body lubes him up, he increases the pace.

"You're so tight," he gasps. "Fuck you feel good."

"Please," I moan, wanting more of him.

Putting one hand under my knee, he pulls my leg up and starts thrusting harder. Roman holds my hips in place so Jax can fully control the angle he enters me at. I can feel my breasts bouncing with each thrust, Jax's face a mask of concentration and lust.

"God, those tits. You look like a goddamn goddess," he grits out.

"I can't wait to fuck those tits," Roman whispers in my ear, only for me to hear.

My breath hitches. I'm not used to someone loving my body the way both of them do. I move my hands to hold on to the back of Roman's neck to anchor myself. Jax moves faster, moving his fingers down to play with my clit as my body tightens in anticipation of the orgasm rushing closer.

"Yes, give it to me, baby. You take my cock so well, like you were made for me."

His words along with his fingers on my clit push me over the edge and I cry out as my body is overtaken. Waves of pleasure wash over me and I can feel my body contracting around his cock, and the sensation sends him over the edge with me. Two more rough thrusts and he groans loudly, holding himself as deep as he can go as he fills the condom.

"Fuck," he whispers.

"Yeah," I agree, words completely failing me.

He pulls out after a moment, takes off the condom, ties it off, and tosses it in the small trash can I keep in my room.

Roman pushes me forward, on my hands and knees, and I hear the foil ripping behind me. My breathing picks right back up, a combination of nerves and excitement. I've never had two men back-to-back like this.

"You still good, baby girl?" Roman checks in with me, his body caging mine in.

"So good," I tell him, pushing my ass back into him.

"Thank fuck," he growls in my ear.

Roman grabs my hair, pulling my head back, and slowly pushes his cock into my pussy. I'm not sure my poor pussy can handle more of this, but I'm not about to ask him to stop. There's an edge of pain with the pleasure, my body unused to so much sensation and friction.

He pumps slowly at first, getting me used to him. He's a little wider than Jax, but still not a monster cock from some of the smut I've read, thank God. His thrusts pick up in intensity, but not quite in speed. He's slamming into me and pulling out so slowly it's almost torture.

"Roman," I whine.

"Mmmmm, yes, baby girl?"

"I need more."

"More? Are you sure? Careful what you wish for," he says.

He picks up the pace and puts a hand around my shoulders to haul me up back into him. My legs are spread wide, and he is in between them, thrusting into me from behind.

"Jax, our girl here says she needs more," Roman says, not slowing at all.

Jax grins. "Happy to oblige."

Jax comes up next to us and reaches his hand down to circle my clit. His other hand tugs at my nipples as Roman continues to thrust into me as hard as he can. Maybe I should have been more careful of what I asked for, but I guarantee if I die from this, it's going to be the best death ever.

Roman picks up the pace even more, still slamming in hard, and Jax matches his pace on my clit. My body is strung tight, completely worn out from the orgasms that have taken over multiple times already, but still trying to get to another release.

"Fuck baby girl," Roman growls in my ear. "You feel so goddamn good. Be a good girl and come for us."

In romance books, you read about people being able to come on command, and I've always thought it was a bit unrealistic. Now, though, with my body molded perfectly to Roman's, his hard thrusts picking up, and Jax's magic finger? Well, I came like a fucking typhoon.

I scream as the orgasm takes over my already worn-out body, and more liquid than I thought possible shoots out from my body in a rush of pleasure and release.

"FUCK!" Roman shouts as he thrusts up two more times and then holds himself as deep as he can go.

He holds me there for a minute and I can feel his cock twitching in my pussy.

"That was the hottest shit I've ever seen," Jax says.

I giggle and look down around us. There is a massive wet spot on the bed.

What the fuck? It looks like I peed all over!

Roman pulls out and starts taking his condom off. I can feel my face flushing red from the embarrassment of the state of my bedding, and I want to go hide.

"Hey," Jax says, grabbing my hand and pulling me down with him. "Have you ever squirted before?"

I shake my head no and bury my face in his neck. He chuckles and tucks some hair behind my ear.

"It's okay, totally normal and honestly fuckin' hot," he says.

Roman speaks up from behind me, closer than I thought he was. "He's right. That was some of the hottest shit I've seen."

"You promise?" I ask, peeking out from Jax's neck.

They both promise, and Roman pulls the comforter off the bed and we all crawl in under the sheets together. My head rests on Jax's chest and his arms circle me, hands running up and down my skin. Roman is pushed up behind me, his nose buried in the back of my neck.

"Can I keep you?" I ask them.

"You already have me," Jax says with a smile and tilts his head to kiss my forehead.

"Me too," Roman agrees.

"Good." I snuggle in with both of them.

#

We spend the rest of the morning snuggling or watching a movie, just passing the time together. Jax and Roman take turns talking about their families and traditions while I share some of mine as well. Turns out Roman's only family is an aunt who lives across the country, so I internally promise myself to always include him in my family. Must be lonely not having parents or siblings. He was cagey about explanations, so whatever the story there is must be painful.

Jax explains his family dynamics and their focus on healthy living. My opinion is that they are a little too focused on that, but I don't voice that out loud. I'm trying to learn about them more, not create fights.

As Roman and Jax talk about previous relationships, my phone buzzes on the coffee table, lighting up with a phone call. I grab it and look at the Caller ID.

"My mom," I say, rolling my eyes to stare at the ceiling. "Pray for me."

Roman and Jax chuckle at my dramatics.

"Hello?"

"Charli! How are you, baby?" My mom coos at me from her side.

I give an internal sigh. "I'm fine Mom. How are you?"

"Oh, I'm just fine, honey, just fine." She waves off my question. "I wanted to let you know we'd like to have family dinner soon. It's been almost a month and a half since we've all gotten together."

"Blame Graham for that one," I tell her.

"Charli, you know he's just busy with work," she scolds me.

"So, does that mean Thomas and I aren't busy?" I challenge, a smile starting.

For some reason, pushing my mother's buttons until she figures out what I'm doing always makes me happy, and this sounds like the start of some fun.

"Oh honey, that's not what I meant, and you know it."

"Do I, Mom? I mean, you always talk about how great Graham is."

"Well, I can't very well tell you how great you are all the time!" She's starting to get flustered.

"You could. It's an option. You just choose to let me wallow in my misery."

Jax and Roman are starting to look alarmed, so I wink at them, so they know it's all good. Jax grins while Roman shakes his head at me.

"Charli, I'm so sorry, honey. You know I'm proud of you, right? You are so good at your job and the fact that you own your home is amazing," she tells me, starting to really get upset now.

"You haven't even been here in months Mom, what if it's destroyed? What if I've been living on the street?" I get dramatic to clue her in on what I'm doing.

"Oh my God, Charlotte, you're just pushing my buttons again. One of these days I'm gonna figure it out sooner and get you back." She's giggling by the end.

I'm flat out laughing at this point, listening as her tone goes from upset, to slightly disgusted, to amused.

"Love you Mommy," I tell her sweetly.

"Love you too, troublemaker."

"What day is dinner? You know Thanksgiving is next week, right?" I ask her.

"That doesn't count. That will have all your cousins and aunts and uncles. How about next weekend? Does that work for you, oh busy, important daughter?"

I cackle. "That's fine mom, I'll be there."

"Bring the boy," she says out of the blue.

"What boy?" I ask. I haven't told them about Jax *or* Roman yet, so I'm not sure who she's talking about.

"Thomas said there was a boy you're seeing. Bring him along. We need to see if he passes."

Shit, I never told Thomas about Roman. How should I play this? Just admit it? It's soon for one person, let alone two people, and I don't know if Roman would want to meet my family. Would my family support two guys? Like, am I going to be disowned for wanting two men?

"Mom! It's way too soon for anything like that," I protest, trying to throw her off.

"You ARE seeing someone!" she exclaims.

"You just said—"

"Thomas wasn't sure, so I figured I'd fish it out of you."

"Crafty old lady," I grumble.

It's her turn to cackle. "Seriously, bring him if he's free. We'd love to meet him and who knows when we'll get together again. You could bring him to Thanksgiving…"

"NO, definitely too soon for that! I'll ask, no guarantees if they will want to come," I tell her, trying subtly to hint at the fact that there's more than one.

"Okay, okay, love you sweetie, get back to being my amazing, successful daughter."

"Okay, stop praising me, it's getting weird now."

"I could never stop telling you what an amazing woman you are and how proud you make me and your father," she says too sweetly.

"This ain't over," I inform her.

"I sure hope not! Love you… wait, did you say 'they'?" she says.

"Ummmm yes? I might be seeing two guys. OkayloveyoutoobyeMom."

I hang up the phone before she can respond and throw my head back against Jax's arm that's around my shoulders. My head turns so

I can look at him. Roman looks over, my feet in his lap, his hands rubbing them.

"Meet the parents, round two?" I ask.

He laughs. "Seems only fair since I had you meet mine. I'm in."

I look over at Roman. "Do you want to come?" I ask him.

He thinks for a moment, his face serious and somber. "Do you want me to?" He counters after a few moments.

"I do," I tell him, almost surprising myself with how firm my answer is. "I'm nervous to explain to my parents that I'm seeing two guys, but you're not a dirty secret. I don't want to treat you that way, and I don't want you to feel that way."

He gives me his rare smile. "Okay then, I'm in."

 # Chapter 22

Roman

Part of me is a bit nervous to meet Charlotte's parents, mostly just standard nerves, but I know Charlotte has said that her brother is really overprotective. Hopefully, Jax and I can get him on our side. Charlotte offered to drive, so I'm sitting in the back seat drumming my fingers on my legs, and Jax is in the passenger seat. It's a bit of a drive, so she has plenty of time to spiral. I look over at her and see her hands tightening and loosening around the wheel as she drives.

"Did you find any other vibrators?" Jax asks her.

"What?" She's caught off guard and completely confused.

"You know, when I had to repair your car, when it was a vibrator? I wouldn't want to get caught *buzzed* driving."

"That was horrible," she says, a smile on her face.

"Made you smile."

"You always make me smile."

"Hey, what about me? Am I just the third wheel?" I ask.

Jax knows I'm joking. I can already see his shoulders shake slightly from holding the laugh in.

"Roman no!" Charlotte exclaims. "Of course not!"

She looks back in the rearview mirror and sees my smirk. Her mouth pops open, shocked. "Roman, are you teasing me?"

"I would never!" I tell her, trying my best to keep a straight face.

Soon enough we arrive at her parents' house, a nice, large ranch in a newer neighborhood. Between Jax and me, Charlotte was too distracted to spiral much, and I hope we can keep it that way for her sake. I take off my seat belt and move my body forward between her and Jax in the front.

"Come here," I tell her.

She leans over and I meet her halfway, placing my hands on her head to hold her where I want her. I kiss her like she's the air I breathe, my tongue diving into her mouth. She reciprocates and caresses my lips with hers, our tongues dancing together. Her hands grasp my wrists, like she's anchoring herself to me.

The moment I relent, Jax grabs her face, his hands on top of mine, and he ravishes her mouth just as desperately. I've never really thought of myself as a voyeur before, but I could watch these two all day. Any time I think of our time with all three of us, I start to get hard. We're all startled out of the moment by a knock on her window.

A tall man stands outside. He has a lean build and has a shaggy haircut for his blond hair. He's leaning down to the window, and Charlotte cracks her door open.

"Can you make out somewhere else? I don't want to lose my appetite. One man not enough for you?" he asks.

"Fuck off Thomas," she says, laughing.

We hop out of the car, Charlotte's face a bit red from being caught.

"Thomas, this is Jax, and this is Roman. Jax and Roman, this is my younger brother, Thomas," Charlotte introduces.

I hold out my hand. I figure a handshake is a pretty standard way to greet someone. Hopefully, he's not into bro-hugs right off the bat. I don't hug. He grasps my hand firmly, and I'm impressed.

"Nice to meet you, man," I tell him.

"Likewise," he replies.

Jax holds his hand out as well. "I'd hug you, but you need to buy me dinner first."

Thomas laughs and shakes his hand. "You guys sure you wanna do this dinner thing? You can still run. Have you told Mom there are two of them?"

Charlotte winces. "Kind of? I hinted, she caught it. I confirmed speaking really fast and hung up."

"Coward," Thomas accuses.

"Absolutely," Charlotte agrees.

"It can't be that bad," Jax tries to reason.

"Oh, my sweet summer child," Thomas says, placing a hand on his chest. "I recommend you run, stay away from the interrogators. Push your buddy here in front of you, so he gets taken first. Save yourself!"

"Why are you all standing in the driveway? Come in already!" I hear a female voice yell from the house.

"Busted," Charlotte says under her breath. "Did you invite Courtney?"

"Yeah, she should be here soon," Thomas says.

"Thank God, we'll need someone with a semblance of sanity here."

"You guys have to be exaggerating," Jax tells them as we meander toward the front door.

Charlotte turns to Jax and I. "We love our parents. They are wonderful people who have always showered us with love. They are also nosy assholes with strong opinions, and Graham didn't fall far from the tree."

"That makes three nosy assholes all focused on you two, my guys," Thomas states.

"Huh, well, I guess we'll see what happens," I say, determined to leave the evening unscathed.

It's hard to believe that whoever raised these two would be difficult to handle. It just doesn't make sense. Then again, I know firsthand how family can disappoint you.

We finally walk in the front door, having taken our time to chat a bit as we moved. Charlotte shows us where to take our shoes off and we hang our jackets up. She laces her fingers of one hand with mine and the other with Jax, and we start toward the dining room.

"Finally!" I hear the same female voice exclaim. "I thought you guys were just gonna stand out there all night!"

We walk into the dining room and see Charlotte's parents setting food out and ensuring everyone has silverware, drinks, and plates. Her dad looks up first, smiling at his children and giving Jax and I the stern dad face. Her mom looks up second and when she sees the three of us standing together, she freezes and shares a look with her husband.

"Jax, Roman, this is my dad, David, and this is my mom, Anna. Mom, Dad, this is Jax and Roman. My boyfriends," she introduces.

I haven't heard her say that out loud yet and I'm pretty sure my heart just started beating in double time.

Boyfriend. I can definitely handle that. I'm all in with her.

"I thought you were kidding!" her mom exclaims. "Oh, my, we will need another setting, I suppose."

Her dad simply looks at Charlotte with the typical dad look of "Really?" but says nothing out loud. Jax and I shake hands and share pleasantries with her father. Her mom comes around the table and I hold my hand out to her when she steps into my space and gives me a quick hug.

"No handshakes here, young man, you get hugs. It's nice to meet you," she says, then repeats the action with Jax and bustles into the kitchen, muttering about another place setting.

Thomas looks from me to his dad. "Who are you, and what have you done with my parents?"

Charlotte's dad rolls his eyes. "Always so dramatic."

"I'm just saying you aren't ever nice to the people I bring over." He pouts.

"You haven't brought anyone over since Courtney, and you two aren't even dating. Doesn't count," Charlotte's dad says, raising an eyebrow at Thomas.

"Not the point." He sniffs and walks toward the kitchen.

"Anything we can help with?" I ask.

"Beer?" Thomas yells from the kitchen.

"No, we've got this. You just relax. We like to lure new people into a false sense of security," her dad says.

"Three please," Charlotte calls into the kitchen before turning to her dad. "Not funny, Dad."

He holds up his thumb and forefinger close together. "A little funny."

The door opens and I hear more people come in. Feet stomping in, the sound of shoes being kicked off, and then they come into view.

The guy is almost a twin to Thomas, but slightly wider and has a few wrinkles Thomas is lacking. The girl is a bit shorter, but not tiny, more average. Her hair is long and blonde, reaching mid-back and tightly spiraled, the way only naturally curly hair can be. Her dark brown eyes hone in on me and Charlotte immediately, and she smiles.

"Charli!" she greets and steps over for a hug.

"Hey, you," Charlotte greets her. "These are my boyfriends, Jax and Roman. Jax and Roman, this is Courtney."

"Charlotte's told us about you. Nice to meet you," Jax says.

"You too, pretty boy." She looks at me. "Or are you the pretty one?"

"Can you behave for one minute?" the Thomas twin grumbles at her.

She turns and sticks her tongue out. "No."

"I am definitely the pretty one," Jax confirms, making Courtney giggle.

Charlotte walks over and gives the man a hug. "Graham, this is Jax and Roman. Jax and Roman, this is my older brother, Graham."

"Nice to meet you," I tell him.

"So… two guys?" Graham asks Charlotte.

"And?" Charlotte puts her hands on her hips, feisty and ready to go.

"Is that really necessary?"

"Are *you* really necessary?" she counters.

"Childish, but true," Thomas adds as he walks back in with beers for all of us.

We settle in to each once the food is out, and Graham wastes no time in serving himself. Soon plates are piled with food and silverware is clinking against plates as everyone digs in.

"So, Charlotte, where did you meet these, um, men?" Charlotte's mom asks.

"Well, Jax repaired my car a month or two ago, and Roman works with him. It all just kind of clicked into place," says Charlotte.

"Seems greedy," Graham comments.

"Just making up for *your* lack of romance," Charlotte counters.

Courtney starts laughing, and it quickly turns into coughing. She waves away concern, saying she just swallowed wrong.

"That a sustainable job? Mechanic work?" David asks.

"Not wasting time, are ya, Dad?" Thomas asks.

"I think it's a fair question. Charlotte needs someone who can partner with her, not depend on her. Especially if there are two of 'em."

I nod, understanding his point. "I get it. It's important to be partners in a relationship, otherwise it causes problems and resentment."

"See? He gets it," their dad says.

"I actually own the car repair shop we work at," Jax chips in.

"So, you didn't, like, go to college or anything?" Graham asks.

I look over at him, trying to determine his angle.

"Yeah, I went to a technical college for automotive repair. We both did," Jax says.

Graham scoffs softy. "So, no real school? Just learned how to do one thing?"

What the fuck is this guy's problem?

"Well, they had an official name. We both had to apply, and we both have specific and specialized certifications, so pretty sure it was a real school," I counter.

"Not a well-rounded education like you'd get at a full college or university, though."

"Graham, don't be an asshole. What they do isn't easy," Charlotte says.

I reach over and grab her hand, trying to let her know not to worry about defending me. I see Jax do the same with a hand on her thigh. She and Thomas both indicated their family is big on "formal" education, so I was expecting some questions.

"Well, the trade school we went to taught me how to be a mechanic. It was one of the best in the state and we have several certifications to show our skills. What did you attend school for?" I ask.

"I have my business degree and an MBA. I'm working as a director for a local business," Graham informs me, sitting up a bit straighter as he speaks.

"Sounds like you're living your dream," I tell him dryly.

"It was hard work and lots of late night studying to get my degree and get to the position I'm in," he brags.

"You don't own the business, though?" Thomas pokes at Graham.

I take a drink to hide my smirk. *Thomas and I are going to get along just fine.*

"So, how long have you had your own business?" their mom asks Jax, trying to divert the subject.

"We just opened. I worked for a few shops previously but never agreed with how they ran things," he tells her.

"Pretty hard to run a business without a degree," Charlotte's dad comments.

"I've managed so far. Did a lot of learning on the job with previous employers and did my research," Jax says.

"Then you just gave your friend a job?" their dad asks.

"Sir, with all due respect, I earn my spot working alongside Jax. I don't take handouts. I worked hard to get where I am," I add.

"Charlotte, I love your hair. Are you planning to change it soon? It looks a little faded," Courtney interrupts.

Charlotte grabs the lifeline. "Yeah, I really like the blue, but it is fading. I'm gonna let it fade a bit more, I think, then try something new. I'd love to do an ombre type look or do a purple/red combination."

"That would be gorgeous!" Courtney exclaims.

"You'd look good with purple hair," I tell her, tugging gently on a strand.

"We could call you Purple Rain," Jax jokes.

"Please don't," she says, laughing.

Dinner continues mostly peacefully, although there are continual comments throughout the night over the lack of "traditional" schooling. I'm impressed that the entire event isn't as unpleasant as Charlotte and Thomas warmed us it would be. Of course, as soon as I think it, things turn downhill. Isn't that the way it always goes?

"So, Jax. Do you think this shop is going to be something you can keep?" asks Charlotte's dad.

The room goes quiet.

"Uh, excuse me?" Jax questions.

"I mean, we've established that you don't really have the credentials to keep a business running."

"So, since I don't have a formal business degree, I can't own a business?" Jax questions, keeping his tone lighter than I could.

"Well, it's certainly going to be harder. Maybe you should consider going back."

"I've done my research. I studied under previous shop owners, like I mentioned. I think I've got this."

"Owning a business isn't a hobby like fixing cars or something," Graham adds.

Oh, cool, my job is now a hobby. Good to know.

"Oh, so you can fix your car when it breaks?" I question. "That's pretty great for you. Wonder how many new transmissions you've put into your car."

"I'm going to level with you, Jax," their dad jumps in. "What you guys do is necessary, but at this point we're just not sure that it's a good idea for Charlotte to be involved with someone who may not be able to hold their own and just hires friends. Office jobs are a lot steadier."

"Dad…" Charlotte chides, her face turning red.

"So that's my cue," Thomas says and stands up. "Good to know work is a hobby unless you have a degree, and you can only support yourself with an office job. Courtney? Drinks?"

"Sounds delicious," Courtney agrees. "Thanks for dinner, Anna and David."

Thomas nudges my shoulder as he walks out of the room. "Come on by. I'll have a drink waiting for you guys."

Charlotte stands as well. "Drinks sound good. Let's go guys."

Thank God, I need out of here.

"It was really nice to meet you, Mr. and Mrs. Hawkins," Jax tells them.

I look at the three people left at the table without speaking. Feels unnecessary. They stare at us, speechless, and I stand with Charlotte. She grabs my hand, and we walk out of the room, Jax not far behind.

Maybe they'll get better with time. Or maybe I'll just be drinking a lot at future gatherings.

 # Chapter 23

Jax

"Fuck me, that was ridiculous," Thomas says, taking another drink.

"It was somethin'," I mutter, grabbing my own second round. The first round of beer went down way too quickly. I may have chugged it. Roman was right there with me.

"I'm sorry about all that," Charlotte says again.

I kiss the top of her head. "It's fine. It's not like you told them to say it."

"Yeah, I just feel bad," she says.

"You can't control what they say," Roman reasons, grabbing her hand.

Courtney chimes in. "Girl, don't even, the amount of shade your parents have thrown at Thomas and I? Those two are set in their opinions. I am a little surprised at how aggressive Graham and your dad got tonight, but I suppose since Charlotte hasn't brought someone home before they were thrown off. Plus, there are two of you and I'm sure that was pretty unexpected."

"You've never brought someone home?" Roman asks Charlotte.

She blushes. "Not formally, no, my parents have met others when they picked me up for a date when I was younger, but I've been pretty low key about dating since I got out of college."

I pull her toward me and give her a kiss. "We are both very honored."

"Gross!" Thomas yells and tosses a napkin at us.

Charlotte starts laughing against my mouth and then makes dramatic noises, rivaling a porn star. Courtney is cackling now, and Thomas is fake vomiting on the floor. We break apart, laughing, and Courtney gives her a high five. Even Roman cracks a small smile.

"Stop being such a baby," Charlotte chides Thomas.

"Look, I don't make out in front of you. You don't make out in front of me. It's an unspoken sibling rule."

"Whatever. If you had a hot guy on your arm, you'd be rubbing that in my face all the time," Charlotte says.

"I'd be rubbing something," he mutters.

I chuckle and hold my fist out; he bumps it and we take a drink. Courtney looks at Charlotte, a bit alarmed.

"Oh no, they're forming a bromance," she says.

"Roman, resist the bromance, stay with us on the side of sanity!" Charlotte pleads.

Roman just shakes his head and takes another swig of his drink. Slinging my arm around the back of Charlotte's chair, I lean back, surveying Thomas and Courtney.

"I was thinking it might be nice to have some people over to my house," I tell the group.

"What for?" Charlotte asks.

"Our last attempted outing didn't go well, and I'd love to get to know Thomas and Courtney more."

"I think that could be a lot of fun!" Charlotte exclaims.

"Yeah, just let us know when and if we're not working, we'll come. We usually work thirds so it can get tricky to get out, but it sounds awesome," Thomas says.

"So, what is it you guys do?" Roman asks. "You said you get a lot of grief over it."

"Courtney and I both work at a factory. We've gotten ourselves promoted over the years to management positions, but we started on the floor."

"Oh, that's cool. You enjoy it?" I ask.

"Honestly? Yeah, it's nice to go and do specific tasks, then head home and not worry about it again until tomorrow. I like moving around a lot, so the factory gives me the chance to move my body, and it's work that needs doing, so I have a purpose. Not just sitting at a desk and doling out orders."

"Rude," Charlotte says, teasing.

"You're really good at it though," he teases back in a patronizing tone.

"You bet your ass I am!"

"I think Anna and David blamed me for Thomas going into more blue-collar work, but it's actually the other way around." Courtney laughs.

"Yeah? How did that go?" I ask.

Courtney smiles nostalgically. "We've been friends for years, and neither of us enjoyed school. We got by, and we knew it mattered to learn, but it was not the highlight of our lives. After I got accepted at the nearby college, Thomas looked at me, told me to not enroll and join him doing hands on work."

"I thought you'd put up more of a fight," Thomas says with a laugh.

"Almost did! I really didn't want to go to school anymore, though, so figured may as well try it. I could always switch it up later if I hated it."

"Seems like the right choice then," I tell both of them, smiling.

"Yeah, it's been good," Thomas says.

"So, what drove you to open your own place?" Courtney asks. "I think it's pretty awesome that you did."

"Thanks, it was a big decision, that's for sure. I spent probably ten years working for other people before deciding that I wanted my own place. Roman had his own issues. Sometimes we worked at the same shop, but sometimes we didn't, and we swapped horror stories. After I decided to open one, it took another year or two to get things rolling, but I just couldn't handle the way a lot of shops rip people off."

"How so?" she asks.

"Using premium parts without asking the customers so they could justify the up charge in service, over-pricing the labor costs just to make a bigger profit, telling customers that optional work was necessary to do, that kind of stuff," Roman chimes in.

Thomas nods. "Yeah, I've had a couple try to pull one over on me. I managed to stop them, but it's good to know there's a shop out there with the goal to not rip people off. I know Charlotte's really happy with the work you did."

I grin. "I made sure she got the best service I could offer."

"I'm just glad you figured out you left your vibrator in my car and that's what was causing the nose," Charlotte adds, twisting my original joke on her.

I throw my head back and laugh, appreciating that she's taking the joke and running with it. I know she was embarrassed at first, so hearing the joke from her makes my heart happy. Courtney and

Thomas join in laughing and pretty soon we're slinging jokes back and forth, work conversation forgotten. Roman even joins in on occasion, which tells me he feels relaxed around Charlotte's little brother and his friend.

We spend the next few hours as a group just chatting and laughing, and I'm glad Charlotte has Thomas and Courtney for family at least. I'm sure her parents and Graham are good to her, but knowing these two are in her corner and will support the three of us is reassuring.

 # Chapter 24

Jax

We pull into Charlotte's driveway, and she parks the car outside. The air is brisk, but not cold yet. It'll probably snow in the next month or so, but we're safe for now at least. I wonder if she has anybody to take care of her driveway. I'll have to check on that and ask around if not. Sure, she's probably capable, but if I can do something like that for her, then I really want to and I'm sure Roman would too.

She looks at Roman and me, a silent invitation in her eyes. Roman and I both wait, forcing her to ask aloud.

"Do you guys want to come inside for a bit?" she asks.

Roman smiles gently at her, an expression I'm not used to seeing on his face. "I think I'm going to head home. It's been a long evening. As much as I want to bury myself in you, I need some space," he says.

She looks down, disappointed. "Oh."

He grabs her chin and forces her to look at him. "This has nothing to do with you, you hear me? You're not getting rid of me that easily."

She smiles, and he nods, satisfied. He gives her a kiss, then backs away, letting me take the lead. I grab her hand.

"I'll stay if you are okay with it still," I tell her.

She smiles. "Of course!"

Roman says goodbye and hops into his truck. Charlotte and I get inside and head for the couch once we put away our shoes and coats. I sit down near the end, grab a blanket, and hold it open in invitation. She smiles and happily snuggles in next to me as I throw the blanket over us both. Her legs are tucked up next to her and her body is leaning against mine, my arm holding her close.

"You okay?"

"I should be asking you that... and Roman," she replies.

"We both told you we're alright. It wasn't the best night of my life, but at least your parents didn't kick me or Roman out. That was basically a declaration of love."

She laughs. "They'll get past it. They have to. I don't want either of you to go anywhere."

"We're not," I tell her, dropping a kiss to her forehead. "Now tell me what's going on in that head of yours. I can see you doing some mini spirals."

"Mini spiral, I think I like that. I'm just worrying over a lot of little things and my anxiety is hounding me, telling me that you'll both eventually leave me, so why let myself get too invested? Morgan is gorgeous, so maybe you want her back or someone who looks like her, Roman will eventually realize I'm not worth the struggle, my parents are assholes, my brother is an asshole, and I don't even know why you guys like me sometimes. Roman had to leave and I struggle to believe it's not because of me. I even labeled you both my boyfriend without even asking, for heaven's sake!"

"Take a breath," I coach her, waiting until she's done to continue. "I have zero interest in Morgan, other than as a friend. I will remind you of that as often as you need. You are not your parents, and

I'm with you, not them. So even if they're awful, you are not. Roman is head over heels for you, and you are worth every minute we spend with you, good and bad. Sometimes Roman just needs space sometimes. He's… not used to being the subject of scrutiny. The boyfriend thing? I'm just bummed I didn't get to call you my girlfriend first, and I think Roman actually smiled when he heard it. As for *you*, you are an amazing human that I am honored to know. I think Roman might just be in this for your breasts, but you'd have to ask him."

A laugh startles out of her and she takes a deep breath, looking at me with wonder on her face. "How are you so amazing at helping me calm down?"

"I'm just that amazing." Tucking her head into my shoulder, she tries to burrow closer to me. I laugh at her. "What are you doing?"

"Trying to burrow as close as I can so you'll never leave," she says, with a laugh.

"How about I burrow into you?" The offer pops out of my mouth before I can even think about it.

She stops and looks up at me, a smile slowly stretching across her face. Throwing the blanket off us, she moves her body on top of mine, straddling my legs, her body firmly planted in my lap. Her lips hover above mine, so close that the smallest shift would bring us together.

"Think you can handle this?" she asks.

"Fuck, I love how confident and sassy you are with me," I tell her.

Grinning, she replies, "Better show me what ya got."

Unable to hold back, I lean forward the smallest amount and our mouths meet, tender at first. Kissing her always feels like a prayer, something sacred that should be done slowly before you get into the main event. Caressing her lips with mine, I get lost in the moment, our breathing increasing in the quiet space as she starts to shift on my lap.

"Up." I smack her ass. "I want to burrow inside you on your bed."

She giggles but doesn't move. "How about we christen the couch instead?" she suggests as she takes her shirt off.

"You gonna ride me, Sunshine?" She nods, biting her lip. "Can't deny you anything," I tell her, and she reaches for my shirt to pull it off my body.

My lips find her collarbone, and I place open mouth kisses along it, moving up to her neck. She tilts her head so I can reach her neck better and I take full advantage, licking and sucking all the skin I can get at. I want to leave her with my marks tomorrow. Her moans fuel me more and my already hardening dick becomes hard as a rock. The shifting of her hips causes zaps of pleasure as her warm center grinds along my cock.

Reaching behind her, I unclasp her bra and slide it down her arms, my mouth finding her nipples as soon as they're set free from their confines. They're hard and ready for my lips to suck and bite. Her head falls back on a moan as I suck hard on one side, twisting her other nipple between my fingers at the same time. Her movements are speeding up, her body priming to detonate. I roll my hips to meet her on the next pass of her heat against me. She gasps and moans at the additional friction.

"You need me to get you off?" I ask, my voice rough and husky with arousal.

Nodding frantically, she tries to move faster. Grabbing her hips, I halt her movement. One of my hands grabs her hair firmly but not roughly.

"I'm gonna make you scream my name. I want the neighbors to hear and get jealous," I tell her, bringing her mouth to mine.

She gasps at the thought, and I take full advantage of her and slam our mouths together, my tongue exploring hers. Our tongues and lips battle for dominance as my hand returns to her hips and I encourage her to rock against me again. We find a rhythm, my hands firmly on her hips, and our bodies roll together like they were meant for this dance.

I rip my mouth from hers and trap a nipple in my mouth again. The feeling of her nipple in my mouth is sheer perfection, and I flick it with my tongue. A keening cry starts from her and I move her faster.

"That's it. Take what you need from me. I'm yours to use. I can't wait to feel how tight you are again. Pound into that perfect pussy until you come all over me."

The last sentence does it as she falls apart on top of me. Her head flies back, and she cries out her release as I keep her moving on top of me, drawing it out as long as I can. Panting, she looks back at me with pure adoration and kisses me softly.

My hands go to the top of her pants, gently pulling the fabric down and snagging her panties with it. Shakily, she stands and lets me pull her leggings all the way off, and I whip my jeans off faster than I thought possible. Grabbing a condom, I hold out my hand for her to climb back up. She starts to lower, but I hold her up. I need to feel her on my fingers, taste her, before I fuck her.

"I need to taste you," I tell her, sliding my finger down to her clit.

"Yessss…" She hisses as I circle the tight bud with my middle finger, putting the smallest amount of pressure on it before slamming my fingers all the way into her.

Her pussy is dripping for me, and I groan, feeling how easily my fingers slide into her. My hands have a mind of their own as I start pumping my fingers in and out of her. I crook them ever so slightly to get her G spot and her loud cry is my reward.

"Jax!" she cries out, eyes closed in bliss.

"You're so goddamn wet for me, aren't you? Just ready and weeping for me to stuff you with my cock."

She cries out, sounding desperate for something more than my teasing fingers.

"Put this on me," I tell her, ripping the condom open with one hand and my teeth.

Her eyes open and she grabs the condom from me, using shaky hands to try to put it on. I don't make it easy for her, my fingers plunging in and out of her, circling her clit, and then doing it all over again. She has to restart three times before she's able to get it on, and once she does I move my fingers direct over her clit and rub furiously.

She's gonna come at least three times tonight.

Her body shudders above me and I feel her cum leaking out of her as she spasms from my fingers. Her mouth is open, a silent scream to the ceiling. As she comes down, I take the moment to collect her juices and coat my cock with them. She meets my eyes and I pull my fingers from her and slowly put them in my mouth, tasting her.

"Fucking delicious," I tell her.

Her body frozen in surprise, and her eyes locked on my mouth and fingers. I seize the moment, bringing her down on me as I surge up to meet her.

I enter her in one thrust, buried to the hilt, and I hold her like that for a moment. Our eyes hold each other and it's a moment I want etched into my memory for the rest of my life. My hips lower back onto the couch, and I bring her with me.

"Ride me, baby," I tell her.

Wasting no time, Charlotte grinds her hips in circles, experimenting with what feels good. The tight heat and her slickness are heaven and my eyes almost cross with pleasure.

"God, Jax," she gasps, her hips coming up and then back down on my cock.

"Your pussy is heaven. Keep going, baby."

The encouragement doesn't go to waste as she bounces, alternating between moving herself up and down and grinding in circles with me buried deep inside. My hands wander up to her breasts that bounce in my face, and my fingers pluck and twist her nipples. Her breathy moans encourage me on and one hand wanders down to her clit.

"Fuck," she moans out.

"That's it baby. Give it to me. I want you to cum all over me, coat me in you. I want to smell you for days on me, knowing it was me that made you cum. I want you to soak this couch, so you're reminded of this every time you sit down." I tell her, rubbing her clit, alternating between soft and hard.

"God, yes! It feels so good!" she yells.

"Fuck yeah you do, baby, I can't hold back anymore," I confess to her, grabbing her hip with one hand, the other still torturing her clit.

I use her hip as leverage as I pound into her from below. She gasps and her hands slam forward to brace herself against the back of the couch. Her mouth hangs open in pleasure, and her keening cries fall out of it with no restraint. Rubbing faster, I can feel her tighten around me. She's poised to fall off the edge and I'm dying to feel her come.

"Come, baby, come all over me and soak this fuckin' couch. You're so goddamn beautiful," I tell her.

One final cry comes out of her, almost a scream, as she detonates. Her muscles spasm around me and hot liquid squirts out of her, soaking my hips and the couch cushion. The combination of her soaking me and her muscles contracting around me cause my own detonation. I feel tingles run up my spine and pleasure shoots through my body as I fill the condom. My cock spasms and twitches as I come, her little gasps of breath are my favorite sound.

She leans down, putting her forehead on my shoulder, panting heavily, an occasional gasp escaping as the twitching of my dick slows down. My head turns to her, and I put my lips on the side of her head, giving a gentle kiss and letting myself bask in the feel of her. Coming back to herself after a few moments, I hear a groan of embarrassment.

"I soaked the couch, didn't I?" she asks, not moving from my shoulder.

I chuckle. "Fuck yeah you did. That was so hot."

She giggles. "Can't wash it like we did with my comforter."

"True, but I now have a goal to get you to squirt every time. Imagine if we get Roman on this mission too, we'll have everything soaked in no time," I tease her.

She giggles again and picks her head up, and looks me in the eye, our faces inches away.

"That was amazing," I speak first.

"It really was," she says with a smile.

Giving me a quick kiss, she pulls herself up off the couch and I hiss as I feel her move off my overly sensitive cock. I pull the condom off and tie it, looking at her. She nods her head to the side, toward the bathroom and bedroom.

"There's a trash in the bathroom, and we need to shower off, anyway," she says.

I mostly keep my hands to myself in the shower, and she insists she's too sensitive for another orgasm, but I'm pretty sure I could get one out of her. I leave it for tonight, not wanting to push her or make her feel like I only want her for sex. We're snuggled up in bed, completely naked. Her ass is pushed against me, and my arms wrapped around her body. A sigh escapes her, and I squeeze her a little tighter.

"You're amazing," I tell her softly, unsure if she's still awake. "I'm so happy you're taking a chance on me."

"Back at you," she says softly, her words a little slurred as she is pulled to sleep.

I close my eyes and follow her to sleep, hoping for dreams of making her come over and over again.

 # Chapter 25

Charlotte

It's been a week since the disaster dinner at my parents' house, and Jax's gathering is today. I'm looking forward to it. I think it's gonna be great to have a calmer setting where Roman and Jax can really get to know Amy and Olivia. We won't have any catty waitresses throwing things off, and I'm feeling more secure with both guys. We've been group texting in addition to our own chats, and they never fail to remind me of how much they like me and I'm happy to share the sentiment back.

Now, if I can just get past the whole Morgan situation. Jax said it's over and I trust him, so hopefully it can stay that way. I need to remember to keep talking myself down when I see her. Jax assured me they've been done for years, and he has no interest, so even if she does, he's not going to do anything.

As I slip my shoes on to grab Olivia, my phone dings with a new text message. I dive into my purse for it and, of course, can't find it. It takes a good minute for me to find it, my frustration increasing until my fingers finally find it and I yank it out, along with several receipts, my keys, and some lip gloss.

Hm. Might be time to clean out my purse.

Jax: Do you have time to run to the store for me? I forgot some stuff but was hoping to do some last-minute cleaning.

Me: Yeah, I can do that. What do you need?

Jax: Aside from your orgasms? Some chips and dessert.

Me: Well lucky for you, I'll give you both tonight.

Roman: I want orgasms. Can I get in on this action?

Me: Make sure you help Jax and you can get one too.

Roman: I already cleaned. That means I'm good to go.

Jax: You cleaned your room. Doesn't count

Me: Lol, I'll leave you guys to your debate, but here's a sneak peek of tonight.

I take a top-down angled picture, so my cleavage is prominent in the shot.

Jax: And now I have to clean and grill with a stiffy.

Me: Pics or it didn't happen

Roman: Send it to your private chat. I already have to see it in person.

I laugh, but Jax doesn't reply right away, so I put my purse back together and grab my overnight bag. We didn't specifically talk about me staying the night, but it's good to be prepared. The Boy Scouts said so. I'm sure they did. As I climb into the driver's side of my car, my phone dings again.

Damn. He wasn't lying about that stiffy. He even put on gray sweatpants today. This man will be the death of me, and what a death it's gonna be.

I respond with a drool emoji. Not wanting to leave Roman out, I text him and tell him I'd be happy to see how he's faring in the pants department. I start the car and leave my driveway to go grab Olivia. She doesn't take long to come out, and plops with a grin into the passenger seat next to me.

"Sup, bitch?"

"Hey asshole. You mind if we make a run to the grocery store?" I ask.

She whines as I pull away from her apartment building. "Do we *have* to?"

"Jax needs chips and some dessert for tonight. You can pick what you want."

She side eyes me. "Even Takis?"

"I'm not gonna eat those, but I *will* buy you your own bag, so you don't have to share."

"Okay, deal, let's do it."

"Let's be honest, you didn't really have a choice."

She holds up her hand, palm facing me. "Let me have this."

"Whatever you need, crazy lady."

She giggles and we do some carpool karaoke on the way to the store. We already have two bags of chips as we peruse down the aisle, looking for the Takis.

"What else do you think we should grab?" I ask her.

"Definitely get some of the wavy potato chips you dip in shit. Those are awesome," Oliva suggests.

"Good call. We'll need to stop by the dip section. Can't have one without the other. Did you find your Takis yet?"

"No, I can't find them-OH FOUND THEM! Now which flavor?" she asks.

"Grab the blue ones. I want you to have Smurf mouth."

She cackles and grabs the biggest bag she can find on the shelf.

As she puts the Takis in the cart, a woman is walking down the aisle, coming up behind us. She gives us a once over and peers into the cart. It seems as though she doesn't understand the concept of personal space.

"See something you like?" I ask her.

She snaps her eyes up to me and leans back. "Just seems like you have a lot of junk in there. Do you really need all that?"

"Do you really need to be in our space? What we buy isn't your business. You should walk away," I tell her, a bit surprised at my forcefulness.

The lady huffs and walks off. My hands shake a bit as adrenaline floods my system and quickly leaves. It's been a while since I had a reason to really step up for myself and it's slightly jarring.

Olivia looks at me, grinning. "Badass." She holds out her fist to pound.

With a soft laugh, I oblige her. "I really want to spiral right now, but I know it won't help anything and I need to get used to standing up for myself more. I'm a badass at work, but I need to get better at badassing it in the real world."

"Look out world, here comes Charli," Olivia teases me as we move down the aisle.

We grab some other goodies as we wander the aisles, laughing and joking as we go, my nerves at the prior altercation gone. We're standing in front of the Oreo display, trying to figure out which kind we want. They have several varieties out right now and obviously we have to debate the merits of each flavor.

I'm holding a package of the ones with three times the cream center than the original variety, and Liv holds the double ones. She looks over at my package with a critical eye.

"I mean, I feel like there is such a thing as too much cream center. There has to be a balance," she says.

"Well, we know the original ones are completely out at least, and no flavors today. Going classic on flavor."

"Definitely classic. I'm gonna vote we go for the doubles. Much better ratio of cream to cookie."

As I'm about to reply to her, a woman comes walking down the aisle, looking at the cookies as she goes. It's the same woman from the chip aisle. She looks at the two of us, holding a package of cookies each, and a small frown comes to her face. Walking over with purpose, she snatches the package out of my hands.

"With all those chips, you don't need *one* package of cookies, let alone two. I'll take these for you. You'll thank me later."

She primly puts the package back on the shelf and reaches for a different one of her own. I'm completely stunned by the entire interaction. Then she turns to walk away.

"What the *fuck* is your problem, lady?" Olivia shouts.

"I'm just looking out for you girls. Too much of that junk food is why you have to buy plus size clothes. I knew it was a problem when I saw the chips and now it's confirmed. Like I said, you'll thank me." She turns and walks away at this point, quite briskly.

My body stands frozen, still facing the cookie display, and I'm pretty sure I'm in shock. Despite my feelings on her level of doucheyness, she's right, though, isn't she? This food definitely doesn't help with what people see when they look at me. I shouldn't have tried to stand up to her before. She knew we shouldn't have all this junk food. Shame crawls through me, starting at my belly and spreading out. I can feel the flush on my face starting and I have no idea if anyone else saw that.

If they did, what do they think? What if they have the same thoughts? What if that lady was right?

Olivia grabs my hand, tosses the cookies into the cart and grabs another package out of what I assume is spite. My world is reeling, and I can feel the weight of anger and shame settling in my chest. I can't really see anything right now. I mean, I can see lights and colors and shapes, but nothing makes sense. It's all just noise as my emotions swirl inside. Pretty sure it's the start of a panic attack.

"Just a few more minutes," Olivia says to me softly.

I'm in a haze as we check out, but I remember enough to at least give my card to the self-checkout machine, so Olivia doesn't have to pay for the food. We get in the car, and she pushes me into the passenger seat. Taking my keys from my purse, she closes my door and climbs into the driver's seat. Faintly, I register the fact that I must be completely numb if she's taken over like this, but it doesn't make sense to me. None of this makes sense to me.

Why would someone actually take something out of my hands and say it's for my own good?

My pulse is thundering as she pulls away from the parking lot and anger finally starts bubbling to the surface above the shame.

Who the hell does that lady think she is? Who gets away with treating people like that? She knows nothing about me. I'm actually in very good health, and even if I wasn't, there's a level of disrespect in that act that nobody should have to endure. I already told her to mind her own business and she just couldn't do that, could she?

I've had this once before and the same reaction occurred, but not quite at this level. I was alone that time at the store, and someone pulled a bag of chips from my cart, giving me the excuse of the chips having too much sodium. I don't understand why people feel the need to insert themselves where they don't belong. They're not concerned about my health. They just want to point out that a fat person is trying to eat the same foods as everyone else.

When I stood up for myself on the chips this time, I thought I had it. I thought I knew how to handle the situation. I didn't, clearly, and now I'm questioning my ability to do anything. We pull into Jax's driveway, and Olivia hops out first. She comes around to my door, opening it to see if I'll come out. I can't move yet; I need more time. I know I'll eventually have to tell Jax and Roman, but my humiliation won't let me do it just yet. I look at her, then back down at my hands.

"Ok," she says softly.

Olivia closes my door gently, grabs the bags from the back of the car, and heads inside. I wonder what Jax is going to think. I haven't really told him about this kind of thing yet, only Roman.

Who wants to be with someone that has this shit happen? Neither of those guys needs drama in their lives, and I'm already bringing it to them without actually doing anything. They'll be embarrassed to be seen with me, and I can't even blame them. I mean, who wants to deal with someone who has my anxiety, let alone dealing with people inserting themselves into our lives?

I feel my heart start to break as I slowly convince myself that the guys won't want to stay. It makes sense and I don't blame them for not wanting to. In my mind, they've already started walking away and my eyes sting as tears start falling down my face.

This sucks. I finally find someone, two someones, I really like, and I just know they're going to walk away. I should actually take the first step and go. Then they don't have to bear this shame. I can just keep it for them. I have enough anyway. Yeah, I'm gonna walk away. It sucks, but it's best.

My car door pulls open and someone crouches down next to me.

"Seems like a weird place to hold a party, but we can always make it work. Never had a car party before."

I look over at Jax, a small smile forming on my face at his ridiculous suggestion. "I'm sorry," I tell him quietly.

Roman pushes in and his hand comes up to grab my chin lightly, and he looks straight into my eyes. "Never apologize for your feelings, baby girl. They belong to you and everything about you is beautiful."

I cry now in earnest, realizing that I had fully convinced myself if they didn't walk away, I was going to. Roman grabs my hands and encourages me to step out of the car, and immediately pulls me into him.

"You're okay, I have you," he reassures me.

We stand there together as I get it all out, the shame, the anger, the grief caused by my anxiety over the idea of them leaving. Jax comes to my back, closing me in between the two of them. The closeness of them creates a cocoon of sorts, and I get myself together.

"Quite the kickoff to the night, isn't it?" I try to joke.

I pull back from Roman's neck where my face was buried and look at each of them. Jax smiles and wipes the tears off my cheeks with his thumbs and leans in for a gentle kiss. Roman kisses my temple as Jax kisses my mouth.

"Let's get inside and we can talk, yeah?" Roman says.

I nod and follow him into the house, Jax following close behind. Olivia has already taken over the rest of the food prep. She's slicing up vegetables, a pile of meat sitting next to her that was clearly seasoned recently. She looks up and gives me a smile and a wink before going back to her task. Jax, Roman, and I move through the kitchen to sit down on the couch.

"Do you want to tell me about it?" Roman asks.

I sigh. "Not really, but I know I should."

"Liv gave us some basic information. She said some lady was a total asshole, but that's about it." Jax tells me.

"So, we had grabbed all the chips and Liv was bringing over her Takis. This lady walked by and made some comment about the chips we had. I got pissed and told her to mind her own business." I started.

"Fuck yeah, baby girl," Roman says, kissing my head.

I smile before continuing. "She went off, and I had a small adrenaline drop from the confrontation, but we kept going. When we were trying to figure out which Oreos to buy, the same lady came up and took the package I was holding out of my hands. She put it back on the shelf and told us we shouldn't be eating that kind of food with the way we look."

I've started crying again, and Roman is clearly pissed off. Hopefully, it's not at me. I don't think it's at me since he said he is proud of me, but maybe not? Jax just looks confused.

"So, then Liv calls her out on it. I was totally frozen. I had no idea what to do. So, I just stood there. Any bravado from earlier just fucking disappeared. The lady doubled down on saying she was looking out for our health and walked away. Liv grabbed the package back off the shelf and I'm pretty sure it was pure spite." I laugh a little.

Jax smiles. "Sounds like her from what I've heard."

"God, you guys, I was so mortified. How could I stand up for myself one minute and then cave the next? What is wrong with me? Then, even though I got angry about it, I figured you both would be done with me after hearing about what happened. So, I started convincing myself I should go."

"Why would I walk away from this?" Roman seems genuinely confused.

"Sunshine," Jax says softly.

"I mean, you guys already have to deal with my anxiety, and now you're going to have to deal with people being assholes to me all the time. You deserve someone who isn't going to drag you down with drama."

"Charlotte, there isn't a thing in that statement that's true. You have anxiety, but that's okay, there's nothing wrong with that. People are assholes all the time. Why would a few more cause either of us to walk away?" Roman says softly.

His words are a balm to my wound, but I'm still unsure if he really grasps how hard it is to deal with this kind of thing. I know Roman understands how I feel when this happens, but is he ready to deal with it himself? Is Jax? It's not people just being assholes, it's people actively shaming me because I weigh more.

"Well, maybe she was just trying to cover her own insecurities," Jax tries to reason with us.

"I'm worried you don't understand what you're walking into with me," I confess to him.

"Unless you're cheating on me, or a serial killer, there's nothing that can make me walk away from this, okay? I'm in it, I want to make this work. Is that fast? Probably. But it's true." Jax says.

Roman nods solemnly in support.

"Honestly, I might even be okay if you were a serial killer, it would depend on who you kill, though," Jax adds.

We laugh while Roman shakes his head with his small smile.

Maybe it'll be okay after all.

Jax shows me where his bathroom is so I can wash the smeared mascara off my cheeks. My makeup is in my overnight bag, which I haven't told either one I brought yet. Since my mascara isn't too bad right now, I decide to touch it up later. Finishing in the bathroom, I open the door to find Roman leaning on the wall across from the door.

"Hey," I say to him, standing in the doorway.

"You sure you're okay?"

I sigh. "I think so, yeah. It just really caught me off guard that she grabbed it right out of my hands. I've had people take things out of my cart, but not my hands."

Roman steps away from the wall and pulls me in close, wrapping his arms around me. "You shouldn't be okay with people taking things out of your cart either. I'm sorry you've had to deal with this."

"Have you ever been so frustrated that you feel like just bailing?" I ask.

"Oh yeah, I've had that," he says.

"What happened?"

He pulls back and looks me in the eyes, then gives me a soft kiss. "Let's go see what else needs doing, yeah?"

What the hell was that? Talk about avoidance. Maybe it's just not a good time. We do need to get things going.

I nod and head toward the kitchen where Jax and Liv are finishing up the prep.

"Anything I can do?" I ask.

"Yes. You can grab a beer and go relax," Olivia responds.

Rolling my eyes at her, I say, "Yes, MOM."

Jax snickers, grabs two beers, hands one to each of us, and kicks us out of the house.

"Roman can help in here. You two go make sure the patio in the back isn't too cold. I started a fire earlier. We have blankets, and there's a space heater too. I think it'll be enough, but I need someone to test it out."

Liv salutes, grabs my hand, and starts to walk out of the kitchen.

"Wrong way," Jax calls as he puts the meat in the fridge to keep until cooked.

"Just testing you," she responds.

"Do you think I don't know where the patio is in my own house?"

"One can never be sure," she says solemnly and adjusts our path toward the dining room, which has a sliding door to the patio in back.

I'm giggling at her ridiculous banter with Jax as we step out and each grab a camping chair. Several have been placed around the fire pit, small tables in between some of them for easy drink holding. They're firm chairs instead of the bagged camping chairs, and it's pretty comfortable. I see a pile of blankets in a clear tote next to the space heater, but not close enough the plastic would melt.

"Eclectic seating, but I'm down with this," I tell Olivia.

"Honestly, matching porch furniture is overrated and over-priced. I like this. It's practical," she responds.

I take a sip of my drink and we sit in companionable silence, just enjoying the quiet and waiting to see if we get too cold. Sighing, she turns to me and looks at me expectantly. My stare stays forward toward the fire.

"What?" I ask.

"Did you guys talk about it?"

"Did you send them out to get me?"

"No, I told them you were upset and would be in soon. Before I could fully set the groceries down, they were both out the door. I was impressed, actually. I figured they'd start pushing each other to get there first, but they didn't."

"Yeah, they let me get it all out and I told them what happened at the store. I managed to convince myself that they were going to leave me after you left the car. I then convinced myself that I should leave if they don't go first."

"Of course you did," she teases lightly.

I smile because she knows me so well.

"Jax took the time to reassure me he's not going anywhere, but tried to justify the woman's behavior. I think Roman got it, but when I asked him what his experience was with feeling so frustrated that you want to bail, he wouldn't answer the question. He was more concerned about my emotions and making sure I'm okay."

"Babes," Olivia says softly.

"I told both of them I'm worried they don't understand what they're getting into with me. Between the anxiety and fat shaming from strangers, it's a lot," I confess.

Liv takes a drink before responding.

"It's a lot if you let it be a lot. I know I've said this before, but there's no shame in your anxiety. There's no shame in your body. Fight for equality for other fat people if you can, but make sure you don't give in to people who think they're better than you. Have your emotions, but move on from them. Don't linger. I know it's easier said than done, but I'm guessing Jax doesn't linger. So maybe he can help you with that. Not sure about Roman, but at least he's supporting you, so you've got some good people in your corner."

"Can you please stop being reasonable and making sense?" I grumble at her.

"Nope," she replies, popping the p and grinning.

Finally, I start to relax, trying to take my friend's words to heart. Moments later, the slider door opens and Amy comes walking out, drink in hand.

"Hey bitches!" she greets us with a smile. "This is a pretty sweet setup."

"It's nice, isn't it? Not too chilly either. I probably should go tell Jax that," I say.

"Make sure you tell him with lots of moaning and a good O face!" Amy calls after me.

I turn and yell, "Pervert!"

Her cackles fill the air as I step into the house, smiling and shaking my head.

 # Chapter 26

Charlotte

The amount of laughter out here is perfect. Everyone has a plate of food and a drink, and conversation flows smoothly with all the groups. Looks like the evening is going to be the success that Jax was hoping for. I'm glad for him, and I'm also glad that people are getting to know each other better.

Olivia, Amy, and I sit near each other, and Morgan ended up near us as well. I was concerned when Jax said he was inviting her, but I'm definitely warming up to her. Roman is sitting closer to Thomas and Courtney while Jax straddles the two groups. Morgan ends her story about being chased by a pig and I stand up, wiping tears from my eyes.

"Holy shit, that's hilarious. Be right back," I say.

I take my empty beer with me and set it inside as I head for the bathroom. Once I'm done, I open the door and Morgan is standing in the hallway.

"You gotta stop following me into bathrooms," I try to joke.

She laughs a little and looks down, almost like she feels awkward.

"Did you need the bathroom? Sorry if I'm blocking it," I tell her, going to move.

"Uh, no, actually, I wanted to talk to you. You probably don't want to talk to me, but I'm hoping you'll listen."

Well, now I'm curious and I'm buzzed enough that my anxiety is nowhere to be seen. I nod at her and lean against the door frame.

This is the second time I'm having a conversation in this spot. Must be a magical conversation bathroom.

"I never meant to make you feel like you need to lose weight. You don't. I happened to, but it wasn't on purpose. I had thyroid issues, so when they removed mine, a bunch of weight dropped off and just stayed off. I was eating mostly healthy before the surgery, so I just kept doing what I was doing and here I am."

"Oh, wow, I'm glad you're okay!"

She smiles. "Thanks. Anyway, I wanted to reassure you I never meant to make you feel you're less than. I just wanted you to know I've had that type of shit thrown at me before, and it's not right. It's not right that now I'm treated differently, and it's not right that anyone who is fat is treated badly at all."

"Thanks Morgan, I really appreciate that. I'm sorry I didn't give you a chance to tell me your full story. I was just so deep in my anxiety spiral I couldn't think," I tell her sincerely.

She smiles. "No harm done, I'm not trying to force us to be bffs or anything, but I wanted you to know what my intent was."

"Well, Ames and Liv might end up pulling you into the circle, especially if you have more stories like pig chasing. I hope you're ready for that."

"I don't think I would mind too much," she replies, laughing.

She starts walking back toward the patio, and I follow. We stop at the fridge for another round, then head outside. I look over to see Courtney taking selfies with Roman and Thomas. Roman is less than thrilled to be included. Glad to see they're getting along. Jax walks up to meet me at the door while Morgan resumes her spot next to Amy.

Jax grabs my face and brings his mouth to mine. I wrap my arm around his shoulders and I hold myself to him. We take the time to explore each other's mouth, as if we don't already know the space intimately. A wolf whistle starts up and Jax raises one hand to flip everyone off. When a round of cheers and laughter rises up we break apart, smiling from ear to ear.

"You staying the night tonight?" he asks me so only I can hear.

"That's an awfully presumptuous question. Neither of you even asked," I tease just as quietly.

"I would love to have you stay the night, if you are willing, and I bet Roman would be okay with it too."

Pretending to ponder, I tilt my head. "Hmmmm I'm not sure that's a good idea. Sets a bad example for my little brother."

"He's a big boy," he says, nipping at my lip.

"Nope, let's not say he's a big boy in sexy voices when talking about my brother. That's a hard pass," I tell him, making a gagging face.

He chuckles. "Well then give me an answer on staying over."

Smiling, I tell him I would love to stay.

He laughs and starts sticking his face into my neck, tickling me with his beard and trying to raspberry my skin. I shriek and shove him off, running away and plopping in the open seat next to Roman. Jax sits in the seat I was previously in and points to his eyes and then to me. I do the gesture back with a wink and turn to see what Roman and my siblings are talking about.

When I look, Roman is already looking over at me. His blue eyes are pensive and serious. He takes a drink and just keeps looking at me. There's a little heat there, but it feels more observational, which he doesn't usually do with me. Thomas and Courtney keep chatting, and it's almost like Roman is just an observer instead of a participant.

"How's it goin'?" I ask him, taking a swig of my drink.

"Fine."

"Good to know where this rates on your levels of excitement. Outdoor gathering with really only two people you know, so yeah, I suppose that could be fine."

"I didn't say the gathering was fine. And you more than make up for me not knowing many people."

"Well, how would you rate it, then?"

He thinks for a moment, like he's actually trying to decipher what a full answer would be. "Four stars."

"Now you gotta break it down for me. You say you're fine, but the party is four stars, so that's a pretty big rating."

"Jax is throwing it so it's automatically two stars, and seeing you makes up the other two. Maybe not as complimentary as you think."

"Hmmmm, since I'm half the rating, I *guess* we can go with four stars. I might have to tell Ames that you don't like her, though."

"Woman, don't throw me under the bus like that!" he exclaims.

I cackle. "What are you gonna do about it?"

He leans in close and beckons me to come closer. I lean in to meet him, and his voice is soft, meant for just the two of us.

"I'm gonna spank that ass until it's red and throbbing."

My breath picks up and I shudder at his dirty words and dark voice. "Promises, promises," I tell him just as softly.

"You've done it now, baby girl. Your ass is mine tonight."

He turns and nips my ear, just barely, but enough for me to feel it. He leans back, a satisfied smirk on his face. I can feel my face flush and I'm sure I have the typical goofy grin you see on people who are smitten. I hear the back door open and close and look up.

"Bethany! I didn't expect you!" Jax exclaims.

Bitch sister herself gives him a wide smile and is holding hands with a guy I haven't met before.

I wonder if this is her boyfriend that couldn't make family dinner. I didn't realize Jax had invited her. Let's see what happens here. I'm tipsy enough that I'm not pissed about it, but I am not gonna hold back tonight. Add on Amy and Olivia, and she might get flayed.

"Hey, sorry to burst in on you. You mentioned the gathering and said it'd be cool if we came by, but I wasn't sure if we could until just now," she says.

"No problem, grab a chair!" Jax says amicably.

"Fuck," I mutter.

Roman turns, eyeing me sharply, and I even see Olivia and Amy subtly glancing over.

"Did I tell you about dinner with Jax's family?" I ask Roman.

"All I heard was that you felt it didn't go well," he murmurs back.

"Well, when *Bethany* over there kept making snide comments about my weight and their mother joined in subtly, it made the evening a bit of a bummer," I say softly, but with a fair amount of anger thrown in.

"Really?" Roman looks shocked, but he doesn't try to defend them. "That's some bullshit. Did Jax say anything?"

"Nope, he tried to say their comments were about my hair, not my weight."

Roman is frowning now. It's a mixture of anger, confusion, and frustration. I reach over and try to smooth out his eyebrows.

"It's ok, family liking me isn't everything," I tell him.

He smiles softly at me and grabs my hand. Bethany and the guy have taken seats near Jax and Morgan. Our little circle expanded a bit to accommodate the newcomers. Jax goes around doing introductions and when he passes by me, Bethany's eyebrow twitches up. Then she notices my hand in Roman's and her lips pinch.

"I'm gonna guess Jax didn't tell her about this," I whisper to Roman.

"Twenty bucks says she makes a scene," he whispers back.

"You're on. I think she's gonna try to shame me in private."

We finally clue back in just in time to hear Jax introduce the guy as Trevor. I hold back a snort, but barely.

Of course *perfect Bethany is with a guy named Trevor. I bet he had blonde tips in his hair in high school. Probably benched 250 back in the day. Ooo, I'm getting salty, maybe I should back off a little.*

I try to talk myself down a bit and settle back to listen to the conversation.

Maybe she's not so bad. Maybe she was having a bad night. And maybe I don't have anxiety. Yeah.

"So, Morgan, you're looking fantastic," Bethany is saying.

"Oh, thank you, you look good too," Morgan says politely.

"It's not easy keeping a thin body. You really have to ensure you put effort into it," Bethany adds sagely.

"Well, I'm not doing much differently. It's mostly the thyroid stuff, and it's not exactly my life mission to be thin," Morgan says, ensuring Amy and Olivia hear her.

I take a peek at Olivia and Amy's faces, and I can see the wheels turning as they listen to the exchange. They both look over at me and I raise my eyebrow to say, "See? I told you." and Olivia smirks.

Bethany fusses over Morgan. "Well, to overcome health problems too, you are definitely a warrior."

"Do you have a lot of health issues to deal with?" Olivia asks sweetly.

Shit, the sweet tone came out. This is gonna go downhill fast.

"Liv, don't you think that's a little personal?" I interrupt.

"Oh, I don't mind, I'm an open book," Bethany says, her tone decidedly less warm as she directs her words to me. "I don't hide things from people."

I roll my eyes internally and let it play out as best I can. Hopefully, I can keep the cat fight out of the circle but who knows? Olivia and Amy are like sharks in the water when they smell blood. Bethany is ripe for the taking to them.

"No," Bethany says to Olivia. "I have worked hard my entire life to stay healthy and ensure my body is in shape. I take a lot of pride in that."

Liv nods sagely. "Yes, I can see how having muscles would keep you from getting a disease that you can't control."

Jax interjects. "Except that one time you had chicken pox."

Trevor chuckles. "I love this story."

"Trevor!" Bethany scolds him.

He shrugs and takes a drink of his beer.

Maybe he's not so bad.

Jax sits up, excited to share the story. Apparently, Bethany had a terrible case but didn't want to believe it, so she kept telling people it was the latest fashion to have red dots all over. She even put red dots all over Jax to try to convince their mom that it looked good. Their mom was horrified, and when she realized the dots on Jax washed right off, she went to scold Bethany but found her on her bedroom floor, wiggling around on her back, trying to scratch it. Jax said she looked like a worm trying to stay alive in the sun.

Everyone is cracking up, and Bethany even cracks a small smile, which impresses me. When Jax launches into another story, it's clear that Bethany has had enough. She looks straight at me and interrupts her brother.

"So, Charlotte, care to explain why you're holding Roman's hand and not Jax's? Right in front of him, too?"

She's clearly hoping to stir something up, despite the fact that Jax has a clear line of sight, and there's no way he would have missed our handholding before she spoke up.

"Oh, I'm dating both of them," I tell her calmly, as if talking about the weather.

"Excuse me?" she says.

"She's dating both of them," Thomas says slowly for her.

I love my brother.

"Are you serious right now? Jax, this isn't funny," she says.

"It's not a joke. We're both seeing her and she's seeing us. It's a mutual arrangement," he says nonchalantly.

"How in the world could you both want THAT?" she exclaims.

"I owe you twenty bucks," I say to Roman, not bothering to lower my voice.

"You can owe it to me later," he says with a wink.

"Seriously, you guys, I can't believe you're attracted to her. She's huge!" Bethany decides to die on this hill.

We all have to take a stand in life. Apparently, this is Bethany's, and she's in for a rude awakening.

"Beth, who I date shouldn't matter to you," Jax says.

Oh cool, he's not gonna touch the fat comment.

"Look, I don't know what your goal is here, but you might want to take your judgy ass and get out of here," Olivia says.

"Yeah, we don't need hate in this circle, so you can apologize, figure out why you hate fat people and stay, or you can get going with your tiny mind," Amy adds.

Courtney holds up her glass. "Cheers ladies!"

Bethany looks at Trevor for support. He stands and looks at Jax apologetically.

"Sorry bro, I guess we're gonna take off. Didn't mean to cause a scene. I didn't really think this would happen," he says.

Jax waves him off. "She's just being dramatic. We can always meet up again soon."

Olivia starts singing Dancing Queen but changes the lyrics.

"She is the drama queen. She can't help herself, she has to cause a scene!"

Amy joins in. "She can bitch! She can whine! But we're having the time of our lives!"

I start to giggle at my friends being absolutely ridiculous. Bethany chooses to walk over to me, and I let go of Roman's hand and stand. I'm not taking anything she has to say with her towering over me. Before saying what she has to say, she gives a look to Amy and Olivia, who smile and flip her off in reply.

I'm a little taller, but she still manages to look down her nose at me. She says, "You may think that this is going to end well for you, but it's not. Jax needs someone who will actually live a healthy life, not drag him down. Literally."

"Bethany, I hope you figure out where this is coming from and go talk to someone about it," I tell her.

"Whatever. Good luck keeping him with Morgan around."

That one… that one hits. I nod at her, then pass around her and walk into the house, keeping a normal pace. Jax has assured me multiple times that he doesn't want Morgan. Morgan has said she does not want Jax. I believe both of them, but when Bethany said that, a crack of doubt appeared. I can feel it widening, and I just need to take some deep breaths and get it sealed back up. I open a door to a bedroom, not wanting to be seen, and sit down on the simple bed.

The room is sparsely decorated, a few photo frames and tools scattered around. The nightstand stand and tall dresser are the only furniture aside from the bed. The queen size bed sits against a wall, so there's only one side to get in and out of. I sit on the edge of the bed and breathe.

I can do this. I just need to breathe.

 # Chapter 27

Charlotte

I must have dozed off or really zoned out, because the next thing I know, someone is walking into the room and I'm blinking my eyes, laying on my back on the bed. Sitting up, my head swims a little and I chastise myself for moving too quickly. Roman closes the door behind him, letting the room fall back into semi-darkness. When I first came into the room, I lit the bedside lamp, and it's what's lighting the room for us now.

He sets my overnight bag at the end of the bed, then rounds it to come sit next to me. No words are spoken as he shifts himself further onto the bed, so his back is against the wall and his feet are pointing to the side of the bed. He beckons me over, so I shuffle back as well. He grabs me and turns me so that I'm sitting on his lap, facing him. I settle in as he looks at me.

"You okay?" he asks softly.

"Yeah," I answer honestly. "I started doubting when Bethany made that comment about Morgan, and I needed some time to make it go away. I fucking hate that people's words can cause me to feel so awful."

"Hey," he says, grabbing my chin lightly. "It's okay, it happens. I'm glad you took the time you needed."

"What happened after I left?" I ask, not sure if I really want to hear the answer.

Roman sighs. "Well, everybody got quiet for a minute after you walked away and then there was a bit of an uproar. Morgan started it actually, calling Bethany a psycho."

I snorted. "Yeah, I think I'm gonna like her."

"She's actually pretty cool," he says with a smile. "So after she started in, Thomas jumped in with the 'how dare you talk to my sister like that?' line. Ames and Liv sat there, just *fuming,* and I'm actually surprised they didn't chip in. Jax… Jax tried to keep the peace."

"What did he do?" I ask, knowing Roman isn't giving me the full story.

"Don't worry about it. Everyone left. Ames and Liv stayed to help clean up, and I think Thomas and Jax are still amicable."

I nod. "Okay then."

"I, uh, I was hoping I could have you for the night, but if you want to be with Jax, I get it." Roman actually sounds a bit uncertain.

I think about it for a minute. While I know I should go try to smooth things over with Jax, Roman soothes my soul in a way I didn't know I needed. He accepts my feelings how they are; he doesn't push, and he's honest with me. His peace is what I need tonight.

"Well, you do owe me a spanking," I tell him coyly, shifting my hips a little.

He chuckles darkly. "Oh baby, do I ever owe you one. I think we can pay up later, though. Tonight is about you."

My heart melts. This man knows exactly what I need. Smiling, I bring my face to his, our lips meeting in a gentle caress, a reminder that we're here together and we're all that matters.

Roman brings his hands up, holding my head where he wants me. I nip his bottom lip softly and he groans softly, seeking entrance to my mouth with his tongue. Obliging, I open, and our tongues meet. Caressing and exploring, our mouths continue to move together, our breathing picking up a little. My hand lands on his chest and I can feel his heartbeat speeding up as we continue to kiss.

He pulls back slightly from the kiss and looks at me. His eyes are searching mine, and I can see the indecision there. I can also feel how hard he is after our kisses.

"Want to make sure we're good," he says.

"I'm good if you are. Do you have condoms?"

"Fuck!"

"I have an IUD."

"Honestly, I haven't had sex in a couple years. No STIs here."

"OK, then," I tell him with a small smile.

Maybe I should insist on tests, but I trust Roman in a way I didn't think I'd be able to with a man.

"You sure?" he asks

"If you don't fuck me, I'll fuck myself and make you watch," I sass.

He chuckles and pulls me back in, slamming his lips onto mine. He slaps my ass and encourages me to start moving on him. Roman drags his lips from my mouth and makes his way down my throat to my collarbone. Nipping and sucking, he finds the tops of my breasts and pulls the fabric of my shirt down.

"There is no way I'm not fucking you tonight. Take this damn shirt off," he says huskily.

Giggling, I do as he asks and pull my shirt over my head. The lust in his eyes when I do is a boost of confidence, and I don't think I can get enough. I reach back and unhook my bra, letting it slide down my body until it's sitting between us. Roman grabs it and tosses it aside, leaning in to suck one nipple into his mouth.

My head falls backwards, a pleased hum coming from my throat. His mouth sucks and nips at my hardened peak and he wastes no time in ensuring the other has similar treatment. Slowly, he pushes my body back, twisting us so that my head lies near the pillows. Positioning himself on top of me, he grinds himself between my legs. In reflex, I pull my legs up and wrap them around him, seeking more friction.

"Your legs wrapped around me is something I've been dreaming of," he says, nipping at any exposed skin he can get his mouth on.

"You need to take off that shirt," I tell him, my voice coming out breathy.

He sits up from my chest and does that damn one handed shirt pull. I'm telling you guys, they practice this. There's no way they don't. It's not natural to do that so smoothly.

My legs untangle from his waist, and I sit up so he has to stay kneeling. Roman's body is more built than Jax, but I know a lot of that is the job and some of it is his own workouts on occasion. He's not a bodybuilder, but he's not an average dude either. My mouth moves across his firm chest, and I suckle at his skin as I move down to his stomach.

It's faint, but he has a V leading down into his pants, and I've always wanted to see that in person. It's as hot as I expected it to be. My hands work at the buttons on his jeans and my tongue traces the grooves in his skin that lead down. Once the top button is undone, I pull down his zipper and reach in to grab what I'm looking for.

He's hot and hard in my hand, and the second I touch his skin, he moans in pleasure. I look up through my lashes and his eyes are locked on my hand, not wanting to miss a second of the action. Roman wiggles his pants down a little and I'm able to pull his hard cock out of his pants. My mouth waters a little, and I can see some precum beading, so I swipe my tongue through it.

"Fuck. You gonna put your mouth on me, baby girl?"

I nod. "Yes."

"Then show me, stuff your face with me and take it deep. I want you gagging on my cock," he says roughly.

I lick him from root to tip, and then suck the tip into my mouth. Spending a moment there, I can taste the precum on my tongue as he continues to make the sexiest noises I've ever heard. He's moaning in pleasure, almost growling at times. A hand grabs my hair, and he forces my head back to look at him.

"Do you need me to stuff you myself or are you gonna suck me down?" he asks.

My body responds to his dirty words, and my panties are soaked. I'm not sure I've ever been this turned on in my life. I respond by opening my mouth, sticking my tongue out flat for him.

He chuckles darkly before saying, "Tap my thigh three times and I'll stop." Then feeds his cock into my open mouth.

I close around him, covering my teeth, and start to suck. Moving my mouth down and back up his shaft, I hear his breathing increasing as I go.

"That's it baby girl, you look so good with that sassy mouth wrapped around my cock."

I moan in pleasure, causing him to hiss in a breath from the vibrations of my throat. My gag reflex is a little sensitive, so I take him as deep as I can, but I can't get all the way to the root. The first couple of times I try, he notices my immediate retreat and doesn't try to force it.

"As good as your mouth feels, this cum belongs in a different part of your body," he says roughly, and pulls me off him. "Get those pants out of my way."

As I shimmy my own pants off, Roman discards the rest of his. Laying back on the bed, I lock my eyes with his. He's not moving, just staring at my body, awe written across his face as his eyes bounce all over my exposed skin.

"You are a fuckin' goddess," he tells me as he shifts his body lower on the bed.

His hands grab my feet, and he moves them apart and sets them flat on the bed so my knees are bent and my core is exposed.

"Such a pretty pussy. Are you wet for me? Is this all mine?"

He swipes a finger through my slit, and I gasp. "It's yours, Roman, it's all yours."

He grumbles in pleasure before thrusting two fingers in me, without any preamble. His fingers fill me up and the friction is what I've been desperate for. There's an embarrassingly wet noise coming from me as he pumps his fingers in and out of my soaked pussy, but I can't find it in me to care.

"You hear that?" he says roughly, lowering his face closer to where his fingers are driving me crazy. "That's mine, that wet, dripping pussy is all mine."

Never pausing on his pumping, he adds a third finger and licks at my clit. I can feel myself winding up to detonate and more juices pour out of me. He rumbles in pleasure and flicks my clit harder with his tongue, speeding his fingers up to match the pace of his tongue. Then he seals his lips around my clit, grazes it with his teeth and sucks *hard*.

My body explodes, a cry falling from my lips in pleasure. Tingles run up my legs and I can feel my muscles contracting around his fingers. He doesn't slow, dragging the pleasure out to the point where I'm ready to cry. Pleasure wrecks my body and I can't get enough, at the same time, I can't take anymore. He finally slows, looking up at me with a satisfied smirk.

"You ready for me, baby?" he asks.

All I can do is nod. Roman chuckles as he moves his body up mine, settling so his dick is sitting heavy between my legs.

"Are you gonna take all of me in this dripping pussy?" he asks softly. "I'm gonna slam into this cunt and fill you up. Your tits are gonna bounce, and I'm not gonna show you an ounce of mercy."

"Please," I whisper, desperation lacing my tone.

Picking up one leg, he wraps it around him, leaving the other bent where it is. He gives no warmup as he slides slowly in. I'm so fucking wet he could have slammed in if he wanted to. His entrance is slow but forceful, giving no hesitation. Finally, he stops, our bodies physically unable to be closer.

"God, your pussy is heaven," he tells me, his teeth clenched. "I don't think I can get enough of it."

All I can do is whimper and flex my hips. I want to be closer, and I can't. It's infuriating.

"You can't take any more of me baby, you already have it all," he says, catching onto what I'm doing. "You need me to move?"

"Yes!" I almost shout.

He chuckles darkly and pulls back out as slowly as he went in, keeping that steady slow rhythm. I arch my back in frustration, wanting him to go faster, and he chuckles again, fully aware of what I'm trying to do. One finger rubs at my clit, and his pace picks up.

"Do you need this? Do you want me to slam into you so hard you can't think? Can't breathe? I'm gonna fuck you so hard you can't even remember your own goddamn name."

"Please Roman, you feel so good," I cry out to him.

He lifts my leg from around his waist to put my ankle over his shoulder, deepening the angle. Once my leg is where he wants it, he pounds into me harder, picking up speed as he does so. The man is an absolute beast, his pace and roughness never wavering.

"Right there," I whine as I feel my orgasm building.

"Is that the spot? You gonna come for me? Soak my cock in your juices and scream my name? Your body was fuckin' made for me, baby girl, you feel like heaven," Roman grits out as his pace speeds up even more, which I didn't think was possible.

As he's pistoning in and out of me, one of his hands reaches back down to find my clit and he rubs it as fast as he can. The pleasure builds until I'm ready to cry with the need for relief.

"Come for me, baby girl," he growls.

A few more thrusts and I do, my body exploding with pleasure, my muscles contracting around his cock. My eyes close in pleasure and all I can do is feel as my body shakes with pleasure and waves of tingles flow through my legs.

"Gonna fill you up, baby. Come so deep inside you that you'll never be rid of me," he grunts. His pace falters and he slams into me one last time, groaning loudly. "Fuck, Charlotte," he says as his groan escapes him.

His body is bowed back, and his eyes are closed in pleasure. My eyes can't leave him like this. He's beautiful in his pleasure, completely unapologetic and raw.

Body straightening, he comes down from his high, and his eyes meet mine. He smiles and gives me a kiss, short and full of promise. Telling me not to move, he ducks out of the room and returns with a wet cloth. Gentle hands clean between my thighs and he kisses me gently as he cleans me up. No heat, just affection.

When we're clean, we get under the covers and snuggle, completely naked. I sigh, my face resting on his chest, our legs intertwined together. This man is under my skin and it's terrifying and thrilling all at once.

"Tell me something," I say.

"What do you want me to tell you?"

"Was your family as full of assholes as mine and Jax's?"

He's silent for a moment, and I wonder if he's going to answer. As I'm about to lean back to look at him and relieve him of the need to answer, he rubs my back.

"Let's go to sleep," he says.

Sleep does sound good.

We relax into each other and lay, unmoving, the rest of the night together. Safe, warm, and completely happy in the moment.

 Chapter 28

Charlotte

The next morning, I find myself wrapped in warm, strong arms. My eyes blink open, and I find myself in a room that is not mine. It takes a moment for my brain to catch up, and then I remember the disaster friend gathering, followed by epic orgasms.

Not a bad way to end the day.

I stretch and feel Roman hold on tighter. I realize we're both naked under the covers. Smiling, I try to pull his arm off me so I can use the restroom, but he is refusing to let go.

"Mine," he mumbles.

"Yours, but I need to pee, and I doubt you want me doing that in the bed."

"Sacrifice of snuggles," he protests.

Playful Roman in the morning. I didn't think playful Roman was a thing, let alone playful in the morning.

I laugh at him and nudge him again, and he finally obliges and lets me go. My overnight bag beckons me, and I dress in the pajamas I brought and do my business in the bathroom. The smell of coffee is permeating the house, so after I'm done, I head to the kitchen to find the source of life.

Jax has coffee made and is rifling through the fridge, grumbling to himself under his breath. I walk over to him and wrap my arms around his waist, leaning over him while he leans into the fridge.

"Good morning," I say to him.

"Hey. Just looking for some breakfast."

"I got something you can eat."

He rumbles with a chuckle, and I smile with my face leaning against his back. We stand together and Jax triumphantly holds bacon and eggs in his hands.

"Classic," I tell him.

A door down the hall opens and Roman staggers out, pajama pants hanging on his hips, and no shirt. He waves half-heartedly as he goes into the bathroom before joining us in the kitchen. Plopping in a seat, he lays his head down.

"Holy shit, you're up," Jax says, a teasing tone in his voice.

Roman raises a hand and flips him off.

"Coffee?" I ask him.

"Black."

"You got it."

It takes me a moment to figure out what cupboard has the mugs, but I find it and pour two mugs of coffee. Mine gets filled with sugar and creamer, and Roman's stays dark. He takes it with a small smile and sips at it.

"Do you want me to pour you some?" I ask Jax, taking a drink of my own.

"Sure, add a couple spoonfuls of sugar," he replies, bacon sizzling on the pan and eggs preparing to be scrambled.

Once the food is done, Jax comes to join Roman and me at the table. The food is put in the middle, and we serve ourselves, and while

I know this is a super basic breakfast, it's probably one of the best I've had. Despite that, we sit in silence, and it feels like the earlier ease dissipates. The silence doesn't feel comfortable for me.

"So, um, Morgan and I had a good talk last night. I think Liv and Ames are going to want to snap her up," I say.

Roman smirks. "Those girls take anyone in."

"They have big hearts!" I protest.

Jax doesn't join in the conversation, although he looks pleased at the comment about Morgan.

"You okay?" I ask him tentatively.

"I don't think so," he says, frowning at his food. "I guess I'm just feeling frustrated about how last night played out."

"Yeah, Bethany wasn't exactly tactful," Roman comments.

"Well, yeah, I guess, but honestly, I'm more upset that you left, Charlotte."

"What?" I feel my stomach drop at his words.

"I just figured you would stay and work through it. You're usually willing to talk things out with us," he explains.

"Okay… I guess I can see where you're coming from. I was trying to keep from having a meltdown, so that's why I stepped away."

"Meltdown from what?" Jax asks, seeming genuinely confused.

I feel a prickle of embarrassment start up in the back of my head and make its way down my body.

How… how does he not know? Did I overreact? Maybe I should have just stayed. Maybe I was the reason the night got ruined.

Roman butts in. "How about the fact that Bethany clearly doesn't like Charlotte or her weight and said in front of everyone that you should be with Morgan?"

My heart warms at Roman's defense on my behalf and some relief helps drive away a little of the embarrassment.

"She didn't mean that. She had been drinking before she came over. Trevor took her home right after and apologized. He didn't think she was that bad when they headed over," Jax says.

"Are you serious right now?" I ask him. I can feel a flush of embarrassment return full force, starting in the back of my head and washing over my body.

Jax looks uncomfortable. "Yeah, I mean, how are we going to work through stuff if you leave? If you had stayed, you'd have known she didn't mean it."

"Did she apologize?" I ask him.

"I mean, she was pretty upset."

"Did she apologize?" I ask again, my anger rising.

"Look, I know my sister—" he starts.

"So, she didn't apologize then," I interrupt him, getting thoroughly pissed at this point.

"Jax, Charlotte has to deal with people who are anti-fat all the time. She has food taken out of her cart and hears snide comments all the time. Your sister is that type of person to her," Roman interjects.

"Come on, man," Jax pleads. "You know what it's like to have a sister you can't control."

Roman's face loses any warmth it might have held. I look over at him, confused.

"You have a sister?" I ask.

"That's not the point," he says brushing me off.

My heart sinks along with my stomach. Jax doesn't believe I have any reason to be upset, and now I find out Roman doesn't think I'm worth telling his backstory to. He let me believe his only living family was his aunt. I'd never force it from him, but he couldn't have at least mentioned his family was alive to me?

Normally, I'd feel insecure and embarrassed. At this point, though? I'm way past that. I can feel myself start to shake from anger.

Roman seems to think he doesn't need to share anything with me. I thought he was honest, but he's been hiding this. What else is he hiding? Jax doesn't think my experiences are valid and still won't admit that his sister hates me purely on principle. My first instinct to run from this was right. I should have walked away; this is what happens when you let people in.

I take a mental breath.

Maybe we can turn this around, though. I'm going to try.

"Sorry, man, that was low," Jax tells Roman.

"All good, I just can't believe you are defending Bethany in this," Roman replies, his face still mostly closed off.

"Charlotte never said it was bad," Jax protests.

"I tried!" I protest loudly. "I told you a few times that it's something I've experienced, but you brushed it off every time."

"So, you decided to just tell Roman about this stuff, but not me?" Jax questions, turning it back on me.

"I told you about the grocery store yesterday and you tried to justify the woman's actions!"

"I wanted you to try to see her point of view. Not everyone is against you, Charlotte."

I throw my hands up in the air, absolutely done with this conversation. I know, I said I'd try. My ability to try today is gone. Standing, I walk to the bedroom and throw a sweatshirt over my pajamas. The set I picked already has fleece pants, so I'm covered from the temperature. Zipping the bag, I move to the living room to find my purse and throw it over my shoulder.

"I'm not talking about this right now. We're clearly all emotional. Let's try again later," I tell them, and walk to the door. Before I can leave, I turn, and my mouth runs away from me for a moment. "Fuck both of you for this shit!" I yell at them, then storm out the door.

Neither of them tries to come for me as I get into my car and pull out of the driveway.

What the actual fuck just happened? Did Jax really try to justify bigoted behavior to me? Does he really think his sister isn't at fault here? How am I supposed to stand there and be told that I'm not good enough just because I weigh more? I'm supposed to just be okay with her trying to argue that Jax should get back with his ex? Who is she to come in and say all the stuff, anyway? Do I really want to deal with his family if they're going to be like that?

This leads me to remember the revelation of Roman having a sister.

Why didn't he tell me? I thought his family was dead. He gave no indication that they were alive. How could he not open up to me when I gave him so much of myself? What else is he hiding from me?

Part of me feels a little bad for yelling at them like that, but when these thoughts pop back in, my guilt dissipates and morphs back into anger and hurt.

When I arrive home, I immediately drop my bag in my room and get in the shower. I need the heat and steam to help me think through what I want to do next.

Is this relationship something I want to keep working on? Is it worth pushing through our first fight? It's already been identified that my ability to try today is gone, so I don't know. Maybe I'll feel better after my shower is done and I'm dressed.

My first instinct is to dress in my sweats and a hoodie, so I give in to the impulse. Comfort is my priority right now. Moving to the kitchen, I find a box of brownie mix and whip those babies up. It's a comfort day through and through.

I hear dinging faintly and realize I haven't looked at my phone yet today. It's probably almost dead. Grabbing the charger from my room, I plop on the sofa, looking at my messages. I've got two from Morgan, five from Amy, and ten from Olivia. Scrolling through, they all have the same message of checking to see if I'm okay and telling me to get in touch with them.

I'm not even sure how Morgan got my number. I save hers into my phone and figure she grabbed it from one of my friends. My brain is not up for talking right now, and I promise myself I'll call them back in a bit.

When the brownies finally finish cooking, my phone rings. I glance down and see Roman is calling. Do I answer? Petty, bitchy me says to leave him unanswered. We don't need that shit in our life. Reasonable me says I should pick it up and hear him out, especially after the way I left their house. I let my reasonable side win.

"Hey," I answer.

"Hey." He sounds a bit surprised. "I, uh, wanted to check and see how you're doing."

"Fine."

Aw shit, now I'm being that girl. *What's done is done.*

"Ah, I see. Um, well, I guess I just wanted to see if we still need to talk. I feel like we've left things kind of rocky."

"Yeah, you could say that. I just–I feel hurt you didn't tell me *anything* about your family or your past. You only ever mentioned your aunt, and it feels like you intentionally let me think your family is dead. So, what else are you hiding from me?"

"I see your point. It's not easy for me to open up, I'll admit that."

"It's not easy for me either, Roman, but I did for you," I point out to him.

"I just–I don't know if I can. My family history is complicated, and I just don't know," he admits.

I nod, closing my eyes. Thankfully, he can't see me trying to hold it together.

"Okay. When you figure it out, let me know. Go figure it out, Roman," I say more steadily than I thought I could.

"Wait, no, I'm not saying I want to be done," he protests, panicking.

"Roman, you just told me you don't know if you'll be able to open up to me. What kind of relationship is that? Go figure it out and we'll talk later. For now, I need to figure out if this is what I want, and I think you need that, too. Bye."

I hang up before he can protest more. Immature, I know, but I don't think I can hear him plead anymore and not give in. We both need to figure out if this is what we want. We've moved fast and I think this is the smart decision, even if the idea of not seeing him again is painful. I'm realizing I should also talk to Jax when someone knocks on the front door.

Opening it, I see Jax standing there, looking bashful and contrite. I stand in the doorway, not letting him in.

"Hi."

"Hey," he says.

"Roman just called me."

"Yeah?"

"Yeah, I didn't realize you would be coming over."

He shrugs. "I didn't want to just call."

We stand there awkwardly for a moment.

"So?" I start.

"So, I guess I wanted to come see if you're okay. You left pretty upset."

"I did. I'm fine. How are you?"

He shrugs again. "I guess I'm okay."

I nod and wait him out.

"I need you to know something," he says to me.

I nod at him to continue.

"Bethany has always been there for me; she's been in my corner since hour one. I just can't see her being a mean girl, or a bigot. I just can't. She's always so nice."

I close my eyes in frustration and take a deep breath. "Okay, I understand that," I tell him.

"I'm glad," he says, smiling with relief.

"What I don't understand is how you could overlook any feelings I have on this. You blow past it and try to make a joke every time or explain away the behavior like it's okay if the reason is good enough.

"Living in this world as a fat woman has meant that anyone I come across is potentially someone who could tell me I'm worthless. I have had people literally yell at me that nobody will love me because of my body. I have had people tell me not to eat something at restaurants. I frequently get stared at in public, as if people can't believe I would dare show my skin in public.

"Add on top of that frequent anxiety and you get the wonderful cocktail that is struggling in social situations. When the spiral is kicked off by comments on my body, it's pretty damn hard to pull out of it because I am reminded everywhere that my body is not welcome.

I haven't even begun to explain to you what it's like trying to function in a straight sized world."

Jax shifts on his feet as I explain to him my life experiences.

Good, I hope he's uncomfortable. It means he gets it.

"So, Jax, go figure out what you're willing to support and why. I don't know that I can stand by and watch you support your sister, who is part of the problem, and tears me down at every opportunity. I don't know if I can be with someone who belittles my experiences. Come find me when you figure it out."

Leaning back from the doorway, I close my front door and turn the deadbolt. The action keeps me from opening it back up and begging him to come in. I know I can just unlock it again, but the action itself is what makes it final for me. I turn around to head back to my brownies, but when the weight of what I've just done hits me, my emotions crash and I fall to the ground, sobbing.

 Chapter 29

Roman

I look at the phone in my hand, wondering what the hell just happened.

Did she break up with me? I don't think she did. She didn't tell me never to call her again. How the fuck did this happen? I know how this happened, my own stupid brain not being willing to open up is how it happened.

Should have just told her I don't like talking about my family and left it there. I didn't though. My family stayed locked away in a mental box, my dirty secret that I don't want anyone to find. A dad who died when I was little. A mom who bailed on us, a sister who pulled the same disappearing act, and thousands of dollars in debt, drowning me slowly. She doesn't need that burden. Or so I thought.

Maybe I should have told her more, but I'm not used to having someone to rely on. My dad died when I was young, and when my mom remarried, I was eighteen, so she basically left me with my sister and took off into the sunset. Haven't heard from her since.

Maybe commitment isn't in me. I want it to be. Charlotte's almost all I think about. I want to be there for her and soothe her hurts. I want her to rely on me for the things she needs. My biggest joy is seeing her happy.

Jax comes home about an hour after I hang up with Charlotte. He left shortly after she did this morning and hasn't been back. It's late afternoon now, and he looks as awful as I feel. Walking in, he kicks his shoes off and just stands in the space between the living room and the dining room.

"You too?" I ask, my voice low.

"Yeah," he rasps out.

His voice sounds like he's been crying, but his face doesn't show any signs of it. My heart breaks a little more at my best friend's pain. Even if he is the one that started all this.

Why couldn't he just see Bethany for the shallow bitch she was being? Normally he's right, and she's not shallow. When it comes to weight, though, she's always been extreme.

"I'm, uh, I'm gonna go hang in my room a while. Don't worry about me for dinner," he says.

I nod, and he walks away.

It feels like I just lost my best friend and my girl. What the fuck is happening?

My heart hurts, and I rub my hand against my chest.

Who do I even have to talk to? I've been so focused on my job that I've isolated myself. I'm alone in my pain and maybe that's where I deserve to be.

The next week is a blur. I can't keep myself from checking in on Charlotte, but I get one word replies and nothing else. I know, I *know* I should open up to her, but what if she bails? That might be worse. If she willingly walks away, I think that might kill me. At this point, it can be my choice and maybe she'll hurt, but I know she'll find someone else.

It's quick, yes, but I'm pretty sure I love her. She has a fire in her that doesn't ever really go out. Maybe it burns to an ember, but she fans it back up and pushes past the bullshit. She has a heart bigger than I can imagine and family and friends who adore her. Who wouldn't adore her once they get to know her?

After work on Friday, I decide I need to get out of the house and hit a bar. My normally clean-shaven face has stubble on it and my hair is mussed, but not in a styled way. I'm sure I look terrible, but I don't have it in me to put the effort in. I go to Jerry's Pub and grab a spot at the bar. Jax and I used to go here frequently, but he's been in as big of a slump as I have been. Haven't seen him unless it's at work. Doesn't seem like he's shunning me, it's like he just disappears. The house holds evidence of his presence, but he's retreated into himself.

I feel someone pull out the bar chair next to me and immediately get annoyed.

There are a million other chairs here and you gotta pick the one next to me? Fuck. I hate people.

The person sits down and clears their throat. "You look like shit," Thomas tells me.

I look over at him, then look back at the bar in front of me. Thomas flags down the bartender, a tall woman with a long braid, and orders two drinks. I couldn't have told you what they were if you paid me $100,000. Thomas takes a drink of his, so I follow suit and wait to see what he's going to say.

"So," he says.

"So."

"Charlotte's in a bad spot," he confesses.

My eyes close and it's all I can do to keep tears in. I don't have any problems with people showing their emotion, but it doesn't feel like I have a right to those tears in front of Thomas. My tears can wait until I'm home.

"Yeah?" I croak out.

"Yep, she won't tell me what happened," he says.

"Ah, I get it. Not sure where the line is here. At what point is this you being my friend vs you being the protective brother?"

He chuckles without amusement. "She told me you guys come here a lot, so I figured I'd come by and see if I can get the story. I'm not sure which one I am right now. I suppose it'll depend on what happened."

His honesty is something I appreciate, so I may as well reciprocate.

"I'm still trying to figure it all out, but the basics boil down to Jax not defending her to his sister, and me not opening up to her. She told us to figure our shit out."

He huffs a laugh and takes another drink. "Typical," he says, his tone annoyed.

"What?" I ask.

"She gets something that could be real, and she finds reasons to make distance and push them away instead of working through it. I bet she got in a fight the morning after the party at Jax's and stormed out, right?"

"Pretty much," I confess.

"Classic Charli. Instead of working through it, she pushes people away. Her first few fights with Liv were like that, too."

"Well, at least I'm not special," I say wryly. "I suppose that's something."

"You are, though," he says, almost angry. "You *are* special to her and she's being a fucking idiot. Self-sabotaging to the max. She usually does this sooner and over smaller stuff, which is why I know she is into you both. Normally it would be something like drinking the wrong kind of soda."

I take another drink, and we sit in silence for a bit. I'm pondering his words, and I have no idea what's going on in his head. He's a good brother, and I appreciate him giving me more insight into Charlotte. That's probably why I find myself telling him what I can't bring myself to tell Charlotte.

"My dad died when I was a kid. My mom wasn't around much since she had to work two jobs, and when she *did* remarry, I was eighteen, so she took off and I've not really heard from her since. Maybe a text once a year, if that. My sister decided she wanted to go to college, so I cosigned her loans and then she bailed. I'm thousands of dollars in debt and my family all left me."

Thomas looks over at me. "Shit, man."

"Yeah."

"You got nobody?"

I sigh. "I have one aunt that sends me cards and insists she'll be there for me. Not sure if I trust it."

He finishes his drink, stands, and puts a hand on my shoulder.

"I can't tell you what to do, man, but at some point, you have to trust. Call her and see. I'll see if I can pull Charli's head out of her ass, but she might need you for that one. Just channel your inner Liv and don't let her go."

Thomas pulls out a twenty and tosses it on the bar. He turns and walks out, leaving me with his words echoing in my ears.

The next day, I'm still thinking about Thomas' words, and I find my finger hovering over my aunt's number.

Do I call? It doesn't feel safe. It feels like she's going to let it go to voicemail and never call back, or her number won't be legit.

I give myself a mental shake and tell myself to stop being stupid about this and suck it up. Not everyone is like my mom and sister. My finger taps the screen where her name rests. It only rings once or twice before I hear her pick up.

"Hello?"

Her voice almost does me in. It's nostalgic and I remember when she would visit during my childhood, before and after Dad passed.

"Hey, Aunt Nat, it's Roman.".

"ROMAN!" she essentially screeches into the phone. "Oh my God, I'm so glad you called!"

My mouth twitches in a small smile. She's always been a bit over the top. "Yeah, me too," I tell her roughly.

"Oh honey, what's wrong?"

"How do you know something's wrong? Maybe I'm just calling to say hi."

"Roman, I know you better than you think I do, and I know you don't call just to say hi. That's not how you operate. Even though I would love if you did."

Damn, talk about an unintentional guilt trip. Or maybe it was intentional; it's hard to tell.

"I was hoping for some advice," I confess.

I hear some shuffling on her end. "Okay, I'm sitting. Hit me. How can I help?"

I give her the rundown on the whirlwind romance with Charlotte and how we left things the other week. The conversation with Thomas gets an overview as well.

"Wow, honey, that's a lot," she says.

"Yeah. I really like her. I think I love her, but I don't know what to do. Everyone leaves and I'm left with nothing. What if she does the same thing when she sees that?"

"Roman, listen closely to me. Your blood family? It's not who you are. It's part of you at your core, but that doesn't define you. They shape you irrevocably, but you get to choose how. You can choose to be afraid of the same pattern, or you can choose to break the pattern and be better. Telling her is the right thing, if you want my opinion. It will bring you closer together."

"How do you know that?" I ask, and I hate how small my voice is.

"It's actually advice I got from your father. He was always terrified of being honest with people, but when he was, it always worked out well. He always had the best advice when we were growing up. Talk to her, be honest, and come visit me when it all smooths over."

"What if it doesn't?"

"Then come over anyway and I'll make you some blueberry pie," she says.

Aunts always know what to say. Now to call Charlotte. I'm in this thing and she deserves to know that no matter what she chooses. I hope like hell she chooses me and Jax.

 # Chapter 30

Charlotte

Once I cry myself out, I drag my body through the shower for a second time and collapse into bed.

If this was the right choice, why does it hurt so much? Oh, because neither of them actually put me first, that's why it hurts. Roman hid his entire life without giving me anything, not even a "I can't talk about it", just nothing. Jax decided that I'm crazy and people don't judge me for my weight. Fuck.

The next day is a blur as I go through the motions and the evening finds me at home with Liv and Ames in my house, chocolate and salty snacks spread on the table, and my hair soaking up a new color. I'm sitting on the couch, lounge clothes on under a fluffy blanket and a plastic bag on my head.

"You wanna talk about it yet?" Amy asks.

"No."

"Do it anyway," Olivia says firmly. I shoot her a death look. "Don't give me that look. We gave you a day to wallow. Well, maybe like twelve hours, but that's beside the point. You gotta get this shit out."

I mean, she's not wrong.

Sighing, I grab a few more peanut butter M&M's and settle in. Thinking about what to say, I pop them into my mouth and chew slowly, putting the words together in my head.

"So, the next morning we started talking about the shit Bethany pulled. Before I really could understand what was happening, Jax was telling me she didn't mean any of it. She was just drunk. Not once did he take my side on how it would make me feel. Then he lets it slip that Roman has a sister."

"Roman has family?" Amy asks.

"I know. He's never mentioned anything other than an aunt. Not even to tell me he doesn't want to talk about them. I mean, I'd respect that, but to hide his past like that, I have no idea what else he's not telling me. Any time I'd ask, he'd blow me off with no explanation."

"Crazy," Olivia comments.

"I just, I don't know… I told them to go figure their shit out and let me know where they end up."

"I mean that's progress," Amy says.

"What?" I ask, having no idea where she's going with this.

"Yeah, you used to just kick people to the curb when things got rough. You gave these guys an opening to come back," Olivia says.

"Wait, what do you mean?" I protest.

"It's your classic move. You pick something to be upset about when you really start liking someone and call it quits when the first argument happens," Olivia says nonchalantly.

"I do not!" I protest. They both level me with a look. "Often."

"Most times you don't even make it past the second date. You've already decided someone breathes too heavy or sips their water too loudly," Amy says.

"It is a THING!" I protest.

"What we're saying is that you find reasons to bail, honey, unless someone holds your feet to the fire like we both have. This friendship would have crumbled at the start if we hadn't. Once we solidified that foundation, we were good. You need to give them a chance to do the same," Olivia says.

I stay quiet this time.

They might be right. A little. I'm not backing down on this one, though. This is indicative of bigger problems, and I can't put myself in the fire like that.

"We just don't want to see you give up on a good thing too soon," Amy says quietly.

"What if I'm avoiding a bad thing, though?" I counter.

"If you were, we would be right behind you... but this one? It's not a bad thing. They hurt you, and they need to get to groveling. We all fuck up, and you should give them the chance to make it right," Olivia says.

"I'll think about it," I tell her, grabbing more snacks. "Can we just watch a bad movie?"

I get the this isn't over look from both of them, but they relent, and we put on *Bloody Bloody Bible Camp*. Nothing like Ron Jeremy Jesus to make the night better.

The next weekend rolls around and it's officially two weeks since the gathering at Jax's. My parents have insisted on another family dinner and Thomas forces me to go, citing the need for "holiday cheer" or some bullshit. By forces, I mean he shows up at my house with Courtney and starts playing obnoxious music until I'm dressed and out the door just to get him to stop. We arrive, Courtney in tow, and head inside.

Looks like Graham's already here. Cool, looking forward to this one. I'm fully expecting a lot of I told you so comments from him.

"If he says, 'I told you so' even once, I'm gonna kick him in the balls," Courtney says softly and we take our shoes off.

I manage a small chuckle and we gather in the dining room where everything is ready to go and we're the last to sit. Nobody mentions how puffy my eyes are or how my hair is up in a messy bun and I'm wearing sweatpants, so I finally start to relax a bit. I went through the whole process of dying my hair purple and I can't even bring myself to style it.

The meal is fine, if a bit quiet, and I move to sit on the couch in the living room, waiting for Thomas and Courtney to be ready to leave. Closing my eyes, I go through all the deadlines I have coming up this week at work and which priority tasks I need to focus on. If there aren't boys to think about, then work is gonna take priority here.

I feel the couch dip next to me, and when I open my eyes, everyone is in the living room with me. Looking at me.

"Well, that's not creepy," I mutter.

"I told them it would be," Courtney mutters back, having grabbed the spot next to me.

"What's up your butt?" Dad asks.

I roll my eyes. "So tactful Dad."

"I think what your father *means*," Mom says, elbowing Dad. "Is that you're clearly upset, and we'd like to see if you're okay. Usually, you're not quite *this* miserable."

"Not sure that's better, but I guess we'll go with it," I tell her.

"I might have already mentioned some of it," Thomas confesses.

"Seriously? Come on, Thomas, you need to learn how to keep your mouth shut," I tell him, only somewhat angry at him.

"I figured it was necessary after seeing Roman at the bar last weekend."

"*Excuse me?*" I sit up and look at him, sitting on the other side of Courtney.

He holds up his hands. "I didn't think it would be a big deal to talk to him. You never said I couldn't. You just said you didn't want to talk *about* them."

I just narrow my eyes at him and sit back. No words for him. He's lost those for now.

Graham sighs. "Charli what happened?"

I look over at him warily. "Why do you care? You didn't like them, anyway."

Surprisingly, he looks completely embarrassed. "I'm sorry for the way I treated them," he says softly.

I put my feet on the floor and lean my body forward, absolutely shocked. "Excuse me? What did you say?"

He rolls his eyes and says a bit more loudly, "I'm sorry I was an asshole."

My eyes turn to look at Courtney. "Mark this day down in history."

She smirks at my joke, but her eyes are glued to Graham, something akin to respect on her face. Normally, those two are like cats and water; do not mix for your own good. She seems... almost warm to him right now. Filing that away for later, I look back and Graham and lean back on the couch cushions.

"I told them to go figure their shit out," I tell everyone.

"What shit? Do I need to go beat them up?" Dad asks.

That earns him a small smile. "No, they didn't cheat on me or anything. Jax just kept defending his anti-fat sister, and Roman refuses to give me anything about his life. I can't stay with people who defend those who hurt me or refuse to let me in."

Thomas coughs and I'm pretty sure the word hypocrite is in there somewhere. I look over at him expectantly. He still gets no words. He holds my gaze, completely unfazed by my silence.

"Charli, you should talk to them," Graham says, seriously.

"What? You hate them," I reiterate.

"I don't hate them, I just—" He sighs. "I just want the best for you, and I let my ego get in the way of seeing anything other than my own success. You seemed really happy with them."

This shifts my thinking more than I think anything else could have. Graham rarely apologizes, and he struggles to see outside his own world. The fact that he's willing to see me and the guys as a good thing has me listening. His apology goes a long way as well.

Mom looks over at Dad. "Relationships can be harder than you think they'll be, but they are worth it, honey. Working through the fear and the anxiety is worth it."

She looks around the room at everyone and tells the guys to get out. They all grumble and whine, but they go somewhere else in the house. Hopefully doing the dishes for Mom. Courtney scootches over a little and Mom moves closer.

"When I met your father, I broke up with him no less than three times," she confesses.

"Really? You guys are so solid, I can't even imagine something like that."

She chuckles. "Really. I was a lot like you. I was afraid of letting go, letting someone in, and I was terrified it would work out."

"Why would you be scared about that?" Courtney asks.

"Because it would mean that my defenses were for nothing, and I may have missed out on other things. If I just kept to my fear, then I knew what to expect."

"I didn't realize you had anxiety that long ago," I tell her.

"I didn't either, honey. I learned about the anxiety after Thomas was born, but even then, it wasn't exactly a popular subject. Your father knew I wasn't okay though, and we figured it out and I got help, like you have." She smiles at us.

Courtney and I smile back, and I'm grateful my mom sent the guys out. They always get so damn awkward when emotions come out. I can't imagine my dad sitting here talking about this.

"So, what did you do? You obviously ended up with him," I say.

She chuckles. "Yeah, we worked out in the end. After the last breakup, he told me he couldn't do it again. I needed to be in or out, and he was right. I was toying with him without realizing it. So, all that fear? I had to let it go."

"Once those boys finish their groveling, talk it out some more. Tell them what you need. You deserve that from them," Courtney adds.

"I'm scared to talk to them, to let them in again. What if this happens again?"

"Then bail," she responds, as if it's that simple. "You tell them what you need. If they can't respect it and fuck up on this level again, give them the bird and walk away."

My mom smiles at us. "Let the fear go, honey. Write it down, say it out loud, whatever you need to get it out of you, and move forward. I think those guys are special, and I think you know it. Letting them back in will be the best decision you've ever made. Plus, if they mess it up, then your dad will have an excuse to pretend he can beat someone up."

That gets a laugh out of me as I soak in their words.

She's right, they are special. Is it terrifying to let go of my anxiety and fear? Yes, absolutely. What happens if I do and they hurt me again? Or if they leave? What if I let go and they don't catch me?

What if they do?

 # Chapter 31

Jax

It's only been a few days without Charlotte and I'm slowly losing myself.

How the actual fuck am I supposed to function without her?

I'm going through the motions, but I have no idea what the motions are. Charlotte's words have been swirling in my head.

Do I brush things off? I didn't think so, but maybe I do. I'm struggling to reconcile who she has seen me be with who I want to be.

My mom has insisted on another family dinner, and the last thing I want to do is see Bethany, but maybe it'll be good for me to go. I'm sure Roman's annoyed with my sulking; if I'm home, then I'm in my room. I don't talk to him at home at all. At work we interact just fine, but the second one of us leaves, it's like we've forgotten how to exist together. We used to be solid, but Charlotte came into our lives and she filled the cracks we didn't see. Now it's like we don't know how to get around those.

Saturday, one week after our fight, I head to my parents' house for family dinner. I'm hoping the girls will be there at least; those two always cheer me up. Plus, Christmas is coming soon, so they'll be asking for all kinds of stuff and that will definitely keep me thinking. Noise hits me as I step into the house, and I'm glad to hear the two little girls making their usual cacophony. Their feet thunder towards me as they run down the hall.

"UNCLE JAX!" they yell in tandem.

I give what I hope is a smile and kneel down so they can slam into me. Their arms wrap around me, and I hold them a little tighter than usual. It's like kids instinctively know you need some extra hugs because they just keep their arms wrapped around me and don't protest the length of time I hold them.

"Hey girls," I say softly.

"Are you okay, Uncle Jax?" Kinsley asks.

"I hope I will be," I tell her honestly.

"We have a spa set up. Come relax!" Abigail insists.

Who am I to deny them? I stand and let them lead me away. As I'm walking down the hallway, I see Bethany as she moves from the living room to the dining room and our eyes lock for a moment. I can't figure out the look on her face, and I break eye contact first. She's the reason I'm in this damn mess, anyway. Suddenly, I realize I'm angry at her. Really angry.

The girls make me lie down and put cucumbers on my eyes. I'm praying they are fresh, but who knows with these two? I can feel one painting my nails while saying how fabulous this color is on me. My mouth smiles involuntarily.

"Uncle Jax?" Kinsley asks.

"Yeah?"

"Where's Lottie?"

"Who?"

"Lottie, your friend you brought over."

"You mean Charlotte?" I ask.

"Yeah. I told my teacher all about her and she said her cousin has that same name and they call her Lottie. I like it so now I'm gonna call her that," Kinsley says.

My smile is full blown now. "I do too," I tell her.

"So where is she?" she presses.

I sigh. "She couldn't come today."

"Will she come next time?"

"I don't know, honey, we got into a fight," I confess.

"Well, you should say sorry and buy her flowers."

"I should?"

"Yeah, that's what Daddy does for Mommy, and it always works," Kinsley says.

"Not that time he spilled his drink!" Abigail protests. "He had to clean that instead of flowers."

I chuckle. "Maybe I'll ask her what she would like."

Kinsley takes the cucumbers off my eyes and looks at me with a critical eye. "Make sure you do. I want my friend back. It can be my Christmas present, okay?"

Bossy little things, but I can't imagine life without them. My mom pops her head in at that point and announces dinner is ready. So the girls and I pack up and head to the table. Dinner is borderline awkward. Trevor came for once, but there's an obvious avoidance of the topic of Charlotte. When plates are cleared, my mom decides that this is the moment to bring it up.

"Where's Charlotte, honey?"

I slowly look over at her. "Took you all of dinner to ask me that?" I question her.

At least she has the grace to look a little embarrassed. "I wasn't sure if you wanted to talk about her or not. I mean, she's not here, so I wasn't sure…"

"She's taking some space, so I guess I am too," I tell her, the fight in me leaving after only a moment.

"Why's that?" Dad asks. "She seemed great."

I look over at Bethany finally and hold her gaze. She starts to look a little uncomfortable, so Trevor saves her.

"Kiddos, why don't you go play for a bit? We're going to do boring grown up talking," he says.

"Do we hafta??" Abigail whines.

"I promise next time I see you, you can do more spa time," I tell her.

She and Kinsley look at each other and decide that the offer is good enough because they stand and start making up games as they walk away. Bethany waits until they are out of earshot before thanking Trevor and looking around the table to gauge the room. For once, I'm not trying to break the tension. I want to understand why my sister was antagonizing Charlotte at my house.

"So, I might have drunk a little too much—" Trevor coughs, interrupting her, and she rolls her eyes. "Okay, a lot too much. I went over to Jax's because he said he was having people over and I could stop by if I wanted. I was a little bold with Charlotte."

I look at her, really look, and realize she's not really sorry. She doesn't sound apologetic, nor does she look apologetic. She hasn't even attempted an apology.

"Bethany, why?" I ask her.

"You can do better, Jax," she says quietly.

"Explain that to me, 'cuz I have spent weeks telling myself that you were just thrown by Charlotte's hair or that you're protective of me. I tried to convince Charlotte you didn't hate her. I told her you're a good person. So, explain to me how I can do better than the best woman I've ever met!" I'm almost shouting by the end.

She huffs and rolls her eyes, looking over to Mom. Mom has the decency to look uncomfortable.

"Baby, you know we prioritize being healthy here. So when we met her, it was a shock, and I probably did not behave my best. Bethany and I made some jokes, and I'm not particularly proud of it, but I also want you to be with someone healthy, honey," Mom says.

Dad is frowning now, taking in all the talking and all the viewpoints. Trevor is quiet, looking at the table, probably pretending he isn't here. He's never been great with conflict and usually avoids it.

"Trevor? I'm not asking you to take sides or get into anything, but are you ok with this?" I ask.

"How is that not asking me to get involved?" he shoots back.

I sigh. "I just mean, am I being unreasonable? Being upset with Bethany?"

He looks over at Bethany. "We talked, and Bethany knows I'm not particularly proud of how she acted at your house."

She sits up straighter. "Am I the only one here willing to say what needs to be said?"

"What exactly is that?" Dad asks.

"Jax deserves someone who prioritizes their health. Charlotte clearly does not. She was also flirting with Roman and holding his hand. Right in front of Jax and he didn't even say anything! Not only is she physically not good for him, but her morals are also obviously shit."

My big sister has always been someone I look up to. She works hard, she's welcoming to everyone she meets, and she helps people who need it. At this moment, though, I'm seeing her imperfect side for the first time without rose-colored glasses.

I didn't realize how judgmental she is. Has she always been this way? Is this who she is when I'm not around?

"Bethany, Charlotte is –was– seeing both Roman and I. We all talked about it and agreed to it," I tell her gently.

She looks at me, shocked. "What?"

"Yeah. Charlotte even told you that."

"I thought she was being catty,"

"The why the hell didn't you just ask me? If you had just fucking ASKED, this could have been completely avoided!"

"She's still not healthy. I had to point that out," she defends.

What Charlotte told me rings through my head. How people judge her every day for looking the way she does. She looks perfect to me, and I'm beginning to see that not everyone will see what I see when I look at her.

"How do you know she's not?" I question.

"I mean, she's fat, she can't be."

"Have you talked to her doctor? Have you seen her recent test results? Do you know her medical history? Did you make a SINGLE FUCKING EFFORT TO GET TO KNOW HER?" I'm shouting now, my despair turning to fury.

"It's one thing for you girls to comment about your own weight and your own eating habits, but it's quite another to project that on someone else. Bethany, we raised you better than that. Your mother has admitted her mistake. I don't understand why you think this behavior is acceptable," my dad chimes in with the best disappointed dad voice I've ever heard from him.

Bethany huffs but doesn't say anything.

"Oh my god, you *are* an asshole. I never realized it," I say.

I stand up from the table and turn to walk out of the dining room.

"Jax," my mom calls out.

"What?" I ask, not turning back to her.

"Get her back and bring her over with Roman. I want to apologize and try again," she says.

I nod. "Okay, Mom."

"Don't let her get away," my dad adds as I walk away.

When I get home, I see Roman's car in the driveway and I'm glad he's here. I hustle into the house and see him on the couch, looking a little less hopeless than he did the last time I saw him in passing. He looks thoughtful, and he's tapping a pencil against his thigh, staring at the TV that isn't on. I walk over toward him and sit in the chair next to the couch where he's sitting. He looks over at me, a faint frown on his head.

"I'm sorry. I should have listened more."

He nods slowly. "I should have opened up more."

"We gonna get her back?"

"I fuckin' hope so," he says.

"Let's do it. Let's make it happen. I can't let her walk away, man, I can't."

A smirk appears on his face. "Okay, let's do it."

I grin at him, and we get planning.

 Chapter 32

Charlotte

I'm still mired in indecision for the next week. I know I should just decide what I'm going to do, but I can't seem to take that step. My anxiety is choking me and while I logically understand that I would feel better if I made a decision, my heart is still so torn.

It's the Friday after family dinner, and I'm sitting on my couch, texting memes back and forth with the girls. Well, they're texting the memes and I'm sending an occasional lol. Deciding I need popcorn, I head into the kitchen as I continue to hear my phone chime with messages. It continues through the popping process, and I'm impressed with the speed of meme swapping.

They are really on top of it right now.

Hopefully, one actually gets a laugh out of me instead of just the letters. They've been amusing, but I haven't actually laughed yet.

When I pick my phone back up, I see two names I wasn't expecting in a chat I haven't used in weeks. Jax and Roman are messaging in our group chat and my mind freezes, more indecision flooding in.

Is this a sign? Should I just start talking? Will everything just be smoothed over? What if they just keep things the way they were? What if I keep getting pushed to the side? What if things get worse?

I stop myself there. I need to not go down this path. Jax has been helping me to stop my spirals, but I can't keep relying on others to do that for me. I grab a notebook and write down all my negative what ifs, then ask the opposite. What if things go wonderfully? After asking the positive "what if" questions on the paper, I grab my phone to see what the boys want.

Jax: You're all we ever wanted

Roman: You're all we ever needed, yeah

Jax: So tell us what to do now

Roman: Cuz we, we, we, we, we, we want you back

Are they…. are they typing me boy band lyrics? The fuck is this?

Amy and Olivia are continuing their meme texts, but I ignore them because Roman and Jax are still going.

Jax: It's hard to say we're sorry

Roman: It's hard to make the things we did undone

Jax: A lesson we've learned too well for sure

Roman: So don't turn off your phone now

Jax: We're tryin to figure out just what to do

Roman: We're going crazy without you

I smile. I can't help it. This is absolutely ridiculous, and I love every second of it. There's one important question, though.

Me: Which one of you is Justin and which is J.C.?

Jax: I'm obviously Justin, I'm the better looking of us

Roman: Fuck you, I'm blonde, I get to be Justin!

Me: LOL you guys are absolutely ridiculous

Jax: I'M ridiculous, Roman's just along for the ride

Roman: I'm down for riding Charlotte, not you

Me: Pretty sure NSYNC wrote a song about that too

Jax: I wouldn't be surprised, I'm gonna need to find that one.

Roman: Can we see you, pretty girl?

Leave it to Roman to cut to the chase. Do I want to see them? Yes, yes I do. Am I ready? Probably not. Will I ever be ready? Remains to be seen. What I do know is that they made a point to reach out, as silly as it was. I should do the same.

Me: Yeah, it would be nice to see you guys if I'm being honest. What are you thinking?

Jax: Wellll you can come here or we can meet you somewhere.

Me: Why not my place?

Jax: Cuz if you decide to leave, you can just go instead of kicking us out.

Roman: We really hope you stay though

Jax: Oh, yeah, we definitely do

Shaking my head at Jax, I make my decision.

Me: I'll come to you. When?

Roman: 10 minutes ago

Me: Okay *smiley face emoji*

I debate putting on some regular clothes, but at this point they've seen me in all states of dress and undress, so I stay in my lounge clothes. I slide my warm boots on and throw on a coat as I head out the door. Before I leave the driveway, I shoot off a text to the girls to let them know what's up. A rapid-fire noise of text message alerts comes in and I silence my phone. I'll face that music later.

By the time I reach Jax and Roman's, my nerves have officially kicked in full throttle. I can feel the ball of anxiety settling in my chest. Instead of spinning on thoughts, I'm getting the physical reaction. I take a moment to do some deep breathing. In for a count of four, hold it for four, breathe out for the count of six. After repeating this a couple of times, I open the door of my car.

The anxiety isn't gone, but I know the deep breathing will help my body calm in a few minutes. Assuming I don't do anything to make it worse.

The door opens before I knock and Roman is standing there, his hair down, touching his shoulders, and a look of almost torture on his face. Tears prick my eyes upon seeing him.

Fuck, I missed him so much.

"Charlotte," he says, holding his hand out.

I take his hand, luxuriating in his smooth, deep voice. He leads me in and closes the door. Jax is sitting on the couch, his legs bouncing like an eager puppy. Our eyes meet and I'm sucked in again, just like the first time I saw him. I'm not sure how I went for weeks without seeing these two. They ground me in ways I didn't realize were possible.

"Baby girl, want to take a seat?" Roman asks.

I nod and sit on the chair, so I don't have their bodies against me, causing distraction. We sit like that in the quiet for a few moments, silently assessing each other.

"So," I say.

Jax is the first one to come out of the semi-trance we've found ourselves in. "Your hair is purple."

I touch my hair in my messy bun and give a small smile. "Yeah, I dyed it the day after we fought. It was time for a change."

"It's nice," Roman adds.

"I'm sorry," Jax blurts out, almost shouting.

My eyebrows go up to my hairline. That was unexpected. I wait for more.

"Um, I'm sorry," he repeats at a normal volume. "I let my view of my sister blind me to her opinion of you. I couldn't imagine her capable of deceit and so I didn't even try to listen to your side or believe you like I should. I know better now, and I'm sorry."

I give him a small smile at the end of his speech.

"It shouldn't have taken our fight to realize this," Roman adds. "For either of us. I'm sorry too. I was so scared to open up to someone that I didn't think of how it would affect you. You gave so much of yourself to me, and I gave almost nothing back. I would like to explain if you are willing to hear."

My eyes are now tingling with tears, and I take a breath to hold them back.

"Thank you both for saying what you said. Jax, it devastated me to know that you didn't believe me when I explained how people act toward me, especially your sister. Roman, it hurt to know that you gave me nothing of your past, not even to say you didn't want to talk about it. It felt like neither of you trusted me, and that shook me the most."

Roman closes his eyes and rubs his hand across his mouth in thought. Jax, being Jax, essentially throws himself at my feet. Sitting on the floor, he looks up at me.

"I will never doubt you again, and I should never have doubted you in the first place. I finally opened my eyes to Bethany's true colors about you, and my mom wants to apologize to you as well. She realizes she was in the wrong."

"Jax, you can doubt me. Sometimes I'm wrong. I just want to have a conversation about the things I feel and…. and I want you to believe me when it's something I know about. You shouldn't just not doubt me point blank."

"Out of the two of us, you are clearly the smarter person, so I'm inclined to disagree with your assessment on being wrong," he tells me with a wink.

I huff and shake my head.

"Baby girl. Can you forgive either of us? I get it if you only want Jax, but I'm hoping we can move forward and be together like we were. Maybe a little wiser now."

My eyes find Roman's and I take a good look at him. He's got some stubble, like he hasn't been shaving daily, but just enough to not be clean shaven anymore. His eyes are hopeful and sad all at once, and I know his sincerity is real. Roman has a depth to him I never expected.

"I want to. I really want to," I tell both of them, and then stand to walk around the room as I talk.

They both patiently wait and watch, Jax still on the ground and Roman on the couch.

"I know the girls alluded to it with both of you at some point, but I don't open up well, or often, to people. I've had enough people walk away from me that it's hard to do it. It's always been hard, if I'm honest. My family and the girls have all also pointed out that I tend to run, and I don't think I want to run this time. So, yes, I want to forgive you guys. I want to move forward with you both. I want to make amends for my own bad behavior. I just–I don't know how," I finish with a sigh.

Jax looks like he's on the verge of tears and Roman looks determined. He reaches back to tie his hair into a bun and stands. Walking toward me, he grabs my hands and steps close. We're basically eye to eye, my head only slightly tilted up.

"Close your eyes," he says gently, so I do.

I feel him gently pull my hands and walk away from me, forcing me to follow him. We walk down the hallway and into a room where we stop. I can't tell if we're in Jax's room or Roman's, but I think it's Jax's. I feel a body come up behind me, hands lightly resting on my hips.

"You don't have to trust us right away," Jax murmurs in my ear. "Let us show you how sorry we are. Let us earn your trust so we all know we're in this together."

His lips meet my neck and my breath hitches as he gently kisses from my shoulder to my ear. A second set of lips starts on the other side of my neck and my head dips back with a moan escaping my mouth.

"How do you plan to earn my trust?" I ask breathily, surprising myself with how turned on I sound.

"First, we're going to worship this beautiful body, and expect nothing in return," Roman says.

Jax jumps in. "Then, we're going to talk and be an open book for anything you want to know."

"Rinse and repeat," Roman finishes.

I smile, leaving my eyes closed.

"What if I want all of you, not just my pleasure, but yours too?" I ask. "Maybe I want to be fucked senseless."

Two groans surround me, and my smile grows. The heady feeling of holding these two in my hand is one of my favorite feelings.

"Whatever you want, you get," Jax says before clamping his teeth down gently on my ear.

I nod my head. "Okay, show me how much you want me. Fuck me."

I can feel how hard both of them already were when they started kissing my neck, and I'm amazed when they get harder. The feel of them against my body makes me squirm with need. My panties slowly get damper the longer they touch my body.

"Keep your eyes closed. Just enjoy us worshipping this perfect fucking body," Roman whispers.

"Let us take care of you. Show you how much you mean to us," Jax adds.

Roman steps away from my body and I lean toward where he was. Jax bands an arm around my waist, pulling me back into him, rubbing his covered cock against my ass.

Thank God I wore lounge clothes. I can feel him so much better with only soft fabric in the way. My back arches and I rub my ass against him, seeking more friction. His hand not holding me snakes up underneath my shirt and starts to tease my nipples over my bra. He lightly flicks them, pulling on what he can get through the fabric.

My breathing picks up, and he suddenly stops, dragging his hands away from my body slowly. A disappointed noise builds in my throat, but before I can say anything, he gently pushes me forward and Roman's hands immediately catch me. I don't miss what that was, a mini trust fall. Although a bit non-consensual, it oddly helped reaffirm some trust that they'll be there to catch me.

Roman's hands cup my face and his lips meet mine, gently and softly. He doesn't push for more kisses, keeping it light and sweet. Our lips stay locked as he turns my body and lays me down on an unfamiliar bed.

Must be Jax's bed. It feels bigger than Roman's.

Rope sneaks around my hands and pulls them up above my head.

"Is this ok?" Jax asks, suddenly near my head.

I nod. "Yeah, it's okay."

A hand pulls my pants down, grabbing my underwear at the same time, exposing me to the air. Then fingers swipe through my slit slowly, gathering the wetness that's spread there. A deep groan reverberates by my legs.

"Fuck yeah, it's okay, she's fucking soaked," I hear Roman rasp, his voice shaking a little.

Moaning, I pull my feet out of the last bit of my pants and spread my legs wide on the bed, showing him everything.

"I don't know what I did to deserve this, but I'm never giving you back, baby girl. You're gonna have to chase me off," he says.

Then he dives in. His mouth plunders my lower lips, licking and sucking anything he can find. No place in my pussy is safe from his exploration. As he continues to lick and suck, Jax grabs the bottom of my shirt. He pulls it up over my head, and I feel the fabric gather at my hands, unable to go further because of the rope.

Jax reaches under me and unclasps my bra. One of the straps comes loose from the band and I suddenly remember my favorite lounge bra is a convertible one; the straps are able to modify to match the shirt I have on. He notices the first strap, and it doesn't take him long to remove the other, allowing my bra to be pulled completely off my body.

He doesn't waste time descending his hot mouth onto my hardened nipple. I cry out at the double stimulation of Jax sucking and nipping at my nipples, while Roman sucks and licks my clit. Roman adds two fingers to the mix and begins to pump in and out, not wasting any time. He pistons his fingers in and out of me, adds a third, and with one more hard suck, my body explodes.

I can feel my muscles clenching around his fingers and my body bows off the bed, shoving my breasts further into Jax's face. Roman's fingers don't slow, and his mouth continues to suck as I ride out the pleasure. I can feel my cum leaking out around his fingers, dripping from my body as I come down from my orgasm.

"Fuck, your pussy tastes so damn good," Roman says, placing open mouth kisses along my thighs. "I could eat you for every meal."

A smile grows on my face at his words, and I can feel a surge of comfort and what feels dangerously close to love swirl around my heart.

"Are you on the pill?" Jax asks me softly.

"IUD," I tell him, still breathing hard.

I hear a delighted chuckle as he moves around my body.

"Roman?" I call out.

"Yeah, baby girl? You okay?" He sounds worried, and it warms my heart further.

"You promised you'd fuck me. I'm still waiting," I sass.

"Oh, you want a fucking?" I hear his voice lower in a bit of a growl.

"If you think you can deliver."

"You bet this sweet fucking pussy I can deliver. Jax, get the lube. Those tits need to be fucked while I take this pussy. You want that baby? You want a pearl necklace?"

Roman's dirty talk always does me in. I feel someone climb into the bed and hear the click of a bottle opening. Cool gel startles me as it drips onto my body, but Jax warms it quickly as he massages my breasts, squeezing them and teasing my nipples. One hand leaves my breasts and I assume he's starting to coat himself in the lube as well.

"Spread those beautiful legs for me, baby girl," I hear Roman rumble as he moves my legs further apart.

Jax's hands come back to my breasts, a little more lube on them, before he squeezes them together.

"I'm gonna ruin this pussy for anyone but us, and Jax is gonna mark you, so you remember who you belong to," Roman says.

"Yes, mark me, keep me," I moan in response, so turned on that I'm almost unaware of what I'm saying.

I can feel the tip of Jax tease the spot between my breasts, ever so slightly in and out, not going all the way. Roman's tip settles right at my opening, slightly in but not quite.

"Ready?" Roman asks.

"Ready," Jax responds before I can.

They slowly thrust in their respective spots together, invading my body and sliding between my breasts. The feel of them moving in tandem makes me want to feel them at the same time in both of my lower holes. Maybe we'll work up to that.

Their movements speed up, not quite in tandem after that first thrust, but the feel of them fucking my body is amazing. I missed it more than I realized, and I'm reveling in the feeling of their hardened cocks gliding in and out of me.

As I lick my lips, I feel the very tip of Jax's cock as he thrusts in as far as he can go. He breathes heavily at the contact, and I make a point to start licking his tip when I feel him moving forward.

Roman picks up speed and intensity. He throws one of my legs around his hips and is holding the other out to keep me spread. The obscene sound of flesh slapping and fluids gushing only drives my desire higher.

"Charlotte, you keep licking me like that and I'm gonna come," Jax threatens.

Of course, I don't stop and after a few more thrusts, I feel his hot cum spray across my collarbone and throat.

"Fuck, she just got wetter," Roman groans.

"I need to taste," Jax says breathlessly.

Before I have time to think, Jax has whipped himself around and his tongue is licking at my clit.

Are they-are they going to touch?

I want to watch so badly, but I promised to keep my eyes closed. His tongue continues to lap at my clit and the feeling of his tongue mixed with Roman's cock is driving me higher than I thought possible.

"Jax, I'm about to go for it. If you don't want to get smacked in the face, then move," Roman grits out.

Jax sneaks in another lick before backing away. Roman takes that as his cue, climbs up on the bed, and starts hammering into my pussy. He's merciless, grabbing my hips to get a deeper angle without missing a beat. Jax has moved to my head and is spreading his cum across my chest.

"I hope every time you put on a necklace you think of my cum spread across you," he whispers into my ear.

"I'm never gonna get enough of this pussy," Roman grits out. "So fucking perfect. Takes my cock perfectly, so tight and warm. I'm gonna come, baby girl, come with me."

His fingers find my clit, and he rubs circles, increasing the pressing slowly. My orgasm hits out of nowhere, and I cry out my release.

"FUCK!" I yell out.

"God baby, yes, YES!" Roman grits out as his hips stutter and he slams home, staying there for a moment as I feel him fill my pussy with his cum.

A moment later, Jax comes in and gently cleans me, starting with his mess and then working down to between my legs once Roman leaves. We pile into the bed in a heap, and it's confirmed that Jax has a king size when we all fit.

We're a complicated tangle of limbs and breath, but I've never felt more comfortable. We snuggle in the quiet, slowly rubbing hands on arms, whispering sweet words and soaking in each other's presence.

"Roman?" I say quietly.

"Yeah, baby girl?" He responds.

"You don't have to tell me about your family if you don't want to."

"Thanks, I do want to tell you. I want you to know all about me. Maybe not right after sex, though." He rumbles a chuckle.

I start to giggle. "Good point."

This feels good. This feels right. I'm not questioning this anymore; I'm going to let the questions go like my mom said and just be with these two amazing men.

 # Chapter 33

Roman – Six months later

Walking in the door, I smile as I hear pounding and moaning from the other room. Glad to hear Jax and Charlotte making good use of our new place. We closed about a month ago and moved in last week.

Since reuniting six months ago, we've made a point to live up to our promises about correcting our mistakes. Jax and I have been working to reassure Charlotte as much as we can to help with her trust issues. Her trust increases daily with us, and she sticks it out to work through arguments instead of assuming things will fall apart. I gave her all the information she wanted on my family, and she demanded I call my aunt more. Aunt Nat was, obviously, delighted with this and demanded we come visit her. We're planning a trip in another month or so.

Jax has opened his eyes more and more to anti-fat biases in the world and if he even thinks someone is going to approach Charlotte, he cuts that shit off fast. She actually asked him to back off a little, let her fight her own battles sometimes. His sister is finally coming around, but Charlotte doesn't trust her still and I can't blame her. She talks to Bethany about her experiences and gives Bethany information on how being hyper focused on health could potentially hurt her girls in the long run.

That caused some problems, but when Bethany calmed down and actually read the information, she agreed. She's been working on her viewpoints, but it's slow going, so Charlotte only gives her surface level information for now when they talk. Jax's parents have made their amends, and they get along fabulously with Charlotte.

Of course, Charlotte and Jax's nieces get along fabulously. They call her Lottie and Charlotte will not allow anyone else in the family to use that name, claiming it's special and just for the girls.

Charlottes's parents have made their own changes and apologized to both Jax and I. The biggest shock was when Graham admitted he was in the wrong. His own insecurities and desire for success made him a dick, and he's been trying more. Sometimes he still comes across wrong, but he's trying. We've all speculated when he and Courtney are going to give in. I'm pretty sure most of his effort is to impress her, but I'll take the benefits of it.

I take a seat on the couch, listening like a voyeur to the sounds of pleasure coming from our room; my dick slowly hardening as they continue. Thankfully, I don't get to full mast before they finish. I did have something I wanted to talk to them about, and a hard cock would make things difficult. My head is tipped back against the headrest of the chair when I hear the door open down the hall.

"Hey, you're home!" Charlotte says happily, and she comes over to sit on my lap.

"Hey baby girl, sounds like you guys had a good afternoon," I tease her, bringing her mouth to mine.

She giggles as we kiss, and when Jax plops down on the sofa, we break it up. I sigh deeply, thinking about the topic I'm going to bring up.

"What's up, man?" Jax asks.

"My sister called the shop today as I was closing up," I tell them.

"What?!" Charlotte exclaims. "What did you do?"

"I kind of froze, and just listened. She couldn't find my cell, so when she saw the repair shop listed in the city, she hoped it was the same Jax from when I was in trade school."

"The fuck did she want?" Jax growls.

"She wants to make amends, I guess," I say.

"What, did she say she's going to pay you back all your money and be a fucking sister for once?" Charlotte says with more venom than expected.

I explained the debt to Charlotte when I told her about my family. She's been wonderful about helping me get my finances more in order.

"God, I love when you get protective," I tell her, grabbing her hair to yank her head back and kiss her neck.

She moans and wiggles her ass on me.

"Hey! Focus!" Jax yells with a smile on his face.

I chuckle and release Charlotte's hair. "She didn't really say what her plan was, just that she missed me, and she was sorry. Didn't give any info on where she was, but she did give me her cell number when I wouldn't share mine. So, I guess the ball is in my court."

"What are you going to do?" Charlotte asks gently.

"I don't know," I reply honestly.

"You don't have to decide right now, man. Think on it and let us know how we can support you," Jax adds.

I nod and smile at them both. "Thanks guys, you're the best."

"I love you," Charlotte says to me, rubbing her nose against mine.

"I love you too, baby girl," I reply.

"Love you, man, just not like that," Jax adds with a laugh.

"Same, bro, same," I tell him and hold out my knuckles.

He bumps them and sits back in his spot on the couch. Not two minutes later, the doorbell rings and Charlotte jumps up, excited.

"They're here!" she squeals.

"Shit, I forgot it's bad movie night," I say, throwing my head back.

"You love it, and you know it," Jax teases, standing.

"I'll come help you with the snacks."

We leave the living room as Charlotte and the girls come out of the foyer. Amy has one of her girlfriends in tow and the four of them giggle and tease as they spread out in the living room. Smiling, I help Jax grab the wine and beers along with the snacks.

"Somethin' wrong with your face?" Jax asks me. "I can see your teeth."

"Fuck off," I tell him, chuckling a little.

"Honestly, it's nice to see you smile more these days. I like it."

"Thanks, man."

We make it into the room in time to see the title screen of *Velocipastor* on the TV.

"A classic!" Jax exclaims.

He's been a lot more supportive of bad horror movies than I have been. I roll my eyes at the movie and groan. They've been trying to get me to watch this one for months now.

"Seriously?" I borderline whine.

Charlotte turns her head to me and widens her eyes while pushing out her lower lip in an exaggerated pout. "Please? It would mean a lot to me," she says, pleading for me to stay.

I sigh and look up at the ceiling. The doorbell rings, so I use that opportunity to chicken out and go see who is here. When I open the door, Thomas is standing on the other side.

"Hey man!" I greet him with a quick hug and step back for him to enter.

Apparently, I'm a bit of a hugger now. It's weird.

"Sup?" he says as he kicks his shoes off.

"She's trying to get me to watch *Velocipastor* again," I say in a low voice.

"You knew this was coming," he tells me.

"If you stay, I'll watch it," I tell him.

"I'll even hold your hand at the scary parts," he says, talking down to me.

"Fuck off," I tell him, laughing.

We find seats in the living room, and I make a point to ensure I'm next to Charlotte. I lean close to her ear.

"You owe me for this," I whisper.

She looks up and whispers back, "You can have total control tonight."

Whelp, there goes all my blood to my dick.

She chuckles, knowing exactly what she just did to me, and we turn to watch the movie.

"Thomas, you still gonna hold my hand if I get scared?" I ask.

"What? You never let ME hold your hand!" Jax exclaims.

"That's because you make it weird," I tell him.

"Facts," Olivia says, pointing at Jax. "You always make it weird."

"Here I thought we were friends, Liv, that hurts. It hurts real deep."

She throws some popcorn at him, which he promptly catches in his mouth. Chuckling, she rolls her eyes at Jax. The two of them have developed a sibling dynamic, and it's good to see someone give Jax back his own shit.

I'm content for the first time in a long time. I'm not hiding away after talking to my sister, and Charlotte has helped me develop a better relationship with my aunt. Jax is growing as a person, and so are our families. It feels like we've built our own family with everyone mixed together.

Fear isn't keeping Charlotte or me from opening up and believing people will stick around. The three of us continue to grow closer and this thing we've built feels steady. Solid.

Fully settling into the moment of bad graphics and terrible plot line, I'm filled and content in a way I don't know that I've ever been. Life is good, and I can't wait to see where it leads us.

A Note from the Author

This book is such a labor of love and support that I don't even know where to start. I want to make sure to call out my husband for being the most supportive person I could dream of. His constant encouragement and willingness to step up and handle the kiddos when inspiration came was invaluable. Honey, I hope you know how much I love and appreciate you. Thank you also to my friend Sarah for helping me get where I am and introducing me to the best editor ever, Scarlett. Both of you have been so patient and supportive. I cannot thank you enough. Shout out to my cousin for the many text and video chats during this process that supported and encouraged me.

I also want to thank you, the reader, for taking a chance on this book. Maybe you hated it. Maybe you loved it. Either way you took time to read it and I appreciate that SO much. There are more stories floating around in my head, so I hope you'll stick around to read them when they're ready to share.

About the Author

Eliza Jonas is a Michigan based author who has dreamed of publishing since she was in the fourth grade. Words have been a constant source of joy in her life and she's excited to share with them with the world. While she never dreamed of writing smut, it feels like the perfect fit for her. She lives with her husband and two children, and reads just about anything she can get her hands on. Especially the smut.